The People Traders

Keith Hoare

The People Traders

ISBN 978-0-9560191-1-0

Revised 2011 V2

Chapter 1

Susan, a big girl for her age, used this to her advantage, pushing smaller girls aside as they scrambled to get out of the school at lunchtime. Many scowled, others muttered threats under their breath. All of them too frightened of this girl to risk a confrontation.

As the girls flooded out, some went to waiting cars, others gathered in groups around the playground, with a few making their way to the park alongside, meeting boyfriends, or just to sit around on the grass eating their lunches.

Susan followed these girls and was soon sitting alone on a park bench, chewing a crust spread messily with peanut butter. She had no real friends; in some ways she couldn't care less, but in other ways she felt bitter towards the popular ones. These were girls who would always wear the top fashions, were often attractive and had parents with pots of money. She, on the other hand, had a father who lived in the pub, never coming home until closing time, and often full of some madcap scheme to make easy money, usually brewed up by others drinking in the bar.

It was one of these schemes that had brought Susan to the park. Her dad had met a man who wanted to talk to one of the older girls from her school. The man had told her dad that he was the girl's uncle, but that the family had broken up through some silly argument. He'd tried to heal the rift between the families but the girl's parents didn't want to know. However, he'd got on with the girl when she was younger and believed, if he could talk to her, she would be the key to bringing the two families together again.

"Who's the girl you're talking about?" she'd asked.

Her dad had pulled an empty cigarette packet from his pocket before squinting at a name written on the flap.

"Karen, Karen Marshall," he'd grunted.

Susan remembered staring at him in shock, "Karen! She's in the Upper Sixth," she'd replied. "What do you expect me to do, just go up to her and say, 'Please, Karen, your Uncle wants to talk to you'? Get real, Dad!"

He'd looked at her strangely. "She's a schoolmate, isn't she? Surely you know her well enough to speak to?"

'Yes', she'd thought to herself, 'trying to speak to Karen's like talking to God'. The girl was a year older and way out of her league, besides being attractive, rich and constantly surrounded by her friends. Turning to him, she'd shaken her head. "Forget it, Dad. I've as much chance of getting her to come with me to meet a man, as you have of winning the lottery. The girl's not approachable by the likes of me. She's stuck-up and normally has her current boyfriend waiting at the school gates. I say current, because she…" her voice changed tone with bitterness and envy, "changes them as often as I change my socks."

He'd gone quiet for a moment, and then looked at her, "Think about it, Susan, there must be some way. Ask her to help you, offer her something, anything, just try, won't you? It's worth two hundred quid and God knows we need money like that."

"Two hundred quid!" she'd gasped. "Why does this man want to pay us that? Surely he could just wait for her after she finishes school?"

Her father had sighed annoyingly. "I told you, the family won't speak to him. He just wants her alone so he can explain his side of the story. The man's convinced Karen will want the family together after she understands how petty the argument was to start with, and then push her parents into mending the rift. Besides, if it was me trying to see you under those circumstances, I'd pay anything if I thought someone could help."

Susan remembered she'd leaned over and kissed him on

the cheek. She'd felt proud of him and although she didn't really agree with the drinking all the time, sometimes his words showed just how much he loved her. "Okay, Dad," she'd replied, "I'll think of something. We'll get that two hundred quid no matter what. I've just got to think how."

It was left at that and no more was said. However, only three days later, an opportunity fell straight into Susan's lap. She'd heard Karen was looking for a CD of one of her favourite bands, but they'd sold out everywhere and she'd been asking around if anybody had it. Normally Susan wouldn't have bothered, they couldn't even afford to buy singles let alone albums, but this was an opportunity that had possibilities and she'd purposely bumped into Karen outside the toilets.

"Sorry, Karen, I didn't see you," she'd mumbled.

Karen had responded, saying it was really her fault then began walking away; after all, they'd nothing in common to carry on any meaningful conversation.

However, she'd shouted after Karen. "Say, weren't you asking around about the 'Fire Birds' latest album?"

Karen had stopped in her tracks and turned to face her. It was the first time Susan had really taken much notice of the girl. What hit her first were Karen's eyes; they were sparkling and the most intense blue she'd ever seen. Her auburn hair cascaded down her shoulders, not straight like many girls, but perfectly cut and shaped round her face. Susan was only five foot four; however, Karen had a good three inches on her and was slim. Even in her school uniform Karen looked decidedly attractive. Instantly she'd been jealous and had hated the girl stood in front of her.

"You've got it?" Karen had asked, bringing Susan out of her thoughts with a jolt.

On her part she'd tried to act indifferently. "Got it last week from Woolly's for my brother's birthday. Want a copy?"

"Of course, if you could do it for weekend?" Karen had replied.

"That's easy, bring a blank CD and we'll record it tomorrow night if you want?"

"Can't I just borrow your CD and I'll copy it?"

However, Susan had been ready for this response. "My brother would kill me. Our only chance is to go straight from school and copy it before he gets home from work. My mum's at work too so there's only my gran, and she's not all there half the time."

Karen hadn't seemed to want to do this. "Tell you what, I'll give you five quid if you record it for me and bring it in tomorrow?" she'd suggested.

Under normal conditions five quid, for her, was not to be sneezed at, but the money offered by the man was far more and of course she didn't really have the CD. "Forget it," she'd replied, "I don't want five quid. I just thought you'd like to come and have a cola or something, and then I could show you my CD collection. But if you only want a copy, I'm out of here."

She'd kept her fingers crossed, aware she needed to play it craftily with this girl, and as she'd turned to walk away, every hair on her head had been tingling. She was aware Karen wouldn't be expecting someone to walk away from her, but had hoped Karen really did want the copy enough to agree to come to her house.

"Susan, wait!" Karen had called. "I didn't mean it like that. It's just that I thought it would be a bit of a liberty to come round and copy it for nothing, that's all. I'd love to come and see your collection, but I meet some of the other girls at seven and I've got to go home for a shower. I also need to get out of these school clothes. We're going to the Bridge later; they've got a live band on tomorrow."

She'd turned back and pretended to look shocked. "That's a pub, you're only seventeen, how do you get in there? The last time I went to a pub they tried to direct me to the children's room, refusing to serve me any drink, except cola."

Karen had laughed. "Tell you what, I'll come to your house and then we can copy the CD. I'll also get changed there and we'll talk about how you can get in a pub under age. Is that a deal?"

"You're on," she'd said to Karen. "I'll wait outside school for you."

"No, I can't do that," Karen had replied. "My boyfriend picks me up on Fridays and we go to his flat. But with me going out he's taking me straight home, so rather than get ready at home, I'll pick my clothes up and be round at your house for half four."

She'd agreed, and now Karen was coming to her house so the money was all but earned and maybe she'd helped a family get together again?

Susan was brought out of her thoughts when a man, who looked in his fifties, took the seat alongside her. She looked him up and down. His black curly hair looked dyed, contrasting with a partly grown, grey beard. His clothes, though smart, had seen better days.

"Are you Susan?" he asked politely.

She nodded. "You must be Frank?"

He turned his head and looked directly at her, then grinned, showing a mouth full of sparkling teeth. "Yes, I met your dad quite by chance in the 'Bull' just off Market Square."

Susan smiled to herself. 'Where else?' she thought, but before she could reply Frank continued.

"I suppose my request to your father seemed strange?"

She shrugged. "It did at first, but my dad explained. Anyway, I've got Karen to come to my house tonight, but don't let me down. You see, the excuse was to record a CD she wants, but I've not got it."

Frank patted her leg and Susan pulled back, thinking he was becoming too friendly.

"I'll be there, Susan, you can count on it. Karen and I have lots to talk about. I'll explain your little deception. Karen will understand, believe me."

Susan frowned, worry written all over her face. "You won't tell her about the money? I'd die if it got round school."

"I certainly won't, the money is between you and me. Anyway, talking of money, your dad said I'm to give you fifty quid up front."

"Yes, have you got it?"

Frank didn't reply, but pulled the notes from his pocket and pushed them into her hand.

Susan's eyes lit up and she clenched the money tightly before stuffing it into the inside pocket of her blazer. 'Some of that's mine', she said to herself, 'now I can buy a half decent pair of jeans.' She grinned at him and stood. "I've got to get back, so I'll see you at about quarter past four. Karen will arrive about half past so don't be late. My dad gave you the address, didn't he?"

"He did, Susan, and don't look so worried, I'll be there. Karen will be so delighted she'll probably thank you and not even bother about the CD."

He watched her go and leaned back in satisfaction, 'The stupid kid fell for it, I should be an actor,' he thought, then spoke aloud as if someone was at his side. "Daddy's done it, darling. You and I have waited so long for this day and I won't let you down, love."

***

Later that afternoon, around four fifteen, Susan opened the back door of her house and Frank entered. Glancing round the room he pulled open a door to a walk-in larder. "I'll wait in here. You put a CD in the computer. Tell her you're already recording it; give her a drink or something. When she's relaxed I'll come and surprise her."

Susan agreed and rushed to put a CD in the drive before opening a computer program that copied CDs.

Ten minutes later she opened the door to Karen, after the doorbell had rung. "Hi, come in, shut the door after you. I'm already recording the CD... Do you want a drink?" Susan asked, before she ran back down the hall to an open door at the end.

Karen entered the dingy hall and her nose wrinkled at the smell. "No thanks, not for the moment," she replied, at the same time pushing the door closed before following Susan. Glancing at the computer running, Karen pulled a blank disc from her bag.

Susan suddenly realised that Karen may want the sound turned up, so she cut in quickly. "It's on mute at the moment because my gran's just gone to lie down. We'll give her ten minutes to get to sleep, and then we can play it as loud as we want."

Karen nodded, offering Susan the CD. "Here's a replacement CD for the one you're using. Tell you what, Susan, if your gran's wanting to settle down, do you mind if I change first, then we can sit and relax for a while?"

Glad Karen hadn't looked too closely at the computer, Susan jumped at the suggestion, asking Karen to follow her upstairs. Leaving her in the bathroom, Susan came back to the kitchen. She could hear the shower running, so she pulled open the door of the larder. "She'll be down soon," Susan said quietly.

Frank pretended to act shyly. "Do you mind going to your room, Susan? Karen and I've got some talking to do and I'd feel a bit embarrassed with you standing there."

"That's okay; I'd feel a bit stupid myself." Then looking very serious, Susan put her hand out. "I don't like to ask, but can I have the rest of the payment now? You know, just in case you want to leave with her and she sees you handing me money?"

Frank nodded, handing her an envelope. "It's all there, Susan, also I've added an extra few quid, just for you, by way of a thank you."

Susan gave a big grin then ran upstairs, slamming her bedroom door loudly. He followed, after first locking the back door and then the front. As he climbed the stairs, his heart was pounding. Stopping for a moment outside the bathroom, a satisfied grin spread over his face. "Right you bitch, come to Frankie," he muttered. Moments later he pushed his shoulder against the door of the bathroom, bursting it open.

Karen spun round in surprise. She'd been drying her hair with a towel and was wearing only a t-shirt and knickers. "Who the hell are you?" she demanded.

Ignoring her question, he just shouted back at her to come with him.

Karen scowled. "I don't know what you want, but you're off your trolley if you think I'm going to come with you, half dressed and with my hair wet. So why don't you get lost before I..." Karen's comments were cut short as Frank moved quickly into the small bathroom and grabbed her hair, forcing her head back, while at the same time clenching his fist and hitting her with all his might in her stomach. Karen instantly doubled up, making a grab at the shower curtain in a vain attempt to support herself, before collapsing on the shower tray and ripping the curtain from the rail. She was struggling for breath and was coughing and retching. He leaned into the shower, turning the water on before following her down. The water was getting in her mouth and up her nose as she gasped for breath.

"You're going to leave this house in one of two ways: Either I beat the fuck out of you or you come quietly,"

Frank demanded, his face inches from hers.

Karen, still coughing and spluttering under the force of the water, struggled round and looked directly at him. She spat in his face. "You can piss off, I'm going nowhere with you," she retorted.

Frank grinned at her. "You are, girl, you fucking are," he demanded, at the same time reaching down and grasping at her knickers, in a vain attempt to drag her out of the shower.

Karen grimaced at his efforts, but she'd no intention of submitting. With one arm trapped under her body, she used the other hand to try and blind him by pushing her fingers into his eyes. Failing at this, she went for his ear, trying to rip it off. But with her hand wet, his ear slipped out of her grasp and she succeeding only in dragging her sharp nails down his cheek. Frank screamed in pain, releasing her to put his hands to his face. This was the break she needed and she quickly scrambled clear in an attempt to get to the door.

Karen gave a scream as he leaned over and grabbed one of her legs, sending her sprawling. He tried to hold her down by throwing all his body weight across her, but he'd the same problem as her, still wet from his drenching, she slipped easily from under him, at the same time grasping at a small table by the toilet to give her extra balance. Bottles and cans flew in all directions. Karen grabbed a can, spraying the contents in Frank's face. It was hair-spray and he spat at her as it touched the injuries she'd made with her nails. With his arms flailing and trying to stop the spray in the small bathroom, he caught her across the head, sending her flying once again into the shower.

"Right, you little bastard, you've asked for it now. I'm going to beat the shit out of you," he screamed, at the same time unfastening his belt.

Karen, still sprawled in the shower, cowered back as the belt was raised, and then seconds later the buckle crashed down, missing her by inches and smashing tiles. As he raised it again, Karen didn't wait for the outcome; she shot out of the shower, crashing her full body weight into him. With his arm raised, Frank lost balance and fell back onto the toilet, smashing the pan. She kicked out, catching him between the legs. That was enough; he rolled up in a ball, the pain of the kick reverberating through his body. Karen scrambled away, yanking the door open before falling outside. She pulled herself up and stumbled, rather than ran; but at that moment, Susan, initially frightened with all the noise, had plucked up enough courage to come and see what was going on. She burst out of her door, barging straight into Karen. Frank, in close pursuit, made a grab at Karen, missed, and caught Susan squarely in the face with his fist. The impact smashed the other side of her head against the door post, and she sank slowly to the floor. Karen scrambled over her, making for the stairs, and, she hoped, freedom.

Grabbing at the front door and finding it locked, she cursed, and then turned and ran through to the back but found that also was locked. Now desperate, she looked at the closed window but couldn't find anything heavy enough to break it with.

At that moment the door from the hall crashed open. "Try to blind me, would you? Now you'll pay for it."

Karen spun round. Frank was stood holding onto the door, blood running down his face. She glanced desperately round the room for a weapon and saw a set of knives in a wooden block on the work surface. Frank saw the knives as well and they both made for them at the same time.

Karen, being closer, won, and pulling the largest knife from the block, she turned to face him. "You're dead if you come any closer," she screamed.

He grinned at her. "Give it your best shot, kid. I'll have it out of your hands in seconds then I'll show you what a knife can really do to a pretty face like yours. I wasn't in the army for nothing!" and he followed the comments with a forced laugh.

She was frightened at these words, and on the edge of panic, tears streamed from her eyes. The fight had shocked her. She'd been to self-defence classes and had even achieved a brown belt, but they hadn't prepared her for reality. There had been lots of room; they'd fought under strict conditions, even with a knife. However, the reality of a stranger threatening to take the knife off her and cut her up, terrified her. Faced with this, the trainer's recommendation to get a weapon, which she had done, was now going sour.

Frank watched her falling apart. She looked nervous, undecided, the arm holding the knife slowly dropping. This was his chance. Lunging forward, Karen saw him coming and raised the knife instantly, catching the pit of his arm. Frank, in pain, pulled back from her and this success spurred her on to go for him again. This time, however, he was ready and punched her hard in the stomach. She fell back, gasping for breath. He was on top of her instantly, at the same time wrenching at the hand holding the knife. She wasn't done yet, and with her other hand she grabbed his ear. This time her hands were dry and she began yanking and twisting it in an effort to rip the ear from his head. Frank was shouting at her to let go as he still tried in vain to get the knife from her other hand. He fell back, in pain from her attack on his ear and Karen struggled away. She was back in control and was not prepared to give in, crawling along the floor before pulling herself up with the help of the door handle and stumbling into the hall. Aware the front door was locked, her only way was up and to barricade herself into a bedroom, so she made for the stairs.

Frank, regaining his balance, grabbed a milk bottle from the side, before following her. He raced up the stairs, catching up as she reached the landing, and made a grab at Karen's t-shirt in a desperate bid to stop her. She was halted in her tracks, stumbling back as he pulled her t-shirt. Then he hit her over the head with the milk bottle and Karen slumped down, unconscious. He knelt at her side and checked her breathing. She was still alive. The girl had given him a hell of a fight and he needed to take stock. Moments later, he dragged her back down the stairs into the kitchen. Quickly, he pulled her t-shirt up over her head and then back down, pinning her arms behind her and tying it in a makeshift knot.

He then stood and looked down at her. "Right, you little shit, let's see you escape Frankie now," he hissed. Walking to the sink and filling a bowl with cold water, he threw the contents at her. Seconds later she came round, coughing and spluttering as the mass of water got up her nose.

"Had enough, kid, or do you want me to take the strap to your bottom?"

"What do you want to do... kill me... is that it?" she gasped.

Frank forced a laugh. She'd had it and all he needed was to dent her ego. "Kill you?" He sniggered and then continued aggressively. "I'm not going to kill you, but believe me today's a day you'll wish I had, that I can promise."

She didn't understand his words. "So what do you want?"

"You'll know in good time. But first you've got a choice. Go like that, just in your pants, or agree not to struggle anymore and I'll let you dress. You see, Karen, you and I need to go for a little ride. We've, or rather you've, a date with a ship, and it won't wait."

She lay there not answering, so Frank moved closer, kicking her in the side. Karen winced at the pain but still didn't reply. He dropped down, his face inches from hers. Karen cowered back, at the same time struggling to release the knot in the t-shirt behind her back, out of his sight. But it was hopeless as the knot was too tight.

"Five seconds and you go like this. Otherwise you agree

to come without any trouble and I'll let you dress."

There was no way out so Karen agreed. At least, she'd decided, there would be time to plan her escape. As it was, with only knickers on, she felt distinctly embarrassed, apart from extremely vulnerable, and he could inflict pain on her body too easily. He untied the t-shirt before standing, allowing her space. She dragged herself up with difficulty, the pain in her stomach making her gasp for breath between bouts of coughing.

He watched and waited till she'd stopped then grabbed her arm. "Now dress quickly, then we go."

With her head throbbing from the blow and the intense pain in her stomach, Karen struggled, clinging to the banister as she climbed the stairs. He followed her up, watching, while she pulled on her jeans and lace-up boots. Convinced now there was no fight left in her, Frank turned away, glancing at Susan. She'd begun to stir. Blood was streaming from a badly cut cheek, her jaw broken after hitting the door post. She just lay on the floor staring up at Frank, the pain so intense she couldn't speak.

Frank moved closer to her. "I told you to stay in the bedroom, didn't I? Now listen well. Tell Karen's father Frank Whittle was here, he'll understand."

He stood and Susan stupidly made a grab at his leg, more for help, than to try to stop him. But Frank glared down at her, giving her a kick in the ribs and another and another, all the time Susan screaming in pain. Then he burst into laughter. "Take a good look," he shouted behind him, "piss me off and I'll break your fucking jaw like Susan's, and that's before kicking the shit out of you. So finished or not, get yourself out here."

Karen, already dressed, made her way past Susan without looking down or saying a word. Where she was going she'd no idea. She now realised this girl had set her up and she hated her for it. At the bottom of the stairs Karen waited by the front door. Frank ran down and told her to place her hands inside the top of her jeans, then he wrenched her belt up tight. Removing a cord from his pocket, he bound it round her, trapping her arms close to her body.

Opening the front door, Frank grasped Karen's hair. "Try to run or shout, kid, and I'll lay you out so fast you'll not know what hit you." He gave a quick look around; the road they were on was deserted, so he urged her forward. At the car he pulled open the passenger door and pushed her inside. He leaned in and unfastened her belt, slipping it out from round her waist. "Get your legs out straight," he demanded.

She did as he asked and he reached down, taking the belt round her legs and threading it through the buckle before pulling it tight, gripping her ankles. He turned to look at her, his face inches from hers. "That'll stop you running. Try it and see how far you get."

Grasping the safety belt, he pulled it harshly across her chest, before clipping the clasp. Then he moved his hand onto her midriff between the jeans and short t-shirt. She winced and he grinned. "Bit sensitive, eh? Still hurts, does it? I want to see your hands inside your jeans at all times. Try to pull them out and I'll punch this little stomach of yours and believe me it'll hurt, perhaps do permanent damage. You wouldn't want that, would you?"

She shook her head and was beginning to feel sick again just at the thought. Frank climbed into the driver's seat and minutes later they were heading out of the city.

***

It was nearly an hour later when Susan's father arrived home. The front door was wide open, which seemed strange. Entering the house he sensed something was wrong.

Shouting first for Susan, then Grandma, he ran up the stairs. Gran was cradling Susan on her lap; the girl was lying motionless on the floor, blood all over her face. Gran knew something was wrong but in her confusion could do nothing about it. He knelt down, gently pushing Gran away, before holding Susan in his arms.

She stirred and opened her eyes; the pain in her chest and face was intense. "Dad?" she whispered.

He moved closer.

"You've got to call the police..." she gasped. "I think he's going to kill her."

He frowned, not quite sure who she was talking about. "Who, darling? Who's going to kill who?"

Susan began to cough, the pain beginning to make her feel sick and dizzy. Her father waited and urged her to tell him what she meant.

"Karen, Dad. The man wanted to kill her. They had a fight and he's taken her. Please, Dad, you must call the police," Susan persisted. Tears came to her eyes and she passed out with the pain.

He laid her down gently on the floor then made his way quickly to the bathroom with the intention of bringing back a wet cloth. As he entered, he froze, staring round the room. It looked like a battlefield; blood was everywhere, the shower curtain in tatters, clothes, bottles and cans strewn over the floor beside a broken toilet. He was visibly shaken; it must have been one hell of a fight, but his first priority was to get Susan to hospital, then call the police.

Chapter 2

Karen felt cold and sick; they'd been on the road for three hours and were now moving slowly down a single-track road somewhere in Wales.

"Not long now," Frank commented.

She looked at him; the blood from his injuries had dried and congealed on his face. He looked evil and these were the first words he'd uttered since setting off. Trying to talk to him a number of times, he'd ignored her, so she'd finally given up. Suddenly the car jerked to a halt. Turning, he released the seat belt, telling her she could remove her hands from her jeans. Karen did as he told her, rubbing them together to restore the circulation. Frank climbed out of the car and looked back inside. "Stay; don't even think about moving. The nearest habitation's about five miles from here and, believe me, there's no way out but up the way we've come down. I'd catch you in minutes then beat the shit out of you. Do we understand each other?"

Karen nodded. She wasn't stupid; she'd seen the terrain, grassland to one side and steep hills to the other.

Just at that moment two figures appeared, approaching from further down the track. Frank went over to them and shook hands with both. She could hardly make out their conversation, but one of the strangers was arguing about money. The other approached the car and pulled open her door. She looked at him. He was a small man of five foot; his eyes were big and round, protruding from his unshaven face as if on stalks. He was definitely not English, Karen thought, but she couldn't decide what nationality.

"The belt, pass me the belt," he demanded.

She reached down and unfastened it from her ankles. But before she could do anything else, he'd snatched the belt from her hand; slipping it round her neck and looping the free end through the buckle, he pulled tight.

"Try to escape and it'll strangle you. Do you understand?"

"Yes," she answered, her eyes wide with fear.

"Okay, now get out of the car and come with me."

She climbed out and he pulled her forward with the belt, stopping her in front of the other man. This man was six foot, clean-shaven and obviously in charge.

"She's a bit scrawny, I'll not get a lot for her," the man commented.

Frank shrugged. "I couldn't give a fuck how much extra you get, you've already got your payment, so do the job," he responded dryly.

The man moved closer; she could smell beer on his breath. He grasped her face in his big hand, forcing her to look at him directly. "Pretty eyes, nice complexion. How old are you?"

"Seventeen," she replied quietly.

He moved his hands down her body and she stepped back in revulsion. The man slapped her across the face without hesitation, "Don't move!" he shouted.

With her face stinging from the blow and tears running down her cheeks, she stood still as he moved his hands over her body.

Frank watched impatiently. "She's well educated, goes to a convent school. Apart from which she's no wimp. I had a hell of a fight to subdue her; besides, she's some kid in bed, I'm told. They'll be queuing up, I can promise you that," Frank commented.

Karen's eyes widened. "I'm not for bloody sale," she replied curtly.

The men looked at her, and the little fat one began to laugh. "You've not told her, have you?" he laughed.

Frank shrugged. "Why should I?" he replied. "Perhaps

you want to enlighten her as to what this is all about?"

The older of the two men nodded his head up and down slowly. "What is her name?" he asked Frank.

"Karen, Karen Marshall," Frank replied.

"Ah yes, I remember now. Well, Karen Marshall, my name's Assam. Perhaps I should tell you a few things as we're going to be in each other's company for some time?" he began. "You see, my partner Garrett and me run this little side-line; we buy and sell things, or to put a finer point on it, we buy and sell people."

The shock on her face was all too apparent, her eyes starting to fill. "There must be a mistake, I've a home and a mum and dad, you can't take it all away," she whispered.

Assam never answered, but snatched her handbag, which Frank was holding, tipping the contents out onto the ground. Then he looked at her for a moment before unclasping her watch and grabbing a cross attached to a small gold chain round her neck. The chain snapped easily and he threw it and the cross to the ground with the watch, stamping on them and all the other personal items from the bag.

"You see, Karen; you did a have a home, a family, even pets. Now your life as it was, is finished. The items you probably held dear, which may have reminded you of that life, are lying in the dirt. So think hard, girl, think very hard, because from this moment, I own you. It is me who decides when you eat, when you sleep and, more importantly, if you live or die."

Unable to understand his words, she stared down at her gold cross, crushed and broken, with her other personal items, lying on the ground. Bravely she looked back up at him watching her, tears running down her cheeks. "Please, may I keep my cross? It was a present from my grandmother who died two months ago. I'm Catholic and I hold it when I pray for her?" she asked, her voice faltering.

He moved closer, his face inches from hers. "You don't seem to understand what I've just said, kid. Now listen well and don't ever talk again, unless I tell you to. You get nothing, nothing I said, and especially not things that have any significance. Do you understand?"

She nodded her head up and down, tears running freely down her cheeks, afraid to answer back at him.

Assam shrugged, indifferent to her distress. "Okay, we take her," he said.

With that, Garrett snatched at the belt, immediately tightening it round the neck and choking her. Hardly able to breathe, he began dragging her back down the path they'd come up.

She started screaming at him to let her go, trying to hold back, but all that happened was the belt tightening round her throat even more. Assam, following behind and watching her struggle, removed a baseball bat from a large pocket inside his coat. Seconds later he struck her across the back of the head. The blow stunned her into silence.

"Struggle or scream once more and I'll hit you again. But next time I'll use some force," Assam shouted into her ear.

With her head spinning from the blow, she stumbled after Garrett.

The track suddenly ended at a steep set of steps leading down into a small cove. At the water's edge a dinghy was bobbing about. Within five minutes they were in the craft. Garrett removed the belt and, sitting on the bench in front of her, began rowing expertly towards a ship some distance away.

She could see as they were approaching; it was some sort of cargo vessel, old, with paint flaking among rusted panels. The two men had turned their backs on her, more concerned with the ship they were approaching rather than what she was doing. Karen had watched and planned. She realised that once on this ship, escape would be hopeless or perhaps impossible. This might be her only chance. A strong swimmer, she'd no real worries about swimming back to shore. All she prayed for now was that they'd not turn to check what she was doing for a few seconds.

Mentally she planned the escape. Her jeans and shoes would have to go; they would drag too much, leaving only t-shirt and knickers. It'd be cold, she knew that, but if she kept going the swim would help keep her warm. Besides, she decided, death trying to escape would be better than the alternative. Reaching down, she unfastened her boots, slipping them from her feet. Then she released her jeans and pushed down the zipper. Now ready, she took a deep breath before standing quickly and throwing herself from the dinghy. The small dinghy rocked dangerously, sending one of the men sprawling into the bottom. The other spun round just in time to see her go over.

Karen swam under water for a short distance before breaking surface, struggling to finally get her jeans off. Now free, she struck out effortlessly towards the shore, often diving deep so as not to give herself away with splashes. A powerful swimmer, this swim for her would have been nothing but for the cold. She'd planned to follow the tide and climb ashore at least half a mile from the cove. However, the constant underwater times, and then the slow strokes on the surface to avoid splashing which might have attracted her pursuers, were taking their toll and she finally decided to come ashore.

The rocks as she approached the shore were dangerous, sea spray rising feet into the air and crashing back, forming a boiling water effect. Holding back a minute and after a particularly high wave, she swam strongly in-between two rocks and then allowed herself to be lifted on the next wave before grasping at the rock. The cold out of the water was unimaginable and Karen began shivering uncontrollably.

She'd also begun to feel dizzy and light-headed, frighteningly close to hypothermia. Her only hope now was to move and keep moving. Scrambling up the rocks, she crouched low, trying to see if they'd followed, but there wasn't a sound. Then, after a few minutes, she was on the move, scrambling through deep grass and following the run of the track. The grass was shorter now and no longer offered a place to hide, so to speed things up she moved onto the track and began to sprint. She'd run for at least five minutes and then her heart sank with the sound of a car approaching fast from behind with its lights cutting through the dark. They would have no difficulty in catching her up. Looking round in panic, she left the road and flattened herself to the grass in a vain attempt to hide.

The car stopped feet from her and the door opened. Frank clapped his hands in applause. "I've got to hand it to you, Karen, you're a resourceful girl. After the beating you took earlier, to escape so spectacularly is worth a medal. Anyway, I hope you liked your little swim and you're not too cold? So why don't you just turn round and make your way back down the path? My friends are waiting there. Unfortunately I don't think they're going to be too pleased, do you?"

She looked up from the ground, her body shivering uncontrollably. "I'm too cold, I don't think I can do that," she pleaded.

Frank turned and reached into the car. He pulled out a car blanket, throwing it at her. "Take this, kid, then back down the track."

There was nowhere for her to go, so without a word she turned and walked slowly back from where she'd come. Frank was right; he'd selected a place which had little or no chance of escape.

The dinghy was back at the cove and the two men stood watching her. She stopped some three feet from them, saying nothing.

Assam grinned at her. "Back are you? You've blown your clothes. We've got none; I'm afraid you're down to what you've got left for the whole trip. So why don't you go back to the dinghy like a good little girl?"

She stood her ground but Garrett had moved swiftly and grabbing her arm he began dragging her, screaming, to the dinghy, but Assam was behind her and pushed her on. At the dinghy, Garrett let go and climbed aboard then grasped both her hands. She thought he was helping her aboard but that was not his intention. He pulled her up tight to the side of the dinghy and then forced her head down by grabbing her hair so she was bent over the side. Assam grinned and unfastened his belt. Then he pulled her knickers to her feet. "Now, little girl, it's time you knew just who's in charge round here and it's certainly not you," he growled.

Seconds later the belt hit her squarely across the buttocks, making her scream in pain. Three times it landed before he stopped. Karen was sobbing uncontrollably.

"Next time you disobey me or my partner and try to escape, you'll feel my belt across your backside again. Each time I'll double the beating, then if that doesn't help, I'll send you for a night with the crew. I think with twelve men away from home and the chance of a young girl for their entertainment, it may just bring out the animal in them, don't you think?"

Never in her life had she been so frightened. She hadn't even known people like this existed, but this was reality. She was alone, unable to understand or comprehend just what was happening to her.

"I'm waiting for an answer, or haven't I got through to you yet? Perhaps a few more strokes will loosen your tongue?"

His threat quickly broke her silence. "I'm sorry, Sir," she stuttered. "I promise I won't be any more trouble."

He stared at her for a moment, still bent over the side, and then raised the belt again. However, by this time Karen had relaxed, not expecting more punishment, so the shock of the belt, not on her now numb bottom, but across the tops of her legs, followed by intense pain, stunned her.

"Next time, I don't want to wait for an answer, do you understand?"

"Yes, Sir," she replied without hesitation.

"Let her go, Garrett," he shouted, and then glared down at her. "I want you in that dinghy, crouched down in the bow now."

She did as he'd asked, climbing quickly into the dinghy. "May I have the blanket back, I'm so cold?" she uttered bravely.

He shrugged indifferently, ignoring her plea, and climbed in after her. Too frightened to ask again, she winced as the salt water washing about in the dinghy caught the sore areas on her bottom from Assam's belt.

Time seemed to pass very slowly; her body was shaking uncontrollably, her head spinning. Resigned to the fact that escape was futile, the effort of the swim, the punishment, and now the cold, was taking its toll. Even as strong and fit as she was, Karen sank slowly into unconsciousness.

Garrett looked at her closely. "This girl's very cold, Assam, I'd better put her straight into a shower when we're aboard. Then just for tonight, stick her in the empty cabin on the lower deck, rather than leave her in the hold."

Assam looked at her for a moment then nodded his agreement. They had by now arrived by the side of the ship and Garrett leaned over, grabbing a cable which he attached to the bow. Assam grabbed the second and attached it to the stern, then after shouting to someone on deck, the dinghy quickly rose and was swung into its holders. Garrett leaned across to her, splashing cold water from the bottom of the dinghy onto her face, shouting at her to wake up.

She opened her eyes, at first not knowing where she was, only that she felt cold, before the memory of her ordeal came flooding back. Garrett gave her no time to think; as soon as she seemed awake he grasped her hand and half dragged her off the dinghy and onto the deck. Then he pushed her through a door, down two flights of stairs and along a corridor, before stopping outside a closed door. He opened it and leaned inside. Turning the taps, he waited until the water ran hot and stepped aside. "Clothes off and inside under the shower. Stay until I return."

She went and did as he asked, pulling the door shut. She'd found a small piece of soap on the shower floor and soaped herself under the hot water, finally beginning to feel warm again.

Garrett came in and stood watching her. She cowered back in the corner of the shower cubicle, embarrassed at him seeing her naked. "That's enough, kid, take this towel and dry yourself."

Although embarrassed with him watching her, she did as he asked, and when dry, wrapped the towel round her body.

"Follow me," he demanded.

At the end of the corridor they entered a cabin furnished with a bunk bed, a chair and a small table with a cupboard below.

"If you're hungry, there's a hot drink and sandwiches. I'll keep your clothes, they need drying. When you've finished, get to bed. Tomorrow you'll be given work around the ship. Talk to anyone and you'll feel the strap later. Believe me, you don't want to take that route."

"Thank you for the food," she replied, still very aware of the risk if she didn't answer quickly enough.

"Let me see your bottom." he asked, at the same time turning her round and pulling the towel up. Karen stood there, afraid to move or object. However, he only looked

24

then let go of the towel before reaching into a cupboard and pulling out a jar. "You're lucky; Assam's belt's not cut the skin, but it's obviously sore, so use this cream, it'll help ease the pain."

She took the jar, at the same time thanking him again.

He grinned. "I'm not a hard man, Karen, play fair with me and we should get on. You're in here for tonight and then it's the hold for you. We have other guests and they are more valuable, but the hold can be chilly so I'll find you an extra blanket if you're no trouble."

Feeling that the barrier between them had softened, Karen took the opportunity to ask questions. "Can you tell me where I'm going?"

Garrett was stood at the door looking at her. "To hell kid... To hell."

A lump came to her throat, tears forming in her eyes. "Why, what have I done?" she whispered.

There was an uneasy silence as if Garrett was choosing his reply carefully. "Nothing that I know of," he began, "but Whittle paid a lot of money for us to deliver you to a people trader. This trader will offer you at auction. You'll go to the highest bidder. That could be a brothel, or perhaps to some man who's after a young girl. Either way, kid, life as you've known it is finished. Perhaps if you're lucky you'll last a year or two, after that," he shrugged indifferently, "who knows?"

She looked at him, her eyes pleading. "Don't you have a family, a daughter? Could you really send me into a life like you describe? You've been paid. I'm positive my daddy would double anything you'd expect to get from this trader. You've only got to call him."

He smiled softly. "Don't try that route, kid, I've heard it all before. Besides, when push comes to shove, parents get police involved and rarely pay. We've a reputation to uphold; ten years on this ship and we've moved all sorts of cargo across the world. You're cargo for us and that's all. I don't want to know the reason why Whittle hates you so much. Perhaps you threw over his son for some other lad? Killed his dog or goldfish? It's of no interest to me. But he's paid for you to be delivered and delivered you'll be. So I'd forget about trying to play on my feelings, I'm not interested. Mind you while we're on that subject, try talking this way to any member of the crew and believe me you will go to a brothel. But it'll be a brothel that couldn't care less what you looked like; the client can always turn you over. I tell you this for your own good. Assam's a past master at cutting pretty faces into grotesque ones."

Watching him as he talked, she realised nothing she said would dissuade him from their own plans for her, so she averted her eyes away from him, staring down at the floor.

"Food, sleep, in that order," then he was gone.

Karen sat for some time, chewing at the huge sandwich filled with cheese, in-between sipping the strong coffee. Resigned to the fact that no white knight was coming to her rescue, she sat there defiant. She'd no intention of being sold, no intention of living the life this Frank seemed to have sent her to. She needed to study the lie of the land, form a plan and keep as fit as she could. She'd skills like swimming, self-defence and had done lots of weekends with her dad in mock combat exercises using paint guns. If she chose her time well, she could possibly escape and use these skills. Before climbing into bed she knelt down, clasping her hands, praying silently.

Frank had stood at the top of the path, watching the ship move slowly into the blackness. At last it was all over. At last his wife and daughter were avenged. He turned and climbed into the car, removing a telephone from the glove box. Dialling a number, he waited until someone answered.

Chapter 3

When Karen's father arrived home, three police cars were already outside the house. He ran in to see his wife and older daughter sitting quietly on the settee. Both were crying, but his wife on seeing him, stood quickly and threw her arms round his neck.

"What is it, love?" he asked gently.

She could say nothing, just sobbed her heart out on his shoulder. A policeman, who seemed in charge, asked a policewoman to look after her, before explaining what had happened.

He frowned. "You say she was abducted, but why? We've not enough money to pay a ransom; I work in the city as a banking adviser, so what reason would anybody have?"

The policeman pulled a cigarette out, offering one to Karen's father, who declined.

"Mr. Marshall, at this point we believe it's a case of mistaken identity. In the school there's another Karen; she's one year younger and is the daughter of a diplomat. Currently this man's working at a very high level on behalf of the U.N. towards peace in the Baltics. We're working on this assumption and believe when they find their mistake, Karen will be released."

He looked for a moment at the policeman, their eyes locking. "Or killed, officer, or killed."

The policeman shook his head. "We don't envisage that, Mr. Marshall. These people are extremists, yes, but the damage to their reputation in killing a young girl; I don't think so. We've also informed the ports and airlines in case they try to take her out of the country. Karen will not leave this country, I can guarantee that."

Just then a police officer came into the room and spoke

quietly to the officer in charge. He nodded his understanding and turned to Karen's father. "Have you ever heard of a Frank Whittle, Sir?"

"I have, but what's Frank Whittle got to do with Karen?"

The officer removed his book from his pocket to make notes then looked at Karen's father. "It would seem, Sir, that a girl called Susan James has mentioned this name a number of times; she kept saying you would know him. Perhaps under the circumstances you'd better explain."

He shrugged, trying to act indifferently. "There's not a lot to tell. Ten years ago I was leaving a sales meeting and there was an accident. Frank Whittle's daughter ran out of a shop with two of her friends: she never stopped at the kerb, but ran out on the road and under my car's wheels. To cut a long story short, I was breathalysed and the result was positive. Frank Whittle blamed me because of that, saying I'd murdered his child. Shortly after the court case, his wife, suffering from depression, committed suicide. Her death really shook him and for weeks he'd ring day and night, threatening to get even. Eventually I had an injunction placed against him. It was more for the safety of my children rather than myself. The man was a nuisance, yes, but I was also worried his hatred would spread to the family. Anyway, he stopped ringing and I heard nothing again, so I suppose the injunction worked."

The officer made notes and looked up. "As a matter of interest, how long has it been since hearing from this Whittle?"

"I don't know exactly, perhaps five years."

"And how old was his daughter when she died?"

Karen's father sat for a moment and suddenly put his hands to his head. "My God, she was Karen's age when she died, seventeen with only weeks before her eighteenth. You don't think he's been waiting all these years to take her from us at the same age as his daughter died, do you?"The officer glanced towards another stood by the door and nodded to him. That officer left the room quickly. He then looked back at Karen's father. "It would seem, Sir, in view of what you've told me, that it may not be a simple matter of mistaken identity but more a grudge abduction. Karen's in greater danger than we first thought. I suspect after what you've told me, the snatch was a very carefully planned action by this Whittle. What his intentions are can only be pure conjecture at this stage."

The room fell silent, everyone considering in their own minds the implications of what had been said. Suddenly the police officer stood. "We'll be in constant contact with you, Sir. I'll have the telephone line tapped and one of our officers will remain here. If you can think of anything out of the ordinary that might have happened in the last few days which may give us some sort of lead or clue, don't hesitate to call me."

With that he left the house and climbed into a waiting car alongside his assistant. "Anything come through yet?" he asked.

"Nothing, Sir, it's as if both the girl and this Frank Whittle have disappeared into thin air."

The senior officer nodded. "He'll emerge, believe me. It's Karen I'm worried about."

The other detective frowned, "Why's that, Sir?"

"Well, Frank Whittle wasn't afraid of leaving his name. In my book it can mean one of two things. One, he's intending to leave the country with or without the girl, if he's not already gone. Two, he hasn't given the right name and Frank Whittle's completely innocent. Either way the girl's life's in great danger."

They fell silent and the senior officer asked the driver to take them to the hospital. He'd decided it was important to interview Susan, now she'd regained consciousness, as to what really happened.

With the senior officers gone, Karen's father sat down alongside his wife. The remaining officer was stood some distance away when the telephone rang. The officer answered it.

"Get me Marshall," Frank demanded.

The officer asked his name. "Just get him, tell him it's about his precious daughter: he'll talk to me."

The officer handed Karen's father the telephone.

"Hello, this is Kevin Marshall here, who am I talking to?"

Frank leaned back in satisfaction. "Marshall, its Frank Whittle. Perhaps you remember my name? After all, it was you who killed my Sharon."

Kevin covered the handset and looked at the policeman standing there. "It's Whittle, how do you want me to play it?"

The policeman spoke quickly into his radio before looking back at Kevin. "They think it's a mobile; keep the man talking as long as possible and leave it to us. We will be able to locate the cell area at least."

Kevin nodded, at the same time he could hear Frank demanding a response. Kevin took a deep breath, trying to keep the panic out of his voice. "I suppose you want some sort of ransom for Karen... Whittle?"

Frank laughed. "Money... Money from you, Marshall? What are you offering? Perhaps a hundred quid, after all that's all they fined you after killing my Sharon? I don't want your money; in fact I want nothing from you except what I have... your daughter."

Kevin bit his lip; he wanted to strangle this man. "Hurt Karen, Whittle, and as God's my judge I'll come after you," he growled.

He could hear Frank laughing.

"I suppose you'll get drunk and try to run me down with

your car, will you? The same as you did to Sharon. Come off it, Marshall, apart from being a child killer, you're a wimp, a gold-edged wimp. Your daughter Karen's not going to die, that for her would be an easy cop-out. She's going to a living hell; everyday of her pathetic life she'll be raped and beaten, never knowing why. All because you, Marshall, hadn't the guts to tell her how you killed my daughter."

Kevin was boiling. "You bastard, Whittle, are you such a pathetic excuse of a man that you'd take our fight out on an innocent child? Why don't you just let her go and let's meet? Alone, if you want; then we'll sort this stupid vendetta out once and for all."

The phone went silent for a while then Frank spoke quietly. "It's too late, Marshall. Way, way too late. I suppose some years ago I'd have just done that, but you don't understand, do you? I lost my only daughter, my wife, my job, ending up on the street. I allowed your daughter Karen to grow to Sharon's age, allowed you to get the same attachment to her as I had to my Sharon. I've watched your daughter for years. In fact I probably know more about her life outside your house than you do. She's not a patch on my Sharon. My Sharon would never have worn skirts inches from her bottom. Neither would she wear clothes that showed all her stomach. Alongside Sharon, your Karen's a tramp," then, to add insult to injury, Frank sneered. "Besides, you probably don't even know your little girl's been sleeping around? But I suppose that's been fortunate, after all, at least she'll know what to do with her clients ten times a day, don't you agree, Marshall?"

Kevin cut in. "You're lying, Whittle, just as you lied about your daughter, Sharon. How you got people to tell the court that she was watching where she was going, when the truth was she ran out straight into the road, I don't know. Now you're at it again, still lying. Karen's a good girl, a lovely daughter; she's studious, swims for her school, goes to adventure club with me, does self-defence, and I'll tell you this, has had only one boyfriend in the last six months. Besides which, Karen's a child, and doesn't jump into bed with every man she sees as you claim. She's not a tramp, just an innocent pawn in your vendetta towards me."

The atmosphere between these men could be cut with a knife. Kevin desperately trying to keep Frank on the line to find out more of what he'd done with Karen. Frank, on the other hand, was enjoying hearing Kevin squirm under pressure.

"I'm going now, Marshall. I know what the next few years are going to do to you and your family and I relish it. It's your turn to live with the pain, the anguish of not knowing just what's happening to your little girl. Who's screwing her at night? If she's dead or alive? Get ready, Marshall, to face years of your wife blaming you for Karen's dilemma, the arguments, the pure hell of knowing what your drunken action has brought on your family and especially your daughter."

Kevin panicked. "Don't cut me off, Whittle; I want to know about Karen, what you've done to her, where she is?"

Frank laughed mockingly. "I suppose you do, Marshall, but that's for you to find out and me..." he stopped for a moment as if in thought. "Well, of course I know, don't I? I'll tell you this though; I've just stood and watched her get her first good strapping across that tight little bottom of hers. Spunky girl, trying to escape, but she's learning, Marshall, she's learning, believe me."

Kevin could hardly control himself. "You're sick, Whittle, tell me what's eating you? A man who claims so much love wouldn't take it out on a defenceless girl," he shouted down the line after finally breaking his composure, realising the man on the other side of the phone was not interested in his arguments to leave Karen out of it.

Frank sighed. "Well, for me, it no longer matters. She's

gone; I'm alone, my job done. Goodbye, Marshall, today is your first day, like Karen, to know what hell is all about. I have a small present for you though; it'll probably arrive in a couple of days, just a reminder of your daughter's secret life."

"Whittle! Whittle! Talk to me," Kevin shouted into the phone, but Frank had cut the line and all that came back was the dialling tone. Starting the engine, Frank pushed it into second gear. Then, carefully turning the car round, he headed off in the direction of the bay. Suddenly he swung the car onto the grass alongside the track and accelerated hard, forty, fifty, the car bumped and crashed over boulders but Frank didn't slow, just stared straight ahead as if in some sort of trance. Minutes later the car shot over the cliff, its engine screaming as the wheels lost traction. Then, as if in some cartoon sketch, the car stopped momentarily in space before falling like a stone onto the rocks below.

Chapter 4

Karen woke when someone shook her roughly. "Wake up, kid," someone shouted in her ear. She turned over, still half asleep, and saw Assam looking down at her.

"There's work to be done," he said, at the same time throwing her clothes on the bed.

She dressed quickly with what little she had, then stood quietly waiting for him to tell her where to go.

"Follow me," he shouted at her as he walked off down a corridor and into a kitchen-cum-canteen.

A man was stood at the stove, cigarette hanging from his mouth, mumbling away to himself. He turned, looked at her, then Assam. "Who's this?"

Assam pushed her forward. "Karen, she's a guest of ours for a short time. Feed her, then put her to work. Any trouble, call me."

The man looked back at Karen and then a smile came across his face. "Take a seat over there, do you want bacon?"

She nodded and moved quickly to the table. Assam picked a slice of bread from the table, then left, stuffing it into his mouth as he went.

The cook handed her a huge sandwich full of bacon and sat down opposite. "The name's Kenny, but everybody calls me Screwer round here. Have you no other clothes than those?"

She shook her head.

He sighed. "They're miserable bastards. Listen, Karen, leave it to me, I'll find you something. To walk around practically naked on this ship's asking for trouble."

She thanked him and he left the kitchen after placing a large mug of coffee on the table. Two minutes later two members of the crew came in, both were grubby and unkempt. One of them stared at her for a moment, grinned and then sat down at her side. "So what's your name, darling?" he asked, putting his arm round her.

She gave him a weak smile. "Karen, what's yours?" she replied indifferently, at the same time pushing his arm away.

He grinned impishly. "I'm Barry, that's Kevin. So where did you spring from, you certainly weren't here yesterday?"

Her face changed to a look of contempt. "Are you putting me on? I've been kidnapped, beaten and dumped on this bloody ship practically naked, and you're pretending that it's some bleeding cruise."

He held his hands up, the look on his face one of confusion. "Hey look, don't get heavy."

Karen was thinking quickly, could it be that this lad didn't know, or was he playing some game with her? She stood and turned her back to him pushing her knickers down a little and to one side. "Are those red marks patterns from the bloody chair? Believe me those are marks from a strap your kind captain decided to use after I objected to being bundled into a dinghy."

She pulled her knickers back and leaned against the wall, looking at one, then the other. They seemed stunned and unable to answer at first, then Kevin cut in. "If that's true, Karen, it's time we had a few words with the captain. Barry and I signed on in Liverpool, but I'm not into this kidnapping stuff."

Just then Screwer came back into the canteen. He seemed taken aback for a moment when he saw the other two. "What are you doing here, the captain would have your hides if he knew?"

Barry shrugged. "We came in for a cuppa, its bloody cold out there. Anyway, this girl claims the captain's kidnapped her, what do you think to that?"

Screwer grinned. "Load of fucking rubbish, she's having you on and you're stupid enough to believe her."

Barry glanced back at Karen. "Show him the marks, Karen."

She did as he asked and Screwer tried to make light of it. "Nice little bottom, girl, I wouldn't go round pulling your knickers down like that, someone just might take it the wrong way. Anyway, those are marks from the seat."

"Just call the police in England and see if I'm missing if you don't believe me?" Karen retorted.

Screwer moved closer to the crew, his voice low. "Leave it to me, lads, I'll see the captain; you're new around here and don't understand the ropes. Mind you, for your own safety, don't mention what you've seen or heard to anyone, and I mean anyone."

With this advice the two seemed unsure as to what to do now. They talked for a few moments then Barry turned to Screwer. "We'll leave it to you; after all, it's the captain's business, not ours."

He gave Karen a weak smile. "Sorry, kid, you're on your own with this," then they both left the room.

"You're stupid; do you want a good beating or what?" Screwer hissed.

She looked taken aback. "What do you mean, what I'm saying is the truth?"

He pushed her down onto the seat and settled down opposite. "Some of the crew don't know about you. If they go spouting to the captain, they'll be put over the side in the night. Believe me, you could have signed their death warrants. This bloody boat moves lots of people like you. It's the only way it can survive. Take my word, we all know what's going on, well the regulars do, and turn a blind eye. It's best that you keep quiet because your very own life's in the balance. There's no way off this tub, no white knight in shining armour, nothing. Shout too much and maybe you will disappear one night, no one's going to miss or notice you're gone. Even if they do they'll keep their mouths shut."

Tears began to form in her eyes. "So I allow them to sell me into slavery for the rest of my life because everybody is only interested in themselves and not prepared to help someone in need?"

He shrugged. "Put it that way, then yes, we will allow him, after all, we have families and they need feeding. You help feed them. Besides, one life's just like the rest, Karen. People adapt, even at home you could be rich, poor, beaten up everyday by some drunken husband. This way you've a chance. Play along and maybe someone will want you so much they'll take you home and give you a good life with children and all that. Otherwise you'll end up in a brothel, opening your legs ten times a day."

She rubbed her eyes. "I'd rather die," she whispered.

He held his hand out and touched her gently. "Death's too easy, and never comes without pain and distress."

He stood and then asked her to help with the dishes. For the next hour or so they said nothing. Karen was deep in thought, somehow she must gain the trust of the two crew members and at least they might call her parents and tell them where she was, or where she was going. Alternatively, they may help her to escape, but in the meantime, she would do as this cook asked and pretend she'd accepted his advice.

It was late when Assam returned. "All right, Screwer?"

Screwer nodded. "Yeh... she's worked well."

Then he turned to Karen. "Come," he demanded.

She followed without a word. Eventually they arrived at his cabin and Assam sank heavily into his chair. She stood, unsure what to say or do.

"Sit," he said pointing at a chair on the other side of his desk.

She sat quickly.

He leaned over to the side-table and switched on a television. The picture was grainy and breaking up but he ignored that and began fiddling with a video. Eventually a reasonable picture appeared. She was confused; they seemed to be watching the news. Suddenly her name was mentioned and Karen's ears pricked up.

"The whereabouts of Karen Marshall, a schoolgirl abducted in a bizarre set-up yesterday, has taken a turn for the worse." The announcer began. "Police have begun lifting the car, believed to be the one used in the abduction, from the sea. The man police were actively seeking in connection with Karen's abduction, Frank Whittle, was found by local fishermen at lunchtime today. The police estimate he'd been dead for at least ten hours. According to sources close to the investigation, police now believe both he and Karen were in the car that plunged two hundred feet over the cliff. Karen's body is not, I stress not, in the car, but the impact burst the doors and, like Mr. Whittle, they believe she was also thrown out. Locals tell us that the currents are very strong and she could be far out at sea or washed, like Mr. Whittle, further down the coast. We have also heard the search is now scaled down and no other persons are being sought in connection with the incident."

Assam stopped the video and switched the now hissing television off. "I recorded that news clip forty minutes ago as we left British waters."

With her head bowed, looking down at the floor and gripping her hands together, Karen was close to tears, not knowing how to reply.

"It would seem you're all but forgotten, Karen, from this day on I own you. I decide if you live or die; nobody else, just me."

She looked up at him and their eyes met. "So what are you going to do, kill me?"

He grinned, showing rows of shining teeth. "Do you want me to?"

Karen shrugged. "Whatever I said you'll do what you want, so why should I bother to answer? That's unless you want me on my knees, begging for my life? That I'll never do and, as you so bluntly put it, I have no life now."

The room fell silent except for the constant background noise of the engines often vibrating items about the room as the ship encountered the resistance of waves, making the engines work harder.

"You know," Assam began, "for a pretty girl like you, life may not be that bad. Plenty of men would want to be with you. So it's really up to you to make the most of what you've got. See it as a challenge and maybe, just maybe, one man will want you enough to think about a family life with you."

Karen sighed, 'The same words as the cook, do they really think I'm going to fall for it?' she thought to herself. Then she looked at him watching her. "You're saying the only choice I have for the rest of my life is to offer myself around like some prostitute, in the hope someone will take pity and want more than something to shag? You've got to be joking, I'd rather die."

Assam smiled. "I've had many girls sit there just like you, Karen, and say the very same words. Listen, sixty percent of women in the world don't get a choice. Many, even when they do, are treated like slaves, often beaten if they object. In your own country it's just as rife as any other. What makes you so special that you'll not dance to the tune? What makes you so certain you wouldn't make the wrong choice?"

She shrugged. "At least it'd be my choice."

He stood and made his way to the door. "Come on, it's time you were locked up for the night."

She followed and they walked along the side of the ship. Suddenly, Assam grabbed her arm and pulled her to the rail. Pushing her head forward over the side with one hand and grasping the back of her pants with the other, he forced her to look down into the dark and murky waters below.

"So you'd rather die, would you?" he shouted into her ear above the noise of the wind. "I'll tell you what; I'm a fair man, I've been paid, so I'll give you your chance to do just that. Mind you this time it won't be like the jump from my dinghy. This, Karen, is a bigger jump, miles from land with the water so cold, in less than an hour you'll be dead. It'll give you just enough time to think about your home, family or whatever else comes into your head before you die. So are you ready to jump?"

Karen stared down into the darkness; her body was shaking not only with the cold of the night, but in fear. He was offering her a get-out, a chance to escape, except it wasn't an escape, it was certain death and Karen didn't want to die like this, alone with a man who hated and despised her. But he was beginning to lift her bodily by her pants, pushing her forward and over the rail. She began to struggle, begging him to stop, at the same time grasping the rails tightly in her hands.

Then suddenly he stopped, and pulled her away from the side, his face inches from hers. "Then it was all talk, this wanting to die, was it? Given the choice you've decided to cling to life?"

She didn't reply.

"I told you, Karen," he screamed at her. "You answer immediately when I ask a question, or isn't your bottom sore enough yet?

"Yes, Sir, I'm sorry, Sir, I don't want the strap again. You're right. I was acting stupid and just saying it. I don't want to die," she answered instantly.

He stood for a moment, looking into her eyes. Through the tears forming he could see the terror he was instilling into the girl. Then, satisfied, he grasped her arm, moving her quickly down the ship and stopping at a hold.

"That's your sleeping quarters. Down the ladder and I'll be back in the morning."

She did as he asked but he stopped her, grabbing her arm just as she started to descend. "Think about what I've said tonight and what's just happened. Have no illusions, as far as I'm concerned, you're an investment. I've already been paid but could make a little more. Make the wrong decision, force me to beat you into submission and you're worth nothing. Perhaps then you'd get your wish."

She looked up at him and their eyes met. "What's that?" she asked.

"To die, what else did you think? Go home?"

Not replying, she climbed down the long steps.

Assam looked down into the gloom. "Choose death, kid, and don't, for one moment, believe it'll be quick. The lads are bound to pay for, shall I say, entertainment. That's until we get close to port, then I'm afraid it's a short swim for you. Mind you, with a few selected cuts to your body the sharks won't waste time in finding you."

He slammed the hatch closed and she heard the grating of bolts. Looking away from the entrance, Karen blinked in the gloom; her accommodation couldn't be much worse. The hold was lit with one bulkhead light surrounded by a wire frame. All around her were packing cases twice her height and two or three metres square. As the ship lurched in the swell, the cases creaked under the strain, giving a constant frightening sound above the noise of the engines. In a corner a camp bed had been laid out with blankets thrown on top. Alongside was a portable toilet, a small table and on top, a tin cup and flask.

She went to the bed, pulled the blankets straight, then climbed inside. The day had been bearable, the work very little. After the first encounter with the two crew members, the cook had kept her away from others coming in to eat. At the same time he warned her not to talk to other crew members about her problems. Assam had lots of eyes and ears, so almost certainly he would hear about it. However, after the conversation and news report in Assam's room, followed by the incident on deck, her confidence was at an all-time low. She couldn't help feeling that what had already happened would be nothing to what the future held for her.

Chapter 5

The following two days were the same; working again in the kitchen, with Garrett coming at the end of the day and taking her back to the hold. However, this time Assam collected her in the early evening and took her back to his cabin.

"There's a shower through there," nodding towards a door, "when you're finished I want to talk to you. We've many things to sort out."

She thanked him, asking if he had a toothbrush.

He pulled open a drawer to his desk, handing her an old used one. "I've no toothpaste," he commented.

"I'll use salt if you have any, my mother always used salt, she swore by it," Karen replied.

He removed a small salt-cellar from his cupboard, passing it her. Just as she was going into the bathroom he called her back.

"The bottom drawer of that chest, Karen," he said pointing at a chest in the corner of his cabin. "Open it, will you? You'll find a brown bag with clothes inside. Put them on after your shower then rinse what you're wearing in the hand bowl."

Within seconds she was standing under the warm cascade of water. It felt good. With working in the kitchen, her hair was full of grease, her body smelling. Quickly drying herself, she opened the bag, but her heart sank. Inside was a pair of knickers so tiny they would hardly cover her, a short-sleeved blouse which tied with a knot at the front, and tight silk shorts. Dressing quickly, she stood for a moment in front of the mirror, combing her hair. Dressed this way she felt decidedly uncomfortable, but with these or nothing, there was no option but to wear them. Going back into the cabin, Assam looked her up and down. "You're looking better; I've a drink here for you."

She thanked him and sipped it slowly. The liquid caught her throat and she began coughing. The drink was neat vodka. "May I have some water with it please, it's too strong like this, I'll be sick?" she gasped.

He pushed a jug of water over to her. "I forgot you're a landlubber, sailors don't water their drinks. What do you think of the clothes then?"

She looked at him for a moment before answering, not wanting to dissuade him from giving her extra clothes. The knickers and t-shirt she'd worn since arriving on the ship were dirty and were clinging, leaving little to the imagination.

"I like the blouse, it's really cool, but the shorts are a bit small for me. I hope you don't want me to wear this outfit in the kitchen tomorrow because they'd be ruined?"

"No, I've found you a pair of jeans and a jumper. The cook was saying you're distracting the crew too much, dressed as you are. He can't get them back out to work," Assam replied, trying to make light of the conversation.

She breathed a sigh of relief. 'Thank God,' she thought. By now she'd drunk nearly a whole glass and Assam filled it again.

He lit a cigarette. "I suppose you've had thoughts about your comments and your desire to die, rather than live, like I propose?"

Karen looked a bit sheepish. "I was perhaps a bit hasty, I really don't want to die but I do desperately want to go home. Can't you at least call my dad? He's bound to come to some sort of deal where you could make money."

Assam took a large gulp of his own drink then leaned back. "You know, you confuse me. Your portrayal of the little schoolgirl at home with mummy and daddy doesn't ring true. How about you clear a few things up before I give you an answer?"

"Like what?" she asked.

He smiled then drew a packet of cigarettes out of his pocket, before lighting one slowly. "I'm a simple man, Karen. I'll ask the questions, you answer and then, perhaps later, I'll answer some of yours."

She shrugged. "If you want, I've all night. In fact I've all my life according to you."

A flicker of a smile crossed his face. "We'll see, Karen, we'll see. Anyway let's see how it goes shall we? Did you have a boyfriend?" he asked indifferently.

She grinned. "Yes, but why do you want to know about him?"

"I said I'll ask, you answer. So what about dancing, did you go to many dance clubs?"

"Of course I did. How many girls of my age don't?"

"You like to dance then?"

She nodded enthusiastically.

"How old was your boyfriend, did he go dancing with you as well?"

She shook her head. "I'd go with my girlfriends. Grant, my boyfriend, is twenty-one and wouldn't be seen dead in the discos we go to."

Assam pretended to look concerned. "If he wouldn't go dancing, which you say you loved doing, why did you stay with him?"

"Why not?" she asked, "it's really cool to have somebody of that age who wants to go out with you, besides, my friends were really jealous," She sniggered. "Their boyfriends were from the boys' school; had no money to take them out and more often than not they'd just hang round the streets, while Grant told me when he got a weekend off, he'd take me to some really expensive place." She frowned, adding a sigh. "He hasn't taken me as yet, you see he works late at weekends and I could only stay out on Saturdays till eleven. The rest of the week I'd loads of homework, or when I did get out, I'd have to be in for ten. Mind you, that will change in July when I leave school. You see we're getting engaged... or," she hesitated, "we would have done."

Assam smiled to himself, the drink was relaxing her; she was moving closer into his trap. "Let's not go down that route, Karen. But this guy interests me, lads at that age, taking young girls out, are more demanding, aren't they? They wouldn't be interested in just holding hands. Wouldn't they expect more?"

She looked confused. "How do you mean, more?" she asked.

He said nothing for a minute, watching her sip the drink. "I suppose I'm saying, what have you to offer him as a girlfriend? You've said it was difficult to go out in the week and he wasn't really available at weekends. Where was this relationship going?"

Karen grinned mischievously. "I didn't say we never saw each other in the week. We did... you see Grant would pick me up from school at least three times a week."

Assam nodded, as if understanding. "But wouldn't he feel a bit stupid walking home with a girl wearing a school uniform? All his friends would rib him for cradle-snatching."

By now Karen was feeling decidedly tipsy, beginning to giggle. "Grant liked me in my uniform; actually he preferred my skirt shorter. So I'd turn the waist over a couple of times. That shortened it a few inches. My mum would have gone mad if she'd known, so I only did it after leaving school and when I was meeting Grant. It was a little short though; I always had trouble not showing my knickers when I sat down."

Assam pretended to laugh. "You mean he's a bit kinky and liked to see your knickers?" he teased.

She looked indignant. "No, Grant loved me. He just said I had nice legs and should show them off."

"How do you know he loved you?"

"He told me loads of times."

Assam lit another cigarette and leaned back. Karen had taken the opportunity to drink more of the vodka, even though she already felt light-headed.

"So this boyfriend, who kept saying he was in love with you, would hang about outside the school. Then he'd walk you home, or did you go somewhere else?"

Karen frowned. "I don't understand what you're getting at, we never walked, he'd a car and always took me to his flat."

"Why always to his flat, Karen? Surely you could have gone to a cafe bar or some other place; after all, he never took you out at night?"

She shifted uneasily; Assam knew he'd hit a nerve.

"How could I go to a bar in my school uniform? They'd throw me out. Anyway, the flat gave us some privacy, we could talk and things."

Assam smiled, he had her now. "Could it be he took you to his flat for sex? After all, the modern generation consider sex as part of a relationship."

She fell silent, not wanting to reply.

"Come on, Karen, it's a simple enough question."

Karen knew it was, but didn't want to answer, so she decided to play it down. "You're trying to say he only wanted me for what he could get. Grant loved me, I loved him and we wanted to be together. We'd go to his flat, yes, but only to play CDs or have a coffee before I'd have to go home."

Assam took another long drag of his cigarette. "But he was a man, Karen, and men take their girlfriends to bed. You're not suggesting he was content just to drink coffee and play records? That will not wash, believe me."

She remained silent, not wanting to go down that path.

"Answer, Karen, I want answers immediately, or it's the strap. Did this man take you to bed or didn't he?" Assam shouted.

"Yes! Yes, for God's sake. We made love, was it so wrong? I wanted to as well, you know. It wasn't Grant; it was my idea, my idea alone. Grant never pushed me; in fact all he wanted was for us to be together. Are you satisfied now?" Karen retorted.

Assam fell back on his seat, stuffing the tip of the cigarette into the ashtray, immediately lighting another.

"Shit, Karen, you didn't want to go to bed with Grant, did you? It was Grant that sowed the seed. Was he going to dump you if you said no? Made out that if you wanted to be treated like an adult you'd got to play adult games? It's a ploy as old as the hills and you kids fall for it every time."

His words stunned her. How did he know Grant wanted to finish? How did he know she'd begged him not to finish with her and said she'd do anything for him?

Assam sighed; he knew he'd hit the right chord now. "I'm waiting for an answer, Karen."

She didn't really want to admit it, so just nodded her head in agreement. The room fell silent; Assam continued to draw on the cigarette, all the time watching her for any reaction.

"What did he like to do then?" Assam finally asked.

Her eyes avoided his. "Grant loved me, what went on between us is private," she replied.

Assam leaned forward, grasping her shoulders, forcing her to look directly at him. "No, Karen, try to understand, from now on nothing that's ever happened in your life's private anymore. I want to know everything that man did to you. I want to know your innermost secrets, your thoughts," he stopped, allowing it to sink in.

"But why, why do you want to know?" she demanded.

He stood and walked around the desk to stand behind her. Karen never moved, terrified he was going to use the belt on her again. However, Assam intended to show her the relationship was just the sordid love affair which he knew it was.

He leaned down; his head close to her ear. "I want to know, Karen," he whispered. "I don't need to give you any reason, but soon you'll understand."

Then he took her hand, urging her to stand and face him. Now inches from her face he grinned. "So was it on the couch, with that short skirt pushed up and the knickers at your feet?" Then he turned her to face the desk, standing behind her, his mouth close to her ear. "Or was it when you were making all that coffee you drank? He'd come up behind you like this and push you face down on the table and take you from behind? Perhaps even make you wear kinky leather gear or handcuff you to the bed?"

Karen's head was spinning not only with the drink, but his words so close to the truth. She raised her hands to her head, blocking her ears. "Stop! Stop, it wasn't like that, I told you he loved me. Grant was gentle, caring. We'd little time; I needed to be home to make the tea in the week."

She stopped, tears were running down her face but Assam urged her on.

"I was doing my exams and had to study at home so I could only get out at weekends and like I said before, he worked. All the time I was torn between Grant and home. I'd have lost him if I'd not agreed. So he'd pick me up in his car and the thirty minutes it normally took to walk home or if I got an afternoon off for study, we'd spend together."

Assam sighed and returned to his seat, telling her to do the same.

"At last, Karen, we're getting the truth. So let's cut the crap and get to the point. What did he have you do on these quick, half hour or so, visits?"

Karen went silent; she'd decided this man was some sort of pervert. Perhaps he liked to talk dirty, got his kicks that way? Should she play his game or leave it at that? She wasn't sure, except if she refused to talk there was always the risk of him using the belt on her again.

"Well, I'm waiting."

She shrugged. "It depended on what time we had and I did tell the truth; often we only had time for coffee. Other times he'd want to take me to bed and we'd make love."

Assam smiled. "That wasn't too difficult, was it, Karen? I think we'll leave your explanation of what you got up to for a few minutes and talk about the other side of Grant Martin."

Karen looked confused. "My Grant isn't Martin, its Johnson."

Assam never replied but pulled open a drawer in the desk and lifted out a large bulky envelope. Karen recognised it as the envelope Frank had given him. She decided it was best not to mention it, so she just watched as he drew out a sheet of paper with a photograph which he placed in front of her on the desk. "Grant Martin, or, as you knew him, Grant Johnson. Is that your Grant in the photo?"

Karen nodded, still bemused with the two names.

Assam continued. "Aged twenty-nine, married with two children, lives in Harlow, Essex, part time barman and other times acts as an escort to people who pay for the privilege."

Karen stared at him, her mouth partly open, unable to reply.

Assam read on. "Hired by a Frank Whittle, he was instructed to attend a wedding in September last year. Am I still on track, Karen?"

"Yes," she whispered.

Assam smiled and looked back at the paper. "Frank Whittle had given explicit instructions for him to meet a girl named Karen Marshall, aged seventeen. He was to spill wine on her then, full of remorse, offer to pay for the cleaning. He was then to deliver it cleaned, to her house, between the hours of four and five thirty, so as not to meet the parents.

Are we still with it, Karen?"

She nodded, stunned at his words. It was as if he'd been there.

"I presume that's how the relationship began, is it? He asked you out and you accepted."

Karen was looking down at her hands, unable to answer. This man was talking about someone she loved, a chance meeting, not as he made out, that it had all been a set-up.

"It's all a lie," she blurted out. "Grant's not married, he can't be. I agree he did spill wine over me and he did come round to my house to collect the stained clothes, besides bring them back a couple of days later. That's when he asked me out. But anyone in my class could have told you that. They all thought it romantic. As for twenty-nine and married; my Grant's twenty-one and single."

He smiled softly. "Shall I go on then?"

Karen nodded slowly, frightened by what he may still reveal.

"The instructions were to bed the girl as soon as possible. Push her to the limit and be dominant if she said no. In other words he was to teach you all about sex and I'm not on about the sex between married couples. He was also to make sure you were seen with him, dressed in your school uniform. There's also a date when he was to take you to the park with him."

Karen wanted to scream, tell him it all wasn't true, but everything he'd described was as it happened.

Assam looked up at her again. "So now we've established this Grant is not what he seems, Karen, perhaps you can tell me just what went on between you two?"

By now she was becoming disillusioned. Every second he was shattering her dreams. However, she wasn't going to fall into any more traps and she remained steadfastly silent. He pulled out another photo from the envelope and handed it her. She looked at it, stunned. Photographed in what looked like a zoo, two children were leaning over, throwing bread to ducks. Her Grant was stood alongside a woman in her twenties, he was holding her hand. They were all obviously together.

"I don't understand, Grant loved me, we were to be married. Maybe he was divorced from this woman and hadn't told me," she whispered, trying to clutch at straws, tears running down her cheeks.

Assam threw another photo down in front of her. "I presume the girl kissing Grant is you?"

She stared at it for some time. She'd been photographed by someone in the park next to the school. Even at her five foot eight, Grant, over six foot, meant she was on tiptoes kissing him. Karen was wearing her school uniform and she could see the reason he'd asked for the shortened skirt. In the photo Grant's hand was grasping her skirt, exposing the knickers that he'd always insisted she wore, leaving little to the imagination.

"Good photo, Karen, but not exactly school approved underclothes, where did they come from?"

She turned her head away, not wanting to look at him directly, and her voice was low. "Grant bought them for me; he said the school ones must have been designed by some deranged spinster. We both laughed so I always changed in the toilets before we met, but when I shortened my skirt I didn't realise it was that bad."

Assam leaned back and smiled, the girl was slowly falling apart. Gone now was the self-confidence, the arrogance. All her dreams of Grant wanting to marry her were gone, but Assam was close to shattering her illusions completely.

"You know it's like pulling teeth with you, Karen. We've now got a so-called boyfriend who buys you silk knickers, has you shorten the skirt and yet is content to play happy families in his flat. Oh, let's not forget he's really married and is being paid to seduce you."

Then he laid, on the desk, a number of photos. They were professionally taken and Karen looked stunning in them.

"These are nice, but expensive I would think, who took these?" Assam asked.

She picked the photos up and looked at them for a moment; then she smiled, relived he'd gone off the subject of Grant. "I won a competition, well not really a competition, more a raffle sort of thing. It was at the shopping centre and a man was handing cards out with numbers on to all the girls. You just had to check in their shop later to see if your number was in the window. The prize was a professional photo. Anyway, when we checked later one of the numbers was mine, but the photographer was so taken with me, as a photo model that is, he took more than the one."

Assam was looking at a receipt attached to the negatives. "Yes, Karen, it would seem he was, except perhaps the two hundred and fifty pounds paid to the studio might have had a little to do with you winning, besides the extra photos, don't you think?"

She frowned. "Why would anyone do that? After all, it couldn't have been Grant, he never got one?"

"Maybe it wasn't a competition? Or if it was only you in it, rather than Grant pay, it was your friend, Frank Whittle, who paid? Could it have been for him to obtain photos of you to send to potential buyers, Karen? Mind you, I'd have been surprised if the studio took these as well," he replied, at the same time pushing a number of other photos in front of her.

Her mouth dropped open. The photos were of her naked, sprawled on a bed. It left nothing to the imagination.

"I think perhaps an explanation for those photos is also

required?" Assam said quietly, throwing at least twenty similar photos showing her posing naked in different positions, all but one, in the same flat.

Karen felt decidedly embarrassed and close to tears; Grant had promised they'd be destroyed and yet this man had every one, some she'd not even known about. She picked the drink up and sipped it again, the alcohol no longer had an effect and she felt completely sober.

"Talk," Assam pushed, "or feel the strap."

Never looking directly at him, she began the explanation. "Grant wanted a photo for the side of his bed. Said he missed me when I wasn't there and with a photo he could look at me any time. I was flattered and brought a snapshot from the family album the next day. It'd been taken on holiday. I was wearing a bikini, so I thought it would be nice for him, but Grant didn't want it, he wanted a more intimate photo. After badgering me for a few days and saying he'd use a digital camera so there'd be no film to go to the chemist to be developed, I finally agreed. One Saturday, when I was supposed to be going to town for some new clothes, I went to his flat. He started making love before I'd even got through the door, and then afterwards produced his camera. I really tried to look sexy for him, but I was frightened and couldn't relax. He stormed out of the flat and I followed. We were driving round. I found myself apologising, telling him I'd no idea how to pose and he could try again if he wanted. In some ways I was embarrassed, but all the time he kept saying how much he loved me and how we should get married, so I just wanted to please him."

Assam had listened without interruption. He now had her doubting the boyfriend's sincerity; soon she'd be in the position to accept his own plans for her. "So when was that taken?" he asked, pointing at a photo of her naked, but outdoors.

Karen looked sheepish. "It was the following Tuesday,

I'd a study afternoon off. He'd picked me up from school and because the sun was shining, instead of going to the flat, we drove out to Duran Woods. Anyway, he stopped the car in the picnic area and we went for a walk in the woods. He seemed to know where he was going and I was happy he'd got over the photo argument and still wanted me to be with me. In a clearing there was this fallen tree and he sat down, I sat on his knee. We began kissing, then he pulled his camera from his pocket, telling me he'd been thinking and this was where he wanted his special photo to be taken. I was stunned he was suggesting I took my clothes off in public and refused, telling him somebody would come and catch me naked, but he insisted it'd only take less than two minutes and there was nobody about. He kept at me, threatening this time he really would walk away if I was that prudish. I didn't want him to leave me, so eventually I relented and quickly removed my clothes. Then he kept making me pose in different positions until he found the one he wanted. It was taking ages and I was terrified someone would come. I was sure he'd messed about and delayed taking the photo on purpose, perhaps hoping someone would come, catch me naked, and I'd be really embarrassed then? After this I'd had enough and told him if he didn't treat me better, we were finished. He held me tight and apologised, said he'd problems in his life and we'd talk about it on the Saturday. He even talked about getting engaged."

"So what happened after that?" Assam asked.

By now Karen had no fight left in her. Every time she tried to make out the love affair was romantic, which she knew deep down towards the end it wasn't, the more Assam shattered her illusions. In some ways it felt better to tell somebody, anybody. The affair had been taking its toll, one moment studying for exams, the next coping with the ever increasing demands of Grant, so she decided to tell Assam just what had been going on.

"After the photos and two weeks before I was abducted, Grant had become more demanding; every time we got to the flat all he'd want to do was make love. I thought we'd sorted out our problems and I was really looking forward to taking him to meet my mum and dad. We'd agreed to get married but his unusual persistence in wanting to make love all the time was getting too much, what with exams and everything else in my life, so I began to refuse his advances. It wasn't that I didn't want him, I did, but I couldn't cope. He was getting more and more annoyed with my refusals and started to become very rough with me. My visions of love, of being swept off my feet and carried to the bedroom on my wedding night, were falling apart. Everything was becoming sordid and ugly. One time he even suggested we did it in the lift, but I wouldn't. He was often so rough I was afraid he'd rip my school clothes, so once I changed at school into my jeans. He went mad, telling me never to do it again."

She fell silent, hoping it was enough, but Assam wanted to push it in her face.

"Not a nice man, this Grant, was he? In fact I'd go as far as to say he's made a bloody fool of you."

She said nothing. In reality she'd known it all along, but it was like being grown up making love to an older man. She felt superior to other girls who could only dream or giggle about sex; she'd never dared to tell them the real truth.

"I suppose," she muttered.

Assam lit another cigarette and took a long draw before talking. "I've some more bad news for you, Karen."

She looked at him, tears coming into her eyes, not really able to take much more.

He smiled to himself, Assam wanted her like this. He wanted her so low that she'd agree to anything, so he hit her hard with his words.

"By now, your parents will have the copies of everything

in front of you, unfortunately so will the papers. They will also have a copy of this video," he said, at the same time pushing it towards her. "It's you and him playing about on his bed. I don't suppose you would like to see it? So it would seem this Frank Whittle was out to get you. His plan, not only to have you abducted, but to ensure your parents felt disgust with their little girl's sexual escapades while they were at work. However, Frank also wanted you to experience life; be sexually aware, even, might I say, experienced, very experienced."

Karen stared at the photos, tears trickling down her cheeks. Grant had promised they'd all been destroyed, she'd even seen him delete the photos on the computer. All the time he'd tricked her and these were the proof of their wild relationship. His constant talk of marriage meaningless, all he'd done was to destroy her life, her reputation.

"So do you still want to go home?" Assam asked with a hint of malice.

She remained staring at the table. "What to? My life's finished, I couldn't look my mum and dad in the face, let alone my friends," she whispered.

Assam stood and walked round to her, placing his hand on her shoulder. "Welcome to your new life, Karen," he said softly. "Now I'd like you to watch a video."

She looked up at him, fear on her face. "Not of me?" she stuttered.

"No, not this time. I might let you see it one day but this is a video of your future, so watch and learn."

The television flickered into life and Karen watched in silence. It was a club type of environment; the girls wore very little and danced seductively around a pole. As a man entered, one girl would break away, talk to him for a few minutes, and then they'd leave and go through a small door. The next part showed a girl dancing in front of a man, removing her clothes slowly and, when naked, first sitting on his knee allowing the man to kiss her, before she moved astride him, simulating intercourse and allowing him more fondling, before moving away as the music stopped. Assam, by the time it ended, had returned to his chair and lit a cigarette.

"It's as simple as that, Karen. I want you to watch that video every night, practise the movements and then I want you ready to perform that with me."

She stared at him, appalled. "It's disgusting, what do you think I am?" she demanded.

He leaned forward only inches from her face. "I know what you are, Karen," he shouted. "It's in the bloody photos spread on the table. It's in the actions you performed three or four times a week for a man twice your age. You're not a naive schoolgirl taken from her parents. Perhaps if you were I might have called your dad, after all, I've been paid and the person who'd arranged it all is dead, but you're not. You left your naiveté in that flat, along with your so-called 'it's disgusting' attitude when you allowed this man to take you in every position he could think of."

Karen cut in. "But I was in love, he was my boyfriend and we were going to marry," she protested.

Assam nodded his head up and down. "Yes, Karen, claim what you will, bury your head in the sand with the excuse he loved you, but even you weren't that stupid. You liked the excitement. You enjoyed the dominance of this man but more importantly, you liked sex. The superiority of doing what you were doing over the other girls at school. If you hadn't, you'd have screamed rape from the rooftop, but you didn't. So is there a need for us to sit and watch the video of you and him enjoying his type of sex, not as you say, yours?"

She never replied, but shook her head before lowering it in shame. What could she say? He might be right, but still in her mind what she did was in the privacy of Grant's flat, not in public, and should have been their secret.

Assam cut in again. "You're an attractive and sexually experienced young girl, Karen. The man who's coming for you will pay good money for a lap dancer of your age. Let me down and so help me, I'll cut you up so badly even a sewer rat wouldn't want you."

Karen sat for a moment then gave a shrug. The man in front of her had won; she, by her own admission, was already a whore. How it had all gone wrong, she'd no idea, but the thought of him using a knife on her face terrified her. She needed to think, to get her life in perspective but this moment wasn't the time to deny him. "I've been a fool, haven't I?" she began. "I'd never been out with a man, just lads larking about before Grant. I didn't understand what he was having me do, at the time it seemed right, a laugh, but it wasn't and I can see that now. But I believed he loved me... and what I was doing was pleasing my man."

Assam banged the table to shut her up. "Cut this hard-done-to story, Karen. Within two weeks you dance or I carve that face of yours."

She shook her head. "I'll do it and I won't let you down. Besides, I've no intention of living a life disfigured just for the sake of not taking my clothes off. Like you say, I've done it often enough."

Assam grinned. He'd trapped her perfectly and she'd fetch a lot of money. Without this evidence a girl like her would need beating into submission; however, strap marks on a body would be of no value to these buyers.

"Do you mind if I go to bed now, I feel sick? Tomorrow I'll start practising if that's soon enough for you?" she asked.

Assam stood and walked to the door. "Come on then. The television will be put in the hold, I'll be otherwise engaged so won't be seeing you again. That is, until you perform in front of me."

Karen followed in silence, before climbing down the long ladder into the hold. Assam looked over the edge. "You'll find jeans and tops on your bed. Also, to go with what you're wearing now, are stockings and shoes. I want the lot, as in the video, Karen, and it'd better be good. Good enough for me to want to screw you. You'll be doing well if you can achieve that because, unlike you, I'm fussy who I screw. Goodnight, don't have nightmares." He laughed and slammed the hatch closed. She stood shivering in the gloom, and then suddenly felt sick. The next few minutes she retched over the toilet before returning to sit on the bed, ashamed of what she'd done. It had always been her secret. Now, with her family knowing, the papers probably splashing it across the front pages, what for her, began as love, a willingness to please her man, would be seen as some sordid sex act between a young girl and a married man. That she couldn't take, she wanted to crawl under a stone and die.

Chapter 6

While Karen worked in the kitchen she heard the crew talking about two other girls who were on the ship, but she'd seen no sign of them. Once Barry, who'd she seen on the first day in the kitchen, was sitting having his breakfast, when cook slipped out to go to the toilet. She'd taken that opportunity to ask Barry if he'd come and talk to her in the hold some time; he'd promised he would, but he'd never turned up. Karen was disappointed, she'd hoped he'd at least come and talk to her.

It had been days since her meeting with Assam. Garrett had taken it on to escort her back to the hold from the kitchen, after allowing her to take a shower each night. She'd sit for hours alone, depression setting in at the hopelessness of her situation. The practising had been simple; the other girls, in Karen's view, were pathetic. Soon she had the routine perfected and it gave her the confidence to be able to face Assam without fear. As for him threatening to screw her when she'd finished, even that she wasn't bothered about, confident anything Assam demanded of her she'd be able to cope with, just so long as he didn't disfigure her. After Garrett slammed the hatch shut and she'd lain down on the bed as usual, Karen sensed someone else was in the hold with her.

She sat up alert. "Who's there?" she called.

Barry appeared from behind a crate. "Shush, keep the noise down, someone might hear," he said quietly.

Karen smiled, relief written all over her face. "Thanks for coming. You won't get into trouble, will you?"

He shrugged. "No, I can get in this hold from the other one through a watertight door. It's empty so it's not locked and the watertight door can only be opened from the other side. Anyway, I've pulled it closed just off the catches. They'll never know I've been here. So what do you want?"

She looked him in the eyes, tears forming slowly. "I just want to go home. Will you help me?"

He shrugged. "What can I do?" he asked.

"You could call the police, if not them, your family and ask them to call for you, anything, so long as the police know I'm still alive and where I am. It's not a lot to ask."

He walked over to the bed and sat down at her side. "I could I suppose, but it's a hell of a risk. If Assam knew, he'd kill me."

She took his hand, gripping it hard. "Nobody would know, Barry. Ask them to tell Customs that the ship's full of drugs. They could then just do a general search and find me. Please, Barry, say you'll do it."

She waited, holding her breath for his response.

"I'll think about it, Karen, but I've a couple of hours to kill, how about us talking for a while?"

"What do you want to talk about?" she asked.

He kept hold of her hand, not letting her pull away. "There's a rumour that you're some girl. It seems you do posing in the nude and other things."

She snatched her hand away and glared at him. "I don't do anything of the sort. I'm seventeen for God's sake. A schoolgirl!"

Barry looked at her. "That maybe, Karen, but you're also a very attractive schoolgirl and I bet you've had a string of boyfriends."

Karen shrugged. "I did have a boyfriend but we've split up. Anyway are you going to help or not?"

He grinned. "More to the point, Karen, what are you going to do for me? After all, you want freedom, I want a woman."

She tried to look indignant. "You've got it all wrong, Barry. I've never posed nude or even made love and I've no intention of doing either," she lied.

He stood up, shrugging. "Okay, have it your way. I came to help; the risks are enormous, but if you're just on the take and giving nothing in return, so to speak, I'm out of here."

As he moved away she sat there, panic setting in. This man was the only chance she had of escape and she'd thrown it away. Then an idea began to form in her mind, with a little effort she might turn things her way.

"What do you expect of me?" she called.

He turned and looked back. "I'd expected you'd be grateful I want to help. Grateful enough to the point that you'd want to cement the deal, so to speak?"

Karen laughed. "Oh, I see; the truth is, it's fuck me and my problems, just screw me and go."

He looked away and began kicking at the bottom of one of the packing cases. "That's a bit harsh, you asked for the help, not me. There are a couple of other girls knocking around but I've no chance with them, they're booked up solid. I've been on this bloody ship for ages and I feel horny, so take it or leave it," he laughed, expecting her to say yes.

Karen looked interested. "Who are these other girls then?"

Barry wasn't inclined to change the subject, so he scowled at her. "They're just a couple of hookers that's all. So are you prepared to take your knickers off or not?"

She remained silent for a moment, keeping him guessing. She now had a plan but would it work? "Tell you what, come and sit down on the chair and I'll make you a proposition," she finally said.

Barry's eyes lit up; the girl was desperate and he could see a fun hour or so coming up. Sitting on the chair as she'd asked, he waited for her proposal.

"Here's the deal," she said shyly.

"Go on," he urged.

"Get me help and I promise you can have me for the

night. That means, Barry, from dusk to dawn. I'll do anything for you, no matter what. Think about it, Barry, I'm seventeen and never been with a man. You'd be getting a virgin and a very grateful girl prepared to play and experiment. How's that for an offer?"

His eyes opened so wide she thought they'd fall out. "You mean it, Karen? You'd really spend the night with me and play out all my fantasies?"

She moved closer and kissed him on the lips gently. "Every word, Barry, besides your fantasies, I've a few myself I'd like to try. I promise it'll be a night to remember."

He sat there for some time without replying. He'd never had an offer like that and it'd be quite easy to telephone home. The ship had satellite communication and he'd already phoned home twice.

"Okay let's do it, get your clothes off," he demanded.

Karen laughed. "Not now, silly, when you've called home for me. Like you say, you've only a couple of hours now, I'm offering a night."

He looked despondent but Karen wasn't finished with him yet. "While you think about my offer, I'm going to give you a taste of just what I can do. We've got Sky at home and when my mum and dad went out once I tuned into a sex channel. My dad watched them when we go to bed, my mum didn't know but my sister and I did."

"What sort of taster?" Barry asked with interest.

She grinned. "I think I can copy what was on telly; you know what a lap dance is? You have to sit on your hands and promise you won't touch. I'm really scared though, so if you don't keep your promise not to touch me, I'm finished and the deal's off."

Barry quickly sat on his hands as she'd asked. "Okay, Karen, I agree, but it had better be good."

She frowned. "I'll do my best, Barry; I'm not a dancer you know, so all I ask is that you call home for me."

"Stop talking and get on. It's the all-night one I'm really looking forward to," Barry replied quickly.

"Okay, but close your eyes till I'm ready then," she said.

Karen went to the bed and got out of the clothes Assam had given her. Stripping quickly, she pulled the tiny knickers on, followed by the shorts and fastened the blouse. With the high-heeled shoes he'd also left, she knew Barry would be stunned. Taking a look at him with his eyes closed, as she clipped her hair back, a smile came across her face. She'd no intention of keeping her promise as the thought of making out with him made her retch, but someone needed to know she was still alive and, if it meant doing a stupid dance, as opposed to him screwing her, so be it.

"Okay, open your eyes."

He opened them and stared at her in astonishment. "Where did you get the clothes from?" he asked.

She tried to shrug it off. "They were in a box in the hold with other clothes. I think they've used this hold before for girls and they'd just been left. Anyway, let's get on with the dance shall we? Don't move your hands though, that's our deal, otherwise I stop and it's all off. I'm scared enough as it is," she lied.

Careful to turn the television picture right down and only the sound up, Karen pressed the play button on the video. She'd decided, with luck, he'd think it was a record. When the music began, Karen stood in front of him for a moment, her eyes locked on his never wavering. Then she began to sway to the music, rubbing her hands gently over her body, before slowly unfastening the loose knot on the blouse. Allowing it to fall to the floor, she carried on moving her hands slowly up her body, exaggerating the movements, moving her hips provocatively as she raised her hands above her head, clasping them together. Then her hands broke apart, slipping slowly back down, pausing over her breasts and pushing them forward, before moving down to the top of her shorts. Barry could only sit there mesmerised, his mouth dropping open. Slowly, but deliberately, she unfastened the side buttons of the shorts, before turning her back on him while she wriggled the shorts free from her hips, allowing them to drop to her feet. Barry couldn't tear his eyes away from her. She turned round and could see him becoming more excited by the second. Then she moved closer to him, sitting on his lap and pulling his head forward against her chest, allowing him to kiss her breasts. She pushed him back and stood, before sitting back down facing him, this time her legs astride his, pushing herself close, moving back and forth, pretending intercourse, before finally kissing him hard. She could feel the hardness in his jeans and smiled to herself. He was hooked. Suddenly she stopped as the music finished and moved away, replacing her blouse and shorts.

Then, with a little girl look and soft voice, she whispered. "Was it alright, I was so nervous that you were going to laugh? You turned me on so much, I want you, Barry, believe me, I want you."

He was shaking. "God, Karen, that was fantastic. Please, I'll do anything, but you can't stop now, you've really turned me on as well," he begged.

She smiled. "That's it, Barry. Like you, I want to do more, but a promise is a promise. So get me out and I'll do that dance as your opener; but when I finish then, not like now with my knickers on, I'll be naked and ready to make love."

"I will, Karen, you can be sure of that," he stuttered, still overawed with this girl's actions.

He stood and she moved closer, kissing him gently on the lips. "Don't let me down, will you?"

He held her tight, moving his hands down her back, slipping inside her knickers and grasping her bottom. Karen let him, for her it was like sealing the deal, but after a few moments she pushed him away gently. "No more please, or I won't be able to stop. Remember your promise and I'll look forward to keeping mine," she whispered softly in his ear.

But Barry didn't want to go, grasping her again, releasing her shorts and pushing them down, with her knickers clear of her bottom. This time Karen was beginning to panic. If she didn't do something now, she'd have no option but to allow Barry to take her.

"I'm really turned on, Karen; you can't leave me like this. Why don't you get these knickers off and let's do it now?"

She pushed him away, pulling her knickers back up, but allowing the shorts to drop to the floor and stared at him, hurt in her eyes. "I will if you want but I've offered everything I have, Barry. I've never been with a man and wanted my first time to be perfect. Shatter it if you want with five minutes on the bed, or give me a night I'll never forget."

She began fiddling with her blouse buttons, at the same time holding her breath, hoping the lie had hit the right spot.

He stood there for a moment, suddenly feeling sorry for this girl standing in front of him. "You're right. I'll keep my side of the bargain. Besides a night with you against ten minutes now is a bad deal in anybody's book."

She smiled. "Thank you, Barry, you won't regret it, believe me. But when you ring, please tell them you've met Karen Marshall and give them the name of the ship and when it docks."

"I will, Karen," and, giving her one last kiss on the lips, he disappeared behind some packing cases and went out. Moments later the watertight door creaked shut.

Karen sat on the bed, relieved that he'd gone for the all-night option. Time was moving on and she'd become convinced that without Barry's call to the authorities, she'd be off the ship in a strange land with no chance of help. The dance had been a risk, leaving her vulnerable when she was down to her knickers, that he might demand to go all the way and she'd have to accept it. As it was, she'd done just enough, leaving her offer dangling. Barry would have the incentive to call. She was also pleased with her performance. Now she could stand in front of Assam with confidence. Before she'd have been scared and embarrassed but now she realised that it wasn't that bad. If she kept her eyes fixed to the man's eyes, she could lose herself in the dance, and not worry about the reality that she would end up dancing naked in front of him.

She lay back on the bed and began to think of home. Grant had seen to it she couldn't actually go home, but forming in her mind was a list of people who would pay for what she was going through. With Frank Whittle dead and Grant's address imprinted on her mind, he would be a start. Susan would be next, along with her family. Then there was the ship's crew. Just how many girls had taken this route into slavery and prostitution? Her list was growing and she'd no doubt it would become longer. Sitting up, she sighed, and getting rid of the dancing clothes, she replaced her t-shirt.

After the first night of feeling sorry for herself she'd decided to keep herself fit, to help her in any escape she might try, and her once fifteen minutes of hard exercise was now an hour and a half. Desperate to stay as fit as possible, every night she pushed herself that little bit more. Astounded at her progress, she'd moved from literally collapsing at six push-ups to an easy fifty and from five lifts on the side of a packing crate, to thirty. Then, running round the narrow passage of the hold, she found even after twenty circuits she wasn't out of breath. Also, if the truth was known, besides keeping her figure, the exercise took her mind off the initial depression of being taken from her home. She'd simply collapse shattered in her bed, falling asleep in minutes, rather than pondering her position for hours on end. Assam and Grant, for that matter, had also helped her self-confidence in facing an uncertain future. She no longer wanted to see her family, really because she couldn't face them anyway. So all that she had left was a desperate urge to be free, an urge to seek revenge and then live how she wanted. Would Barry really make the call or would he just say he did, expecting payment? She could only take the chance that he'd keep to his word, but it didn't mean she intended to keep to hers.

Chapter 7

The next night when Garrett collected her from the kitchen, they didn't go back to the hold, but instead he took her to Assam's cabin. Assam was sat at his desk, deep in thought. He didn't acknowledge her when she entered and Garrett pulled the other chair out, telling her to sit down. Karen sat there nervously; the atmosphere in the room was oppressive.

Eventually Assam looked her directly in the eyes. "Tell me about Barry?"

Her heart skipped a beat, had he been caught? Had he told Assam what she'd asked? She'd no way of knowing, so decided to act dumb. "What about him?"

Assam shook his head slowly. "Karen, Karen, have you not listened to anything I've said? A ship's like a tiny village. Nothing happens here without me knowing. We have cameras in holds, even telephone calls are recorded. So, I ask again, what went on between you and Barry and just what did you want him to do?"

She sighed; what was the use of lying, he probably knew already? "He was in the hold and told me it was all round the ship that I pose in the nude and was a good screw. Told me there were other girls onboard but he couldn't get a look in, so he wanted me. If I agreed, he said in return, he'd tell my parents where I was."

"And did you let him? Screw you, I mean?"

She shook her head, "No I didn't. I did ask him to call home though; you can't blame me for that."

"You danced for him, why was that?"

Karen was beginning to panic; Assam knew everything, she was sure now. "I wanted him to call, but he was still demanding I paid in advance by going to bed with him. I knew if I let him have me, he'd never call home, so I came up with the promise of him spending the night with me rather than ten minutes. After all," she said cockily, "if he'd succeeded, how could he take me up on the promise when you'd all have been arrested at the dock? But to show my word was good, I gave him the dance for a taster. Besides, it allowed me to practise my dance in front of someone, just to see if it was okay. I stopped at removing my knickers. I'm not that stupid."

Assam grinned. "You're a clever and resourceful girl, Karen, perhaps I underestimated you?"

He stood and moved round the table. Karen cowered back, expecting him to strike her, but he didn't. Instead Garrett came up behind and pulled her head back with her hair. She screamed, but Assam slapped her face hard.

"Shut up, close your eyes and open your mouth," he demanded.

Relieved he wasn't going to strap her, Karen did as he asked. There was the rustle of a bag and a few seconds later she felt a soft round sweet thrust into her mouth.

"Chew it, Karen, chew it and swallow it," Assam whispered into her ear.

She chewed the revolting item which seemed to be coated with some sort of sugar, then swallowed it quickly, no longer wanting to keep it in her mouth. However, as soon as she'd done that, Assam pushed another in. This time the sweet tasted bitter and she very nearly threw up before swallowing it, yet again, with difficulty.

"How do you like the taste of those, kid? They've been specially prepared for you, by your friend Screwer. But you've not quite finished, I've just one more thing I want you to taste," he laughed, thrusting something long, hard and sticky into her mouth. "Why don't you give it a good suck, perhaps you can tell me what it is," he demanded.

Assam was still holding the end, so she sucked a little and then licked around with her tongue as he'd told her. The taste of the burnt, hard covering, mixed with a bitter taste, was confusing; she was convinced it must be drugs or poison?

"Still confused, Karen? Then give it a good bite, chew it, then if you don't know, I'll tell you."

She opened her eyes; Assam was inches from her, a sickly grin spread over his face.

"Bite, bite hard and chew it or you'll feel my strap," he shouted.

She bit into it and an oozy, bitter tasting liquid filled her mouth, making her choke. Assam pulled the rest from her mouth and clasped his hand over so she couldn't spit it out, annoyed at her delay. "Chew it, I said chew it, or God help me, I'll beat the fucking shit out of you," he screamed at her.

By now Karen, convinced it was poisoned, began tugging at his hand, trying to pull it away from her mouth to spit it out, but Garrett grabbed both her arms, wrenching them tight behind the chair she sat on.

"Swallow it, swallow it," Assam hissed in her face.

Finally she did before he again forced open her mouth, pushing the rest of the obnoxious thing into it. Then, pulling her head back with her hair, he clasped his hand over her mouth again so she couldn't spit it out. Karen, her eyes wide with terror, felt helpless, waiting for the pains or whatever would happen before she died.

"Was it good, that? Think I've poisoned you? Waiting to die, Karen, wondering how it'd feel?" Assam mocked. "Sorry to disappoint you but it's not poison, it's something more, should we say, personal. You see, Barry called England for you, I didn't tell you that, did I? They know you're on this ship. That's good news, don't you think? Unfortunately for you, the bad news is you're leaving tomorrow, so you won't be here. A little earlier than planned, I agree, but no matter. A boat will pick you up before we dock. So the ship will be clean as a whistle. Your Barry won't be on board, of course.

You see, we had a little accident today. God knows what happened as he just seemed to want to jump over the side; it may have been the pain, who knows? It was tragic, we could do nothing."

He stopped for a moment, allowing it to sink in, at the same time not releasing her mouth. A black sticky liquid was beginning to dribble between his hands. Assam ignored it and carried on his little story. "Mind you, I'd got myself a problem; just how were you going to keep your promise to him for calling England? I'd considered taking his place, or perhaps giving you to the crew, but that wasn't fair. After all, it was a contract between you and Barry. Screwer came to my rescue; you see, I didn't know Barry had this little fantasy that you'd give him a blow job. You know the sort of thing, you'd probably done it many times with Grant when you were at that time of the month. Is that what he'd have you do then, eh?"

She was staring up at him, unable to move or speak, the obnoxious substance still dribbling out between his hands and down her throat. Terror was still in her eyes and she still believed, no matter what he'd said, that she was about to die.

"So did you? Did you give him a blow job?" Assam screamed at her.

She closed her eyes and nodded. How Grant had got her to do it she couldn't remember or even wanted to, but he had and she felt desperately ashamed.

Assam grinned, moving his mouth close to her ear. "I knew you had, Karen, Grant really had you dancing on the end of strings, didn't he? But I'm diversifying; we were talking about Barry and how to keep your promise to him. It was a problem really, so I decided at least to keep one of his fantasies for you to perform, so to speak. Mind you, you'd probably have been very disappointed; he'd only a tiny one, not more than four inches erect, I'm told. Not enough for a girl with your experience." Then he shrugged indifferently.

"Anyway a promise is a promise and while Barry is no longer of this world to ask it of you, I decided to let you suck it anyway."

Her eyes had widened as the realisation of what was in her mouth suddenly sunk in. She began to retch at the thought, struggling to escape and spit the obnoxious thing out, but Assam and Garrett gripped her hard.

"Yes, kid, it's Barry's fantasy. His balls you've eaten, his dick you licked and sucked before you bit into it, chewed then swallowed, and the rest's in your mouth. Screwer's very good with the knife, you should know that. And after a little light grilling, with its special sugar coating, it was ready for you. Poor Barry didn't know what hit him. Stripped on the deck, then held down, Screwer had it off in seconds. Pushed in his face before he'd even known we'd taken it. I'm surprised you didn't hear the screams, but believe me, the sharks soon shut him up. What do you think now, is the debt repaid?"

She could only stare at him. The revulsion of what he'd done to Barry, and now to her, made her stomach churn. He suddenly let go and allowed her to spit what was left of the penis out onto the floor. Karen was coughing and desperately wanted to be sick, staring at the bloody mess on the floor that they'd forced her to eat.

"Go into the bathroom and wash your face. Be sick if you want, then I want you back in here," he shouted.

Karen didn't need any urging and stood quickly to go.

Assam shouted at her again. "And take that thing with you; flush it down the toilet unless you want to keep it, perhaps to suck on it again later?" he barked.

She scooped the remains from the floor and ran and seconds later her head was over the toilet. She had never been so sick; retching hard, trying to be even sicker to get the things out of her stomach, the taste in her mouth acid and bitter. Tears streaming down her face at the very thought of what Assam had done.

Eventually, after five or six minutes she returned, very subdued, and sat down again. Resigned to a strapping, she glared at him. "You sick bastard, strap me all you want but Barry didn't deserve to die. Then to stick that thing down my throat, how low can you sink?"

Assam thrust a drink in front of her. "Drink, it will kill the taste."

She took it without a word, swilling the liquid around in her mouth, but it didn't, the bitter taste still lingered.

"I'll allow that outburst, Karen, just this once," Assam began, "but always remember, it was you who signed his death warrant when you asked him for help. You knew that I warned you days ago and yet only twenty minutes ago in here you were saying how clever you were to get him to do it. So don't come with your 'holier than thou' shit. But the problem I now have is, what's your punishment?"

Karen shrugged. "Strap me, kill me, I no longer care!"

Assam leaned back as if in thought. "I suppose not. You're probably feeling pretty bad at the moment, aren't you? Anyway you've a choice. It's Screwer's birthday tonight; he's fifty. I want you to dance for him at his party like you did with Barry. Refuse, then I give you to the crew, followed by at least ten strokes of the strap. I prefer the latter because you're shit and use people no matter what the risk to them. But I'm a businessman and badly marked girls have lower value, although someone would still buy you."

She remained silent. She despised this man in front of her; given the chance, she would kill him.

"I'm waiting; dance for Screwer, or I give you to the crew, followed by the strap with a long swim to shore, it's very simple."

Karen shrugged. "I'll dance; I'm not a fool, you know."

Assam grinned. "I know you're not and believe me I won't forget you. I'm only sorry Frank Whittle had already made arrangements. I'd have found a far more fitting future for a girl like you."

Garrett touched her arm and she stood, ready to go. Assam pulled a small box from his drawer, placing it on the desk in front of him. "It's a birthday party, Karen, so you should give him a gift after your dance. Tell him it's a gift from you and Assam said he is to use it this time and not leave it on the shelf."

She took the box, but Garrett snatched it off her as they left the cabin. "I'll give it you when you've danced. Go and get a shower, wash your hair and tie it back. Smile, don't scowl at him, remember it's his birthday," Garrett said, and then walked away.

Garrett wasn't there when she came out of the shower but with nowhere to escape to, she returned to the hold and dried her hair. In some ways she didn't mind the dance, it'd worked for Barry and five or ten minutes playing up to a man of fifty was far better than Assam's belt.

***

Garrett came at nine and he led her back to the dining area. She could hear music and laughing and began to pull back as they approached. Garrett urged her on into the room. Eight or nine of the crew were sat about drinking. There was a chair in the middle of the small room and Screwer was being urged to sit in it.

"Screwer, Assam's arranged a present for your fiftieth. Karen's agreed to perform a lap dance for you, so let's have some sexy music playing on the stereo," Garrett shouted.

As the music started, Karen began her dance. This time it was slow, with each item of clothing she removed timed to match the music. At times she squirmed over him, kissing him gently, and eventually, like with Barry, she slipped the shorts to the floor. The men in the room were chanting "knickers off, knickers off", so before sitting astride him, she turned away, allowing her knickers to fall slowly down her legs to the floor and wiggled her bare bottom at him. Then she turned and sat astride his closed legs, simulating intercourse. As the music stopped, all the crew who'd been urging her on, shouted and hooted, with lots of clapping. Karen felt on a high; she'd done it, and now it was over.

Garrett handed her the present.

Kissing Screwer on the cheek, Karen pushed it into his hands. "It's a gift from me for your birthday, Assam said you were to use it immediately and not let it hang about, or something like that," she said.

He started unwrapping the outer paper, only to find another layer underneath. He did it again and again, becoming more frustrated, thinking he was being made a fool of, then suddenly from the final tiny box he drew out two black condoms.

"Why, Karen, I never thought you cared so much for me? It must be all those bacon butties I've given you? But Assam couldn't have given me a better present," Screwer shouted, at the same time beginning to unbuckle his belt. "I think you're right, girl, I should use one immediately and the other certainly won't be hanging around, I promise you."

Karen's eyes widened in alarm, the words of Assam ringing in her ears as she realised that she'd offered herself to Screwer. She tried to move away and leave the room but Screwer had other ideas.

"The table, bring the table. Don't let the bitch leave," he shouted.

While it was fetched, four of them made a grab for Karen, lifting her high in the air, parading her round the room before laying her flat on the hastily moved table, her legs dangling down one side.

"Warm her up for me while I get this bloody thing on," Screwer shouted.

She lay there with her eyes closed tightly as someone started to kiss and fondle her breasts. Another was rubbing her gently between the legs, exciting her sex organ and dampening her with her own juices.

"She's ready, Screwer, she's ready," everyone was chanting.

"At last," Screwer laughed. "Get ready for the shag of your life, kid, and find out why they call me Screwer," he boasted.

Moments later she could feel Screwer slowly sinking deep inside her, his hands gripping her hips as he began to work back and forth. Try as she might to block this abuse of her body out of her mind, and even telling herself that this was rape, she couldn't. The effort of trying to add sexual overtones in her dancing had raised the adrenalin level in her body so high, that now her body was reacting to this man.

At the same time, she could hear him offering the other condom around for whatever money he could get and many men were bidding for it. Suddenly, the deal done, Screwer was beginning to climax, his body slamming into hers, with the men in the room egging him on. Then he was finished, withdrawing slowly, her body still shaking under the onslaught, but for Karen it wasn't over.

"Turn her over, turn her over," someone was shouting. "I want her turned over."

Hands grasped her body, quickly turning her face down and her arms forced forward above her head, keeping her down flat on the table with her legs dangling over the edge. She could feel a man behind trying to enter her and she began kicking out wildly in a vain effort to stop him, but the man began laughing, smacking her bottom hard until she stopped kicking. This was Grant's way and she'd hated it, the position she likened to that of an animal, rather than an act of love.

Karen was angry with herself; she was being raped but

try as she might her body was accepting it and she'd no control. She could hear the man shouting, feel him banging harder and harder into her, as he, like Screwer, came to his own climax before it was over. Then she felt the man withdrawing, leaving her body to relax. Another shouted it was his turn but she could hear Garrett's voice above all of them.

"Assam gave two condoms, you all had a chance to buy one and this man won, so that's it for the night." Then, turning to look at Karen still being held face down on the table, he pushed the men away and told her to follow him.

Karen didn't need asking twice, she stood unsteadily, her legs weak, and her entire body still shaking from the abuse. Gathering her clothes as quickly as she could and not delaying even to replace her pants, she ran out of the room after Garrett.

"Thank you for stopping them," she gasped, as she caught him up."

He turned and scowled at her. "Forget thanks! As far as I'm concerned I'd have left you to the crew, but Assam's word's law round here and I do as he demands. Think yourself lucky, Karen, if I'd had my way you'd have followed Barry over the side."

They arrived at the hold and Karen held her hand out and touched his arm. "All the same, thank you. I didn't ask for any of this, you know; you can't blame me for trying to get home. What happened to me in there is my future; would you want it if you were me?"

He looked at her for a moment, Karen thought she saw some pity in his eyes after all his big talk, but he said nothing and urged her down the ladders.

Once in the hold, he called down to her. "You won't be working in the kitchen tomorrow. I'll collect you late in the afternoon. Someone will bring you food in the morning. Tonight, for your own safety the hold will be locked. The crew has a taste for it now and there is a lot of drinking going on tonight. Unfortunately you were a bit of a hit; some might decide to pay you a late call if I don't take these precautions."

She said nothing and Garrett slammed the door shut and slid the lock, then it was all quiet. Karen sat on the bed, surprised she wasn't breaking down in tears. She'd been raped but couldn't get worked up over it. It was as if she'd accepted this possibility since coming on the ship and knew she couldn't do anything about it. At first, the beating and the knowledge that her mum and dad would know what she'd been getting up to, had devastated her. But her determination to still go home and face the music, after the deal she'd made with Barry, had given her real confidence that rescue was an actual possibility and the nightmare would soon be over.

The reality of the last hour had knocked that out of her. Now she could only feel hatred for Assam and all the others who'd sat back and allowed this to happen. She wanted to kill them, to see them beg for their lives. But Karen was also a realist, aware that these thoughts were just a way of letting off pent-up frustration at not being able to retaliate, and of having to accept and do whatever was demanded of her. More importantly, until she was rescued, if she ever was, would tonight be the pattern of nights to come, where she'd be forced to perform a dance before being raped again and again?

Why wasn't Garrett coming for her until the afternoon? Was she really leaving, or was Assam's talk of her leaving the ship a lie? The more she pondered, the more she was convinced he'd not finished her punishment, because of Barry, and from now on intended to offer her up to more of the crew, as he'd promised, if she'd stepped out of line, before killing her. Karen shuddered at the thought, before tears began to run down her face. The next moment she was sobbing her heart out, finally beginning to realise, either way, just what the future really held for her.

Chapter 8

Karen blinked in the strong sun as she came on deck. After only being below decks, she'd not realised they were somewhere much hotter and warmer than England. Her fears that Assam still had an intention of further punishment, when Garrett came to collect her in the afternoon, didn't materialise. She'd been waiting in jeans and jumper which she usually wore when working in the kitchen, becoming more and more convinced there was to be a repeat of last night as the day wore on. However, when Garrett collected her she was taken directly to the shower room. He then waited outside until she'd finished and handed her a t-shirt, knickers and hair clips to tie her hair back. After she'd dressed as he'd asked, they made their way down corridors towards Assam's cabin. Karen had begun to hold back, now convinced she'd been right and was on her way to Assam's cabin to have some other obnoxious thing forced into her mouth, before being raped once more. But he urged her past his cabin, carrying on down the corridor.

When she arrived on deck, there were two other girls already stood some distance away, watching her. They both looked tired and one of them, a blonde girl, had a bruise on the side of her face. She was small, around twenty and quite large. The other girl was Karen's height, medium build with short-cropped, brown hair. Somehow Karen recognised her but she couldn't think where from. Karen could just about see a small boat approaching at speed. Assam came out on deck, looked over the side, then walked across to Karen, at the same time grinning like a Cheshire cat.

"Stupid girl, weren't you? Fancy giving Screwer the condoms and saying they were from you. What did you expect him to do with them, blow 'em up like balloons?" He began laughing, before turning away from her towards the other girls.

Karen glared at him. "Laugh all you want, but you'll pay for what you had done to me last night," she replied bravely.

He stopped for a minute, turned and walked back to her. Then he put his arm round her shoulder urging her to walk with him to the side railings of the deck, away from everyone else standing around. Suddenly she was very scared for replying. Assam just stood at her side looking out across the still water.

"Karen... Karen... brave words, but it shows you are still a very naive and arrogant girl, when even after last night, you still have not leant when to keep your mouth shut. How about I delay your departure for an hour, after all, you must be expecting a punishment for threatening me? It'll give me time to call the crew up on deck and ask them to bring your favourite table? Then perhaps I'll choose five to take you this time and we'll see how well you cope, shall we?"

A cold shiver ran down her body, she couldn't believe what he was threatening her with. Her eyes began to water as she turned to look at him, desperation in her voice. "I'm sorry, you're right, Assam, it was a stupid and naive remark. You've treated me well and I deserved what happened to me last night, because of Barry." She looked away, her voice faltering. "I've been sat alone in the hold all day, terrified my punishment had not finished and wondering what was eventually going to happen to me. I just said it, without thinking, to give me a little self-confidence, that's all. I didn't mean it, you know that? I'm begging you not to give me to the crew. Take the strap to me in punishment for my remark. In fact anything else you want to do to me, I'll accept. But I'd rather die, truly this time, than be raped by so many men."

Karen stood quietly, looking back up at him, as tears now began to run down her face. Inside she was falling apart, not sure what more she could say that might change his mind from handing her to the crew. Inside she was praying he'd accept her apology, but at the same time a plan was forming in her mind.

Assam waited a short time to allow her real fear to continue, and then smiled to himself. He enjoyed seeing this proud girl squirm. Placing his arm again round her shoulder, he pulled her close to him, speaking quietly in her ear. "Yes, Karen, I believe this time you would rather die. But I told you when you came on my ship; the option to die does not come easy, so first the crew, then die, is that what you want? But while you think about that, don't even consider the option of jumping ship; you'd not get on the first rail before we stopped you."

She swallowed hard; this man seemed to be able to read what she was considering, except... he was wrong. She was very confident now in the open and not confined in a small cabin space; with her self-defence, judo and kick-boxing skills, they'd not succeed in holding her. However, she decided to try once more in changing his mind, before attempting the rail. This was not the place to make her escape. She had every intention of escaping... yes, but to go home, not to die. "What more do you want me to say, except apologise and promise never to talk back again?" she whispered. "But if you won't accept my apology and my only choice is to be raped before I die, then go ahead, provided you keep your promise after, to kill me?"

They stood there for a few minutes, Assam saying nothing as he watched the small craft steadily approaching the ship. He had placed himself in a difficult position by threatening her with rape. This girl would not accept that option. Karen was different to the normal girls he carried, well able to give the impression of a very feminine and weak girl, except he knew she wasn't. She'd accepted the rape too quickly as if she knew he wouldn't go through with it. To try to hold her, now she was on deck, would be difficult. She'd retaliate and they would not be able to restrain her. She'd almost certainly jump ship, injuring or killing herself in the process, and perhaps others, in the attempt. Besides which, the buyer carried the balance of his payment and wouldn't appreciate a girl who'd just been raped and so wasn't able to work immediately, or possibly dead.

"I'll accept your apology and ignore your naive comment this time, Karen; you've worked hard, done as you've been told and I agree, paid for your stupidity with Barry. Don't, because of this reprieve from a punishment, ever believe I'm soft. I'm not. But I accept you said it, without thinking, to keep your spirits up. But never answer back to me again in that way. Next time I won't even offer you a chance to apologise."

While she'd been stood waiting for his reply, she'd already decided her route. Assam no longer had an arm around her shoulder; a punch to his groin and perhaps a flying kick at Garrett, if he attempted to stop her, would be sufficient to give her the time she needed. Then a sprint to the far side of the deck and she'd be over in seconds, diving deep without taking a breath, she'd never surface alive, that she was sure of. However, if he was offering her a get-out, she would take it; after all, committing suicide was her last resort. "Thank you, Assam, I'll remember your advice and never say anything so stupid again," she replied quickly.

Their eyes met for a moment. He could see there was little sincerity in hers, now certain she'd already decided, before accepting the punishment earlier, to jump. However, he smiled, grasping both her shoulders. "Then dry your eyes, Karen; when your new owner checks you over, do everything he asks without objection and more importantly, smile, don't scowl. Do this for me and your naive comment is forgotten."

"I will, Assam, I won't let you down, I promise."

He said no more, but pushed her away and then walked over to the little blonde girl. She started to cry as he talked to her and he hit her hard across the face. "Shut the blubbering or so help me, rather than get a lift, you can bloody swim to shore," he shouted.

The girl fell silent immediately, but Assam was distracted when Garrett shouted that the man had arrived. Karen looked at him carefully as he appeared from over the edge. He was small and fat, gasping for breath after his climb up the ladder onto the deck, and carrying a large bag. She couldn't decide his origin.

"Bloody funny time this, Assam. What's wrong with the normal arrangements, that bleeding sun's been baking me," he cursed.

Assam grinned; he'd not mentioned the Barry incident and only told this man that he'd been advised the ship might well be searched for weapons or drugs and he couldn't keep the girls on board so he could collect in port. "It's worth it, Saeed, believe me. You will like the girl, besides, like I told you over the radio, I've two more as a bonus," he said, at the same time offering him a drink from a tray held by Garrett.

"Yes, so you said, but I'll decide if they are a bonus or not?" Saeed replied as he took the drink offered to him.

Saeed looked at the three girls while he sipped his drink. His eyes rested longer on Karen and then, when he'd finished, he handed the glass back to Garrett and walked over to her with Assam following.

"This is Karen, the girl you've really come to collect, Saeed," Assam said as they approached her.

Saeed pulled a picture of her from his pocket looked at it, then at Karen. "Are you Karen Marshall?" he asked.

"Yes, Sir," she replied with a smile.

"I'm known as Saeed not Sir. You can call me by that name, if I decide to take you. First I need to satisfy myself that you have no injuries and are in good health. I'd like you to sprint to the far end the deck, then walk back towards me slowly, with your arms at your side."

He stood watching as she sprinted to the far end of the deck then began to walk back to him.

"This is a bit over the top, Saeed, she's only destined for the brothel, not running a race," Assam said quietly.

"You will understand, my friend, in a moment, but from now on in our own language please," Saeed replied.

By now Karen was back, standing in front of him.

"Remove your t-shirt and knickers," Saeed demanded.

She quickly removed her clothes, handing them to him with a smile and feeling embarrassed with others watching her. But at least he'd not told her to remove them before sprinting up the deck.

Saeed passed the clothes to Assam, then came closer to her. He grasped her head with his hands, turning her one way then the other as he looked inside and behind her ears, noticing her already pierced earlobes. He pulled back slightly. "I'd like you to smile at me?" he asked.

As she smiled, he studied the line of her teeth, satisfying himself that they were perfectly in line. "Thank you. Now open your mouth wide."

She did as he asked and he peered inside, pulling her cheeks away from her teeth, so he could check the condition of her back teeth. The smell of his bad breath so close made her want to retch, but she held her own breath and didn't move.

"Have you ever used drugs?" he asked letting go of her head.

She shook her head. "No, never."

He took each of her hands one at a time and carefully looked at her nails, besides checking along and under her arms for any signs of needle marks. "Lift your arms high above your head and spread your legs apart slightly."

She quickly did as he asked, not flinching as he walked

round her, rubbing his hands over her body.

"You can put your arms down now," Saeed said, then he looked at Assam. "*Have you had to punish her while she's been on the ship?*" he asked in their language.

"*Yes; I had to use the strap before she came on the ship, Saeed, there was no option after she tried to escape. The girl needed to be punished or any threat in the future would be meaningless. I was careful and only gave her three strokes on the bottom and one to the top of the legs. Garrett checked later and said her skin was sore but hadn't broken. You should understand, this girl would not have accepted continued captivity without instilling fear of another, more vicious, strapping if she stepped out of line. But she hasn't and she has worked hard.*"

"*I see, that could be a problem,*" he said. "*This may mean me having to change my plans, if there's been any permanent scarring.*" Then he reverted back to English. "I'm told you were punished with a strap. So I'd like you to turn round, Karen, spreading you legs and bending down as low as you can, so I can check there's been no scarring."

She did as he asked, feeling particularly violated when he grasped her buttocks, pulling them well apart, while he inspected the surface of each buttock. However, she never moved or verbally objected.

"You can straighten up now and face me," Saeed said to her, then looked towards Assam. "*You're lucky there's no scars. I never strap a bottom, Assam. I always keep the strap to the top of the legs, not directly on the bottom. It's more painful, believe me, and while sometimes the strap makes the legs bleed, it never leaves any permanent scars.*"

"*I will remember that, Saeed. But what do you think of her? I think this girl is the best we've had this year. She's looked after herself, very fit and it shows. I've had her spend her rest time practising hard as a lap dancer, besides, as you know, she's already experienced in the ways of pleasing a man. She will be very popular with clients and is more than ready to work tonight, if you want?*"

Saeed nodded his head up and down in agreement. *"You're right; she's far better than I expected, needs a little more colour, besides smelling nicer, but that's easy to sort out. Mind you, taking her to a brothel, as was arranged with my English contact, is no longer the intention. This is why I wanted to check her very carefully, particularly where you strapped her, besides making sure she didn't limp, had good teeth or used needles. The professional photos from England have aroused much interest and I've already received bids close to forty thousand dollars. This is big money for a girl, Assam, but these buyers want the best and by what I've seen, we have very close to that in her. This Saturday she'll go to the highest bidder, so come by my house on the next trip and whatever I raise, above the original five thousand offers from the brothels, there's twenty percent in it for you."*

Assam smiled to himself, extra cash was always acceptable and he was relieved he'd not had to beat her into submission.

Then Saeed looked back at Karen, "Bend your head forward."

She bent her head down and Saeed began to remove the clips holding her hair up. Then he handed them to Assam. *"She used only four clips?"* he asked, continuing to run his hands carefully through her hair, feeling if she had more.

Assam looked across to Garrett. *"Well?"*

"Yes, there was only four," Garrett answered.

"That is good," Saeed replied. *"I can't be too careful with an intelligent and obviously fit girl like this. Whatever she tells you will be a lie. So you need to count in and count out what you give her. She'll use people and anything you fail to take back off her she might be able to use as a weapon. It is those occasions, my friend, we can lose a great deal of money when she's found out and has to be severely punished."*

Assam was now glad he'd said nothing about Barry. Saeed was right about this girl using people. He himself had made a mistake, believing she was under control. But a girl like her would never be under control, pretending naivety with her natural sexual attraction to ensnare a man.

By now Saeed had opened the large bag he'd brought up with him from his boat. Quickly he removed knickers, t-shirt, shorts and a jumper, handing them to her. Then he pulled a hairbrush from his pocket, handing that to her as well. "You're coming with me, Karen. Get dressed quickly, then brush your hair."

"She has clothes, Saeed," Assam said. *"You didn't have to bring any."*

"Yes I do, Assam. I've already checked her body and hair very carefully. By bringing my own clothes for her, I know she carries nothing I don't know about. Besides, the girl would be very cold later if all she had to wear was what she had on when I came aboard."

Assam laughed. *"You're getting soft, Saeed, giving them a jumper to wear as well."*

The two of them moved over to the next girl, Assam telling her to undress. Saeed inspected the girl, but not nearly as carefully as Karen and again he brought out similar clothes from the bag for the girl to wear, telling Garrett to collect the brush off Karen and give it her. The little blonde girl was next and when Saeed touched the side of her face with the bruise, the girl pulled back, so he slapped her face. "Get your clothes off," he demanded.

She refused point-blank and this time Assam slapped her. "If he says strip, strip," Assam demanded, raising his hand again.

This time the girl didn't hesitate and then stood there shivering while Saeed inspected her, tears running down her face. Karen was appalled; nearly all her body was bruised, some even festering from lack of attention. She was glad Assam hadn't taken the strap to her more than once.

Assam quickly cut in, still using the language the girls couldn't understand. *"She was trouble, Saeed, wouldn't do a bloody thing. We had to control her after she kicked a door down and tried to climb overboard. I'm afraid Garrett got a little carried away,"* he said quietly.

Garrett glared at Assam. *"Me! It was you that beat the kid up."*

Saeed held his hands up in horror. *"Enough! I don't want her anyway. I've no sale, believe me. Bleached blondes with poor teeth and already getting a big arse are no use for me. Besides, the wounds will take too long to heal. I'd have to feed her for weeks; I'm not a bloody hospital."*

"You can have her for free, she can't stay on the ship. Like I said, we could have visitors tomorrow," Assam said.

He shrugged. *"That's your problem, Assam. I'll not take her and that's that."*

The look of annoyance on Assam's face made Karen want to laugh, but of course she remained steadfastly silent, showing no emotion. Although she couldn't understand them, it was obvious something was wrong, but she wasn't prepared for what happened next.

Assam turned to Garrett and shrugged, still speaking in the language only they understood. *"You heard Saeed, we've no alternative,"* Assam said.

Garrett walked over to the girl and took her hand, talking to her softly as if trying to comfort her. She picked her clothes up to dress, but he stopped her and they walked towards the side rail.

Karen thought there must be a problem and she was being returned to her cabin, but Garrett stopped at the rail. He leaned on it, facing out to sea. The girl was at his side and they were talking. Garrett began pointing to something and the girl leaned against the rail, trying to see what he was showing her. He stood back still pointing with one hand as he moved behind her. She was still gazing out, trying to see what he'd seen, when he took a large knife from his inside jacket pocket with his other hand. Swiftly, he grabbed her hair, then, forcing her head back, pulled the knife across her throat. The other girl screamed while Karen watched, speechless, as the girl sank silently to the deck in a fast-forming pool of blood. Then, bending down, Garrett pushed her body between the rails; a splash came seconds later as she hit the water.

Saeed shrugged, handed Assam a large bundle of currency, and turned to the girls. "Over the side and into my boat. Try to escape and it's a twenty mile swim. You'd not get far, by now the water will be alive with sharks from miles around, hungry for human flesh."

The two girls did as he asked and sat together in the large craft. He climbed down and rummaged in a box, removing a chain with an ankle ring attached. He tightened the ring round Karen's ankle, before threading it through the seat support, and fixing it with a padlock.

He looked up at her. "Just so you don't get any ideas about jumping overboard again, Karen. So just settle back and enjoy the ride, it'll be dark when we arrive."

He went through to the forward cabin and started the engine and soon they were speeding away from the ship. Karen turned and looked at it. She could see the name 'Towkey', Panama, on the stern and memorised it. This was a name she wanted to remember.

The girl sat by her, touched Karen's arm to catch her attention. "The name's Debbie, Debbie Malloy. Have you been on the ship for long? I didn't know anybody else, apart from Jane, was aboard. Why did he put a chain on you? Have you, like Jane, been a bad girl?"

Karen looked at her for a moment, then shrugged indifferently. "Karen, Karen Marshall. I've been on that bloody ship since leaving England. So where did they pick you two up from then?" she asked curtly and without any emotion. Karen trusted no one anymore and the last thing she wanted was a hanger-on when she made her break.

"We were brought on for a party when the ship was off Southampton. Jane and I do an exotic dancing type of act. You know the type of thing, a bit of dancing followed by a quick strip then on to the next show."

Karen sighed to herself, that's all she needed, a good-time girl out for a quick pound or two.

"So what went wrong then?" Karen asked, trying to inject some interest in her voice.

Debbie laughed. "We accepted a drink after the act, it's usual, just being friendly, that was all. Anyway, I woke up in the same cabin as Jane late the next day. By then the ship had sailed and they promised they'd drop us at the next port. The catch was we'd have to earn the fare home. Jane wasn't on the game. She was just a stripper so she refused. Refusal didn't mean much; she was passed around the crew anyway and got a beating when she wouldn't perform. She's a kid at home and a boyfriend, so it was understandable, I suppose."

Karen looked carefully at the girl. "What about you, why didn't they beat you then?"

Debbie laughed. "I saw it as an opportunity. I've earned nearly four hundred pounds on that ship. Mind you, when they killed Jane I got a bit nervous, I was worried in case it was me next. You know, for my money."

Karen couldn't believe what she was hearing, the indifference to her friend being killed. But Karen was also thankful for them being there, convinced that if it hadn't been for these two girls she'd almost certainly have been forced to entertain the crew a great deal more than she had last night.

"Have you any idea what this is all about?" Karen asked.

"What do you mean? For me it's just a lift to the mainland."

"Lift to the mainland!" Karen sniggered. "You and I have been bloody sold to that thing driving this boat. Didn't you think it strange that he had you remove all your clothes and look at your teeth? It's a funny request by someone who's just taking you to the mainland."

Debbie grinned. "I did that for Assam. He told me last

night the man liked to see girls naked, so as he'd kindly agreed to take me, he asked if I would indulge his fantasy. I told Assam it seemed strange, but Assam asked me to humour him, so I did."

Karen laughed. "So you think he's going to let you go? You're off your trolley. More like you're on the way to some brothel to be screwed God knows how many times a day the same as me. But this time there's no pay, no escape... That's until you're no longer any use, or they've got replacements, then who knows what will happen, killed perhaps, like they did Jane."

Debbie said nothing for a moment and then shook her head. "He's probably not going to let you go? After all, he really checked your body. I'm surprised you didn't object when he made you bend over, I would have done. Anyway I'm out of here when we dock."

Karen wondered if it was she who was going mad, or was this girl so stupid that she believed everything Assam had told her. "What about Jane then?"

"What about her?" Debbie asked.

"They've bloody killed her, cut her stupid throat and you sit there as if on some sort of Sunday outing."

Debbie glared at her. "Listen, Karen, Jane and I were partners. I told her a few shags would be neither here nor there. God, I've had five men in a single session and come out laughing. We had a cruise, not very posh I grant you, but I've been fed, earned money and for my part, had some wild nights. So Jane got herself beaten up, and then killed; do you think I'm going to report her death to the pigs? I've seen many girls beaten up for not doing what their pimps tell them. Okay, I admit I don't know one that's died, but Jane's income was her body. She should have looked after it, forgotten her scruples, morals, whatever you want to call them, and got on with the job. Mind you, I'd have had to share the crew more, reducing my money, so I wasn't pushing it."

"But she's got a child, a mother and father. You mean to tell me you're going to say nothing, not even to her boyfriend?" Karen cut in.

Debbie grinned. "Why should I? He's some man, Karen, and I'm the girl for him. He just doesn't know it yet."

"And the kid, what's going to happen to that?" Karen asked.

Debbie shrugged. "Go to her parents, I suppose, I don't want it hanging around the flat with me and Terry."

Karen leaned back; this girl was callous, stupid, and deserved everything she got.

"So how long have you been on the game then? You look a bit skinny to me, in my experience men like something to get hold of," Debbie suddenly asked when Karen had not responded.

Karen looked at Debbie, her eyes wild. "I've never been on the game, as you so nicely put it. I was kidnapped and raped on that bloody ship."

Debbie shrugged. "How can you call it rape if, according to you, you're on the way to some brothel? That's what they do in those places, Karen, they shag you, so you'd better start to learn quickly that what's between your legs is all men want. Treat them good and they'll treat you well; you'll have regulars, boyfriends, in fact. I've got loads. Treat them with contempt though and get ready for a taste of what Jane got."

Karen felt deflated, she'd at least hoped her initial assessment of Debbie was wrong, but it seemed not. "I don't suppose you'll call my parents for me when you get home then?" Karen asked quietly.

Debbie scowled at her. "I'm not into the hero bit. You see, the pigs and I don't get on that well; in fact, they've locked me up a few times so they're hardly likely to believe anything I say anyway. If you want, I'll ring one of your mates. You know, just tell them I've met you and where you're likely to be going."

Karen sighed. "It's okay, don't bother. If you're not going to at least tell someone in authority, I'll take my chances. I'd hate to be reliant on some friend going to the police. I could imagine their reaction."

"What would that be?" Debbie asked, interested.

"Think about it, Debbie. They go to the police, tell them they had a call from someone who wouldn't give a name or anything, about a girl supposedly dead. Not sure where she is except somewhere in the world. They'd lock them up for wasting police time and throw away the key."

They said nothing for a while then Debbie stood. "I'm going to have it out with this bloke. Get the crack, so to speak." With that she moved forward and left Karen totally bemused after the conversation.

Five minutes later the boat's engine cut and they began to drift in silence, with only the splash of water on the sides of the hull from the light swell.

***

Karen hadn't seen Debbie or the man for over an hour and, besides getting very thirsty, began to wonder if she was the only person left. Eventually the engine started again and minutes later Debbie climbed out of the cabin.

"It's all sorted, Karen," Debbie began, as she settled down alongside her. "Saeed's arranged to drop me off at his mate's. I need a passport and he's got one for me. You're to go with him to his house. I'm not completely sure but it seems he's got some sort of sale on Saturday and you're in it."

Karen glared at her. "That's bloody big of you. I'm to be sold and you're on your way home. I suppose the hour or so I've been sat here without so much as a glass of water, you've been eating, or whatever?"

Debbie apologised and ran back into the cabin. Moments later she appeared with a cola. "It wasn't easy, you know."

"What wasn't?" Karen asked.

"Me and Saeed," Debbie replied, then looked indignant. "He wanted me to go with him. Didn't realise I was only a passenger and not like you. Mind you, when I told him what I did, for a living that is, he wanted me to prove it. I've had some men, but he's way down the league. Anyway, what the hell, at least he'll arrange a passport and things. I suggested if he dropped you off as well, you'd probably agree he could have us both together, you know the sort of thing?"

Karen sighed; the girl was on another planet. Then, as to performing together for this man, she shuddered at the thought. Glancing at Debbie she gave a weak smile. "Thanks, Debbie, but it's a good thing you didn't, I'd have strangled the bastard. Anyway, I'm not into exhibitions. I've only just finished with a man who should have had sex as his second name. So the thought of dropping my pants for every man promising to help me escape is naive and stupid. I'll accept it's more than likely I'll be raped a number of times until I've planned an escape. Unlike you, it won't be business, love or anything else you want to call it. Neither will I volunteer, without some sort of threat to my life, or like Assam, wanting to cut my face up."

Debbie shrugged. "I get paid; it beats working for a living."

Karen laughed. "That's as maybe but those who take me will pay with their lives."

The conversation died and Karen gazed out at the endless sea. It was becoming dark and she could see, on the horizon, speckles of light which she assumed must be the coast.

"Did he say where we were going, what country or

anything?" Karen eventually asked.

Debbie shrugged. "Not really. Just that they were in a civil war or something and we'd have to travel at night. It was a dangerous country with different groups of soldiers fighting each other."

It was Karen's turn now to worry this cocky girl. "So with all this civil war going on, just how do you expect to get out? Get real, Debbie, even you've been duped. The funny thing is he's even had you for nothing."

Debbie gave her a sickening grin. "It won't wash, Karen, you're just jealous I'm going home and you're not."

"Of course, if it was true you were going home, I'd be bloody jealous. Except I very much doubt you are," she retorted.

Suddenly they were both brought out of their conversation when the boat started to slow and they could make out dark, steep cliffs looming up. Within minutes the boat had stopped completely, twenty yards or so from the beach. Saeed appeared from the cabin.

"We're here, it's as close as I can get so you'll get wet, I'm afraid. If you both get your pants off and roll your t-shirts up, I'll give you polythene bags to keep them in, then you'll at least have dry clothes to wear in the car," he said, at the same time unclasping Karen's chain.

She stood and stretched; should she try to escape in the water, she asked herself? Unfortunately for her, Saeed had other ideas. He pulled a belt from his pocket and slipped it round her neck, threading it through the buckle, and quickly pulling it tight. He gave her a sickly grin. "Get any ideas about trying to escape and I'll drag you to shore, maybe even choke you if you resist."

Karen said nothing; perhaps it was for the best. She needed to get the lie of the land anyway.

After a struggle in a fast flowing tide they all eventually came ashore. Saeed urged them up a steep path and he pulled open the boot of a very old car, handing both of them old towels. Five minutes later they were on the road, Karen with her wrists handcuffed to the bar of the car seat. Any conversation was impossible with the noise the car was making. They passed very few buildings, some obviously occupied, often with single bare lamps, before they entered a small town. The houses were all painted white, the foliage tropical. Because of this Karen decided, they were somewhere in the Mediterranean. Suddenly the car swerved into a small street, lit only at the far end by a single low power bulb hanging over the top of a door. Stopping, Saeed climbed out and moving quickly round the car, forced Karen to lean forward with her head on the dash. Then he unclipped the handcuffs, wrenching her arms behind her back and handcuffing her wrists. Then, slipping the belt back round her neck, he pulled her out of the car. He looked back at Debbie. "Come on, you as well, this is where you get your passport," he shouted.

Debbie followed quickly while Saeed banged on the front door for some time. It opened and two men were standing there. They spoke in a language Karen didn't understand but they seemed to know Saeed and opened the door wider, allowing them all inside. The two men stared at the girls, walking round them, talking fast and furiously to Saeed.

Saeed was shaking his head and pointing at Karen, at the same time grasping Debbie's hand and pulling her forward. "Get your clothes off," Saeed hissed at Debbie.

She stared at him for a moment, then frowned. "What's all this?" she retorted.

Saeed grinned. "You want a passport, they want payment, but before that they want to see what they're getting, so please yourself. The alternative for illegal entry into this country is prison: prison for at least two years."

She sighed and removed her clothes. One man came

close and rubbed his hand over her body, then nodded.

"Go with him, the deal's done," Saeed said quietly to her.

Debbie grabbed her clothes and followed the man, ignoring Karen who stood watching. However, he was only gone for a couple of minutes. When he returned without Debbie, the three men laughed and made their way to another door.

"Come, we eat before moving on," Saeed said, releasing the handcuffs and belt. "Don't think about trying to make a break, the doors are locked and in this house, they also have big sticks to deter any girl from wanting to leave."

The food was a mixture of bread and cold meats with plenty of cheap, bitter wine. She sat with them but, because none could speak English, she was ignored. Eventually, with the meal finished, one of the men pulled a huge bundle of notes from his pocket, handing it to Saeed. They shook hands and Saeed stood to go but not before handcuffing her and once again slipping the belt back round her neck. A few minutes later Karen was in the car again, handcuffed as before.

He grinned at her in his usual sickly way. "The precautions are just in case you get any ideas, Karen. I wouldn't want you attacking me while I drive, would I?"

She said nothing, he'd probably done the right thing, she thought. After seeing what had happened to Debbie, alone in the car would have given her the chance she was waiting for. He walked round to the driver's side and, after cursing the car a few times as it refused to start, they were on the move, leaving the small town behind. Karen decided to try to find out what was Debbie's fate.

"There isn't any passport is there?" Karen asked.

Saeed laughed. "Astute kid, aren't you? Have you any idea what one would have cost? Besides, she's good at what she does so it'd be a pity to waste those talents. The girl's very valuable and I've made a lot of money. Anyway that kid knows the ropes and she'll do all right there. Mind you, if she refuses, then they can be very persuasive, I can tell you."

"And me? What's to happen to me then?" Karen asked slowly.

He glanced over at her, grinning. "You, Karen, are a different proposition. I had an offer for you in there. In fact it was a surprisingly good offer. Tempting as it was to make a quick profit from Debbie's buyers, I refused. They even offered a hundred dollars to use you while we ate. But I'm not a hard man, Karen, I allowed you to eat. Besides, life in a brothel wouldn't have been your sort of life. I can do far better for you."

"Why do you think being a prostitute is any sort of life then?"

He shrugged. "Women are prostitutes all their lives. From the day you learn what it's for, you use it to sponge off men, opening your legs on occasions when you think our interest is waning."

"We bear your children and even you were a child once," Karen replied.

"Oh yes, I know that, but ask yourself why? It's not for us, it's for your own gratification, yet another way to get money from us."

Karen fell silent as the car began to move quicker now he'd turned on to a better kept road. Her curiosity as to what he had in mind for her was overwhelming, so she decided to try again. "Anyway," she said, "you never told me what your intentions are for me. I suppose it means you get paid a lot of money, while I get to be raped or beaten for the rest of my life?"

He didn't reply for a while and Karen thought he'd either not heard her or chosen to ignore what she'd said. However, Saeed wasn't ignoring her; he'd been contemplating how to approach the answer in order to give himself an easier ride. The last thing he wanted was confrontation; it leads to injury and reduced money. So now, as they'd turned onto the main road and the ride had become smoother and quieter, he began to speak. "You could be beaten and almost certainly you'll be raped, as you like to call it. I prefer to say you'll be loved and looked after, but that's a matter of interpretation. You see, Karen, in this country there are many rich men. They live lonely and quiet lives, out of the spotlight, unable to leave the country for one reason or another. They want companionship and yes, someone to lie down with at night. Four such men have seen your photo and are prepared to bid for you. For me it's business, for you it's your life, your future. These are hard and dangerous men. Treat them like shit and retaliation will be swift and painful. Treat them as you would a lover and the rewards are great. Debbie, on the other hand couldn't do that. She's used to men, used to being shagged many times a day. For her it's not and never will be, love. For you it's a new experience and I think, if the truth was known, you'd prefer to have just one man in your life. Maybe this will not be a person you'd choose, but in many countries there are arranged marriages. Even the man has no input then."

He fell silent, waiting for her to respond. As Karen had listened, tears began to fill her eyes. In some ways she hadn't accepted Assam's ramblings that she'd never go home. Her own plans had kept her spirits high, such as escaping, seeking retribution from the men who'd raped and beaten her; that all seemed stupid and naive thinking now. She felt sorry for Debbie, even though the girl was a prostitute, she was still entitled to choose how and where she lived, no woman should be a prisoner for life. Now she found her life was really to be the same, just dressed up differently. Debbie may be able to convince someone to help her, men will fall in love with her and she'll use that power. But in her own case this won't happen, the man will have bought her, own her, and have no intention of letting her go.

"You're very quiet," Saeed eventually said.

She looked across at him, tears trickling down her cheeks. "What's there to say about your so-called plan? Did you know I'm eighteen on Friday? I'd saved up for three months to buy a dress. There was to be a party in the church hall. All my friends would have been there. I was even going to bring my boyfriend for my mum and dad to meet," she stopped for a moment, rubbing her eyes. Then she continued, her voice low and shaking. "Now I've nothing. Assam threw away what few items I had in my bag, photos of my mum and dad, my sister. Assam even ripped the chain off my neck. It had a cross attached to it that my grandma gave me when I was confirmed and he stamped them into the ground. I'm dressed like a tramp and have been raped, besides being told that my boyfriend was paid to seduce me. Or, according to Assam, teach me how to perform in bed. My only future is to become someone's plaything until I'm too old or he's offered a sexier, younger girl. Then what happens? I suppose if I'm still attractive to men, I join Debbie, or like Jane, have my throat cut. What do you want me to do? Fling my arms round you and thank you for saving me from a brothel?"

He shrugged indifferently. "Nice speech, Karen, I'd clap if I wasn't driving, but let me give you a few things to chew over in your room when we arrive. Forget home, forget your family, memories are a luxury you now can't afford to have. On Saturday night you'll be sold to the highest bidder, have no doubts about that. Remember this man wants you enough to outbid everybody else. He'll expect loyalty, a girl capable of accepting his love and will give something in return. It's not ideal I grant you. I suppose you'd visions of falling in love with a boy, getting a house, having children, your choice. This man is the same; you are his choice, and he's taking you into his home, where he'll feed you and clothe you. He's rich enough not to expect you to work in the kitchen but that I can't be sure of; anyway it's certain you'll want for nothing. Maybe he'll let you bear his child, who knows? As for you thinking he'd change you when a new younger model came along, that's up to you. Give him love and respect and men look no further. These men are not fickle, flitting from woman to woman. Those sort use the brothels. What I'm saying is a woman's age is not detrimental to these men because they're looking for companionship as well. However, give him problems, mope about thinking of home everyday, don't respond to his affections, and you risk losing everything. Then yes, he may dump you with Debbie, he may slit your throat like Jane, but that's up to you, Karen, you alone."

She sighed to herself; to her it was obvious, that as with Assam, he was trying to make her accept her fate, so he would have an easy life without resorting to beating her. She could well understand it was easier and more lucrative if the girl being sold was unblemished and not obviously difficult or aggressive. So she decided to bide her time, see just who this man was, then, when he believed she had accepted her life, she was determined to retaliate, how... she'd no idea, but she would never accept having her freedom taken away.

By now the car had slowed and they turned down a narrow street in a town they'd entered a short time ago. He parked outside a weather-beaten house, paint peeling off a door built into the wall. Saeed inserted a key in the lock, pushing the door open. Then he returned to the car, released the handcuffs and again demanded she leant forward, placing her hands behind her back, before reattaching the handcuffs to her wrists. He was taking no chances with this girl. Slipping the belt around her neck, he practically dragged her though into the house, slamming the door quickly shut behind them. They were in a small courtyard, a central entrance in front of them with windows around to two floors. The ground floor windows had fancy curved vertical bars, the upper ones similar but not so elaborate.

"This house dates from the seventeenth century. It was then used as a prison; I've converted it but retained some of the features. You'll notice every window is barred. The only entry to the house is from this courtyard and with eight foot walls, escape is perhaps not impossible, but improbable. Your room is on the top floor." He gave her a moment to look round and then pulled on the belt. "Come, it's time you were locked up, there will be a hot drink waiting in your room for you."

They went quickly through the hall and up some narrow stairs where Saeed opened a door, urging her inside. He took her over to the bed and told her to sit. Pulling a chained leg iron from under the bed, he attached it to her ankle, then removed the handcuffs.

"Use the pot under the bed if you want the toilet. Your chain will just reach the dresser where there's a bowl of water for washing. You've travelled a great deal today; you're probably tired so I'll bid you good night." With that he slammed the door closed and she heard the lock click.

Completely shattered, she drank the warm drink, washed her face and collapsed on the bed. Within minutes she was asleep.

Chapter 9

Karen woke when the door opened and an old lady, followed by Saeed, came into the room carrying a tray. Saeed dragged a small table and chair from the far side of the room and placed it close to the bed, then the old lady put the tray on the table. "You will eat everything and completely finish your drink my mother has prepared. I don't like waste. Leave any and you only get half the amount tomorrow," Saeed demanded.

While she chewed the large roll filled with cheese, Saeed settled down in an easy chair watching her, saying nothing. The old lady waiting at the door came over when Karen finished the last of the roll, checking also that she'd finished the hot drink completely. Then, after nodding to her son, she left the room. Saeed stood and walked over to Karen, who was still sitting at the table. He carried a baseball bat and hit the table hard, startling her.

"Listen and listen well. I know all about your past, your self-defence classes and other so-called training. In this house you'll be restrained with an ankle iron at night and where you sit during the day. When I move you from room to room your hands will be handcuffed behind your back. You'll do as you're told without delay and never answer back. Keep to these rules and we'll get on, break them and I'll lay about you with this bat. You'll at the very least be badly bruised, maybe have a broken bone or two, either way you're no good for sale in that condition and I'm not prepared to feed you for weeks until the bruises are gone, or the bone's healed. I'll take you immediately down to the local brothel, it's the pits, and their clients pay little and expect a lot. A broken bone or two is the norm and you'll be worked at least ten hours a day, maybe more if they are busy. Do we understand each other?"

"Yes I understand, I'll be no trouble," she replied.

"That is good, but there's one more very important point to remember. You'll be searched regularly, by my mother. Try to hide something on your person, be it just a pin slipped in the hem of your clothes and I'll treat it as a weapon you intended to use on us. Believe me, a threat like that to my elderly mother, or even me, whatever you're worth in good condition, would be meaningless. You'd be beaten within an inch of your life, then taken out into the desert and left to die. Death that way, without water and shade from the afternoon sun, would still take many hours. Enough time for you to contemplate your stupidity."

At that moment Saeed's mother came into the room carrying a tray, which she placed on the table. Opening a waterproof sheet, the mother laid it out on the bed then went over to her tray. Picking up a razor and bowl containing shaving foam, she stood waiting.

"Now we have an understanding, my mother will begin to prepare you for the sale. She is very experienced and after first removing your body hair, she will work oils into your skin. By Saturday your skin will no longer be white, but golden, similar to light sunburn, hairless and silky smooth. You will also smell very nice. My clients like their girls presented this way and even in their home, both shaving and oiling of your skin will be a regular part of your preparation for your owner's enjoyment, so you always look your best. When she's finished, unlike my other girls, you will be allowed to sit in the lounge downstairs. I will give you a book to read to help pass the time. After a light lunch you'll be brought back up to this room and my mother will apply more oils. You will then be taken into the garden for some fresh air, but out of the sun, as the oils at first can react and burn you. Finally, after dinner and before you're left alone for the night, very light oils will be applied once again."

He watched her for a moment, she was listening but she seemed to be struggling to keep her eyes open. Saeed smiled to himself. With his mother in her late seventies, himself overweight and unfit, he was determined not to be caught unawares with this very capable and fit girl, so he'd added a sedative to her breakfast drink. Now he could see it was beginning to work, her reactions obviously slowing down fast. Reaching down, he unclasped the leg restraint, then looked up at her. "Remove your clothes and lie on the bed," he demanded.

Once Karen was on the bed his mother worked quickly. First using a razor, she expertly removed Karen's body hair, followed by hair removal cream for shorter hair on her legs and arms. Waiting a short time she wiped it off then turned Karen over onto her face, doing the small of her back and legs. Finally she stood away, satisfied. Saeed had, in the meantime, returned to the chair, holding the bat in one hand and gently tapping the other hand with its tip, carefully watching Karen all the time. Seeing his mother had finished, he sat up. "Go in the bathroom and shower, Karen," he shouted. "It is important you use much soap and wash yourself well."

Karen had lain quietly while Saeed's mother had worked on her, but now her head was spinning as she tried to sit up. She was not able to understand what was going on around her. She could hear someone telling her to go and shower, but try as she might, and acutely aware if she didn't, Saeed would use the bat, she couldn't. Her legs didn't seem to want to work. Then someone was at her side helping her up, and moments later she began to get herself together with the shock of cold water cascading over her body. Then it was switched off and Saeed's mother was at her side with a large sponge, lathering Karen's body with lots of soap. She rubbed her all over vigorously, before turning the shower back on and leaving her alone. After a few minutes Karen came out from the bathroom, still dizzy and holding onto the door pillar. "I don't feel very well; can you help me please?" she asked.

His mother, dried her down with a large towel then helped her back onto the bed, placed small bottles at her side and poured a little on her tummy before working the oils into every part of Karen's body. The sweet smelling oils made Karen feel even more light-headed and detached from what was going on.

Eventually the mother stood back then turned to her son. "I have finished," she said in her own language.

Saeed stood and walked over. Looking down at Karen he could see she was asleep. "I think we may have overdone the sedative, mother, perhaps at lunch we should reduce it to half. Today, rather than take her directly downstairs, I'll leave her here for a time and let her sleep it off," he said to her, in their own language.

His mother nodded her understanding, passing him the ankle restraint and placing a sheet over Karen's body to keep her warm.

***

Karen awoke an hour or so later, she felt cold and, at first, wasn't sure where she was, then everything came flooding back as to what Assam had said. She lifted the sheet in trepidation, looking down at her body, and couldn't believe what the woman had done, making her feel decidedly exposed and embarrassed. Tears began forming in her eyes; everyday that went by, the direction of her future, as some sort of sex object, was becoming more and more a reality and she didn't like it. She decided it was getting close to the time when she must make a bid for freedom before she was locked away in some man's house, or was sent to a brothel. However, much as she wanted to do that, she knew she was in a strange country, couldn't talk the language, and would have no idea where to go. This problem was highlighted even more, because since coming to Saeed's house, she was feeling sleepy and lethargic all the time

A short time later Saeed returned with his mother to find Karen lying on the bed. Her mind had been drifting, trying to plan, but was still coming out of the effects of the drug, so everything she thought about seemed jumbled up and hazy.

"Are you feeling better, would you like to come downstairs?" Saeed asked.

"Yes I feel a lot better, thank you for asking. I suddenly felt really dizzy and wasn't sure what was happening. Do you have something for me to wear, I'm really cold even under this sheet?" she asked.

The mother bent down, unclasping the restraint round her ankle, then when Karen sat up she handed her a thin cotton shirt and clean knickers.

Saeed had stood back, keeping hold of the baseball bat, watching. "From now on that's all you wear during the day, but the nights can get a little cold so I'll have another blanket for you," he began. "You will be given clean clothes each day. Now please get dressed, then place your hands behind you back."

She dressed quickly and Saeed handcuffed her, then she followed the mother downstairs with Saeed following behind. Karen sat down in the lounge and the mother fastened her leg to the settee while Saeed unclasped her hands and handed her a book to read. She had read a little, the sedative only just beginning to wear off, when they gave her a small plate of biscuits and a cold drink for her lunch. Then they waited a short time for the second sedative to take hold before taking her back to the bedroom for the next session and leaving her asleep on the bed. Saeed returned around three in the afternoon and she was taken into the garden, then after dinner at seven in the evening she was returned to her room, more oils applied then left chained to the bed. Karen waited for a short time, then, convinced they were not going to come back, she began her workout, determined to remain fit and close to her peak, ready for when she could make her break.

The daily routine, over the next four days, of shower then oils was the same; each time they added a sedative to her breakfast, eleven o' clock drink and evening meal. On the Friday morning, the day before the auction, she was sitting in the lounge as usual, when Saeed joined her, taking a seat opposite.

"My mother's done a good job. You are more than ready, how do you feel?"

Karen shrugged. "The oils make me sleepy and light-headed, so it's nice to sit outside in the early evening and get some fresh air."

He nodded slowly, happy she believed it was the oil and not a sedative that was affecting her. "Yes, the oils are a little heady. Anyway, you need to know what is to happen to you now. Tomorrow will be filled with potential buyers calling to meet you in advance of the sale. I will leave you alone with each of them for half an hour, but will only be in the next room. They will talk to you, maybe some will ask you to stand and remove your shirt, even want you to walk up and down. You will do that without objection and anything else reasonable they ask of you, but they don't own you yet and you must refuse and call me if they want you to remove your knickers, or make sexual advances towards you. You're obviously attractive and have a nice body, but this meeting is not about that, this meeting is your only chance to make a good impression and sell yourself as a person, show that you're intelligent, a good conversationalist and most importantly, someone they would enjoy being with. Ignore them, scowl at them, and you might not sell. That would be bad news for you, Karen, as I'd have no other option but to accept offers from brothel owners. Believe me it is not a route you want to take. The auction takes place Saturday night. A number of sales will go on before you, mainly for the brothel owners, meaning you will be last on. I will come for you. The brothel owners will hang about hoping you don't sell and can buy you cheaply. What I'm saying now is for your own good; providing you've made a good impression and are sold in the sale, the successful bidder will want to take you immediately. If you haven't made a good enough impression then the brothel owners will be the only ones left. No matter what, you will be sold in the sale, have no doubts about that, so it's up to you who that will be. Either way, travelling clothes will be provided, and you'll dress quickly and be ready to go after payment. Have you any questions?"

Karen didn't say anything. What was there to say, soon she'd have a new owner and a new life.

"I was looking at your details in readiness for the sale and remembered you mentioned it was your birthday," he suddenly said, bringing her out of her thoughts.

She smiled. "It was yesterday, but thank you for remembering."

"I have friends in tonight, Karen. We'll celebrate your birthday with a drink. Perhaps you will dance for us; Assam says you're very good."

Her heart sank; tomorrow would be an ordeal and tonight she just wanted to be alone. However, there was no point in arguing. This man wasn't to be argued with; he'd drag her there if he wanted to.

"I'll dance for you, of course, it's just that I wanted to be alone tonight. But I've not got the clothes from the ship for the dance."

Saeed brushed her objection aside. "We have suitable clothes. Girls sold here are sometimes dancers and will perform prior to the sale. My mother will sort you out. Now I must return you to your room as I've many things I need to do. You will dance for me in the big lounge at nine-thirty."

After he'd chained her back up in the bedroom, she could hear Saeed calling his mother. Twenty minutes or so later she appeared carrying bundles of various garments. "Choose what you want to wear, then please fold the rest up afterwards. I will bring shoes for you later," she said, before leaving the room.

Sitting down on the bed, Karen rummaged through the assortment. Eventually choosing a particularly sexy g-string type of knickers with matching bra, a very short red silk skirt and a silky black top fastened with tiny buttons down the front. She stood for some time at the mirror, practising unfastening the buttons. With little else to do it passed the time, so she was glad she did. The buttons were more difficult than she'd imagined and she would have looked stupid without perfecting the knack of releasing them easily. Finally, happy with her routine, she flopped on the bed, lying back and staring at the ceiling.

Her mind was drifting back to home. Tomorrow would have been the day of the party, her eighteenth, and she'd been planning it for months. It seemed so long since she'd been taken, but in reality, only a few weeks. Her friends would be all going out tonight, as usual. They'd be stood at the bus stop now, planning the night. Starting at the Cafe Bar where the drinks were half price for girls, then, slightly drunk, they'd pile into the Kingsway just before the cover charge time came into force. She'd probably already be forgotten, just a mate that once went around with them. Some may even be happy she wasn't there, less competition for them. Karen laughed to herself; they'd no idea about life. She'd had a lover, been raped and was to be sold into a life of sex and mens' pleasure at just eighteen. It sounded terrible and probably would be, but without any other option on offer, maybe if she threw her heart into it, life wouldn't be so bad. In some ways she'd be proud if someone wanted to pay for her, after all, from now on it'd be only sex. Besides, whatever Assam had said about Grant, she'd been in love and had wanted Grant to be her first lover. Karen still had the memory of that first time so vividly in her mind. She'd been scared, desperately scared. Not just of what would happen, but no man had seen her naked before. She'd been afraid he'd laugh at her small breasts, her thin legs and feel her shaking with fear and anticipation. Grant had been gentle, caring and held her tenderly in his arms, allowing her to relax, before taking her to heights she could only imagine before.

Brought out of her dreams when the door burst open, Saeed's mother stood for a moment and then came to sit by her side. She was carrying a bottle and two glasses in one hand, shoes in another. "As you've been a good girl and it was your birthday yesterday, you will drink with me your health, yes?"

Karen grinned and took a glass from her. The mother filled them both to the top. "Your good health. I hope you've much happiness, Karen, you're like I said, a good girl and shouldn't be here," she whispered in broken English.

Karen sipped the drink, it was something she'd never had but it tasted like cherries. She asked what it was but the mother could only give a complicated foreign word.

Then the mother's eyes lit up. "You want I read your hand? My grandmother had the gift; she spent hours with me, then one day I too could see."

"I'd love that," Karen said, her eyes shining. "Once I had my palm read in Blackpool, she'd said I'd have a long life. I suppose she couldn't foresee that this was going to happen to me."

The mother looked carefully at her hand and then up at Karen, her face full of fear. "You will have a long life, much happiness," she lied, but Karen had read her eyes.

"Please, I want the truth. I'm terrified of the future; if it's death at least it will be a release of some sort."

The old lady pushed her hand away and spoke slowly in French, so Karen could understand. "You shouldn't have been brought here because you bring death and destruction. It follows your life; many will perish because of you. I pray to God my Saeed's not among them."

Karen tried to make light of it. "I'm just a young girl, how can I bring death and destruction? Besides, nobody can really tell your future. Perhaps you're confused. Okay, one man died because he tried to help me, I agree, but I wasn't there and the other was murdered by Garrett. Both weren't my fault," Karen retorted.

The old lady clasped her hands together, looking down at the floor. "What has Saeed done? What has Saeed done?" she kept muttering. Then she stood and moved slowly to the door; in Karen's eyes the woman had visibly aged.

"Please don't go, tell me what am I to do? I don't understand your words, I've done nothing," Karen pleaded.

The woman turned, tears running down her face, her eyes sad. "It's in your hands, Karen, all there for those who can see."

Karen stared at her. "See? What for God's sake, just what can you see?"

The mother seemed at first to ignore her pleading but as she made to leave she stopped, keeping her back to Karen, mumbling in French. "I see only death, Karen, only death."

Then she was gone. Karen sat there stunned, not understanding her words or what they had to do with her. She finished off her glass and refilled it. By the time that was empty she felt better, even perhaps a little drunk, but she didn't care. The dance would be easier; she'd be indifferent to them watching and perhaps a little more fluid in her movements.

***

At about nine the mother came up for her, saying nothing, just releasing her ankle iron. Saeed came into her room and grinned. "You look nice, Karen, good choice of clothes," he said, at the same time turning her round and handcuffing her. "Now down the stairs quickly."

Karen had not been in this room before. A small platform was set up in the centre, tables and chairs surrounding it. She knew this must be where she was to be auctioned. In the room were six or seven men, all smoking and making the atmosphere heavy, stinging Karen's eyes. They'd been playing cards and now were stood around waiting for the entertainment. One handed her a drink and she took it gratefully.

Saeed, following her in, had taken a chair and placed it on the platform. "When you're ready, Karen," he called to her, at the same time sitting down on the chair, grinning.

She nodded, giving him a weak smile, then drained her glass. The others stood around the platform and one switched on a CD player. Karen told Saeed to sit back and place his hands to his side. Then she stood slightly away from him, keeping her eyes locked on his. As the music began she slowly began to move, swinging her hips and allowing her hands to move gently over her body, eventually moving closer and closer to him before sitting on his knee, rubbing herself gently against him. At the same time, she was slowly unfastening the buttons of the blouse, before standing and allowing the blouse to fall to the floor. Turning her back she wriggled her hips a bit more then pushed the short skirt down to join the blouse. Slowly, and she hoped seductively, she unfastened the bra before turning to face him, holding the bra tightly to her chest then allowing it to fall to the floor. This time she moved closer and sat again on his knee, with her face close to his and she whispered quietly into his ear. "Do I keep the g-string on, Saeed, or do you want me to go all the way?"

Saeed was enjoying her dance and turned his head, pretending to kiss her ear. "It's enough for these people, Karen, finish your dance with them on please."

She did as he asked and carried on for some time, finishing, as she'd done with Barry, astride his legs, pretending intercourse, before finally kissing him on the lips. All the men clapped and one handed her a drink, another, her clothes. Karen thanked them and made to leave but Saeed asked her to stay and sit at his side. They all returned to the card game and soon they were pouring money onto the table.

An hour or so passed; she'd watched them for some time and was fed up, sitting cross-legged on the floor, sipping another drink. The tone had changed now, becoming agitated, as the stakes seemed to go higher. Saeed was sweating as money was piled high on the table.

"I raise you one thousand," someone said.

Another pushed his stake into the centre.

Karen became more interested as the stakes went higher. She wasn't sure of the value and even the one's who'd already dropped out had their eyes fixed on the table. Eventually it was down to Saeed and another. This man was tall, well dressed and quietly spoken. They were talking English and he pushed another pile to the middle.

"I raise you five thousand, Saeed."

Saeed seemed restless, unsure of what to do. Then he made a decision. "I'll accept the five thousand and call you," Saeed answered.

The man frowned. "Money, Saeed, where's the money? You know the rules, no credit."

Saeed threw his arms in the air. "I'm out of money; I have no more in the house. I'll write a note, how about that?"

The man shook his head. "No money, you lose," he spat, and made to pull the money forward.

Saeed panicked and asked the others to cover him but they all declined. Then he looked directly at Karen. "Her, she's worth forty thousand. She'll be my guarantee," he said with satisfaction.

The man looked at Karen then back to Saeed. "In this bet, she's worth the call, no more: lose, Saeed, and I keep her."

Karen's eyes widened. Saeed was desperate to stay in the game so was offering her. If the man won there'd be no auction, she'd belong to him. However, her fears were dispelled with Saeed's next words.

Saeed held his hand up. "For the night only. The girl's worth too much to give away. You may have her for the night."

The man laughed. "Five thousand for one night, Saeed? I could have twenty nights for that sort of money. No, I keep her if you lose."

Saeed looked around; everybody was waiting expectantly for him to respond. The table was covered with money, and at the turn of the cards it would be all his. Only a tiny doubt ran through his mind. What if he lost? The buyer's coming tomorrow and Karen would not be here. Saeed began talking in his own language, a language Karen couldn't understand.

"Hussein, I'll gladly give you a girl from tomorrow's batch if I lose. Keep Karen for the night as your insurance for payment but she must be returned tomorrow. Her owner's coming."

Hussein raised an eyebrow. "Who's her owner?"
"Sirec."

Hussein stared at him. "She's Sirec's girl?" he stuttered.

Saeed nodded. "Karen doesn't know it, but the advanced client meetings for her have been cancelled. I have other girls to replace her. Sirec sent Jordan, his man who looks after the villa, to purchase her. I had no option but to accept his price, as you know, what Sirec wants he gets; Sirec will kill me and possibly you, my friend, if she isn't here when his man comes to collect her."

Hussein nodded slowly. "I'll take the deal, Saeed. If I lose, so be it. If I win, I take the girl as security until tomorrow. Then she is to be exchanged for another to be auctioned on my behalf and I keep the bid."

Saeed sighed with relief, he'd won anyway but he had to be sure Karen would be safe. "One other thing, Hussein."

"That is?" Hussein asked.

"She must not be beaten or marked in any way. The girl's already prepared by my mother. Sirec knows she's perfect and without marks. Mark her and it won't just be me you'll answer to but Sirec himself."

Hussein shrugged. "I am not afraid of Sirec," he replied somewhat bravely. "Although you have my word, she stays with me until tomorrow, to do as I will. That's of course, if I win."

Karen listened, trying to understand from the few words she'd picked up, but she couldn't. However at that moment, Saeed reverted to English.

"The deal's done. If I lose, Karen, you're to stay with Hussein as my surety to the debt. Do you understand?"

"Will I be safe, or raped?" she whispered.

Hussein cut in fast. "I rape no woman," he retorted.

Karen smiled weakly, then stood quietly at Saeed's side. She was praying he'd win and she could go back to her room. Already nervous about tomorrow and the potential buyers she was to see, she just wanted time alone to compose herself, besides think what these buyers really wanted of her. Should she be quiet and submissive? Alternatively, should she be her usual confident and talkative self? Karen had no idea and was terrified that they'd reject her, leaving only the brothel alternative. She was brought out of her thoughts when Hussein turned his first card; it was a ten of spades. Saeed turned one; his was a Jack of diamonds. Then Hussein was next with another ten. Saeed felt confident the man had a pair the same as him but a lower number. So, confidently, Saeed turned his second Jack.

"I think I win, Hussein?" Saeed hissed with satisfaction.

Hussein raised an eyebrow. "Why is that, Saeed?"

Saeed shrugged. "Look, I've a pair higher than yours," he laughed.

Hussein grinned. "You would, of course, if my last card wasn't a ten, Saeed, but you see it is. Surely that's three of a kind and beats you?"

With those words, Hussein threw the last card on the table so all could see. Saeed stared dumbfounded at the three cards, his mouth opening and shutting like a fish. Hussein stood and pulled the money towards him, pushing it into a polythene bag, then he turned to Karen. "Come, it's time I left," he said to her, offering his hand.

She took it gingerly, following as he left the room. Saeed, suddenly getting his voice back, ran after them. "Here, handcuff the girl, she's prone to trying to escape and she must be back tomorrow, Hussein, we have a deal," he demanded.

Hussein glanced at Karen. "You want me to handcuff you or do you promise not to try to escape?"

She shrugged. "That's up to you, you're a man, I'm only a girl. How could I escape you?"

He grinned then looked at Saeed. "I don't need handcuffs, Saeed, she won't escape me and she'll be returned to you tomorrow, if you have my money, that is?" Then they left.

Outside, he opened the passenger door of an old car parked behind others. Karen climbed in and he ran round the other side, climbing in alongside her. Soon, after a few tries, the engine fired and they were turning out onto the main road.

"Your name's Karen, where do you come from in England?" Hussein asked.

"Manchester," she said.

He didn't reply for a time until they'd slowed at a crossroads. Then he glanced across at her. "How old are you then?"

She was looking down at her hands, playing with her fingers, becoming more afraid of what might happen to her tonight. However, she decided perhaps if he thought her younger than she really was, he may treat her better. "I'm sixteen nearly seventeen. It was to be my party tomorrow night. My dad had booked a room in our town."

He'd no time to reply as at that moment he turned into a small drive. In front of her was an old house, badly in need of paint.

"We're here, shall we go inside?" he asked politely.

She looked at him for a moment, why had his manner changed? At Saeed's he was harsh and, on the drive, trying to be interested in her but without any real compassion. Deciding she'd never understand these men, she sighed and pushed open the door. By now Hussein was round her side and grasped her hand gently, but firmly, not giving her the opportunity to run. He pushed open the front door and they went inside.

"Hussein, who is this?" A woman's voice came from behind. Karen spun round to see a woman of about forty coming through a door. Hussein went to her and kissed her cheek.

"We have a visitor, Rias, I sort of won her at cards with Saeed."

She glared at him, then Karen. "I'll have no prostitute in my house, get rid of her now," she shouted.

Karen looked indignantly at her. "I'm no prostitute,

thank you," she retorted.

"Ha," the woman responded. "I suppose decent women walk round dressed like you then?"

Hussein cut in to stop the potential fight. "She's right, Rias. The girl's English, one of Saeed's deals. She's been sold to Sirec and Saeed made her dance for us tonight. I don't think what she's wearing would be her choice."

The woman stared at Hussein. The very word Sirec sent cold shivers down her spine.

"She's a Sirec girl, are you out of your mind, Hussein? That man would kill you if he even knew she was here."

Hussein started to talk to her in their own language, the woman shaking her head and throwing her arms about, close to hysterics. Eventually she calmed and looked back at Karen. "You will stay with us tonight. We have a spare bedroom but I need your promise."

Karen frowned. "Promise? What sort of promise?" she asked.

"That you won't try to leave and you'll tell Sirec how well you were treated," she replied softly.

"Who's this Sirec?" Karen asked.

The woman didn't reply at first but urged Karen to follow her into a small kitchen. Then she passed her a drink and asked her to sit. "Sirec is a wealthy man in these parts," the woman began. "He has eyes and ears everywhere and even if you did escape and go to the police it would do you no good. They, like everybody else in this country, are corrupt or supplementing their pay from people like him. If Sirec has decided he wants you then you're lucky, very lucky. You'll want for nothing and will always be protected. So when my stupid brother said you belonged to Sirec, you can understand my fear? Anyway will you promise not to try to escape, for me and my brother's sake?"

Karen smiled and touched the woman's hand. "Where could I go? Besides, I don't want you to get into trouble."

Rias thanked her and they spent some time talking, Karen telling her of her ordeal. She then asked Rias if she could use her telephone and ring home. She promised not to say where she was; in fact she'd no idea where she was, just wanted to talk to her mum. Rias sat for some time, staring at Karen. She felt sorry for the girl but the fear of Sirec finding out was very real. Hussein had come in on the end of the conversation.

"What do you think, Hussein? Dare we risk it?" she asked in their own language.

He replied in the same, not letting Karen understand. "Tell her 'maybe tomorrow'. It won't be possible, of course, but it will save us any trouble tonight. Besides, let her do this and Sirec's bound to find out or the girl may mention it to him, then we're dead."

Rias sighed. "You're right, of course, I will say tomorrow she can call, giving her an excuse, but it won't happen as you'll leave early and take her quickly back to Saeed."

Karen was disappointed she couldn't call till tomorrow, accepting Rias's explanation that in this area, phone calls abroad are through switchboards that close down at night. So after a small piece of cake with a glass of wine, they showed her to her room for the night. She lay there for some time, their words about this man who possibly was to bid for her tomorrow was spinning round in her head. Eventually she dropped off. She'd not been asleep more than an hour when someone clasped a hand over her mouth and whispered in her ear.

"Karen, it's me, Hussein, don't make a sound. I want to talk to you," he whispered.

Then he removed his hand from her face. "Rias is sleeping. Do you still want to call home then?"

"But Rias said I couldn't call till tomorrow."

Hussein grinned. "She didn't tell the truth, she was

trying to protect the family in case Sirec found out. I can arrange it, mind you I want something in return," he said quietly.

"What's that?" she asked cautiously.

He tried to shrug indifferently. "I won you tonight; Saeed said I can do what I want with you, so long as you're returned tomorrow."

Karen's face darkened. "So?" she said slowly.

He touched her arm. "I want you, Karen, I couldn't sleep for thinking about you doing that dance round Saeed. I want you so much."

She sighed to herself. She suspected this might happen but had hoped when she first met Rias, she'd been his wife, not his sister. However, Karen wasn't so naive as to say no, just yet. Although Barry had called, she'd now left the ship and that was nearly a week ago. If they'd known where she was, someone would already have come, and they hadn't. She needed this call home to tell them where she was going.

"If I agree to what you ask, I have conditions of my own," Karen replied quietly.

"Conditions? What are these conditions?" he asked.

"I want more than just to call home, like I asked your sister. I want you to give me this man Sirec's address, so I've a chance of some help. Besides, I also want to call before we do anything."

Hussein's eyes widened. "You ask a great deal, Karen, wanting Sirec's address. But the call, can't it wait till the morning?"

Karen sniggered, her voice scathing. "So I'm letting you fuck me on a bloody promise. You're off your trolley if you think me that stupid; I call first, otherwise I'm not interested."

Hussein was taken aback with the girl's words but he wasn't going to walk away, after all, she'd practically agreed. "How do I know how good you are, you may be hopeless?"

She smiled at his crude attempt to have her with just a promise to let her phone. "Hussein, believe me, if there's one thing I can do well and I mean well, it is to please a man. The man who taught me was good, showed me how to excite a man, besides take me in every position, you... could imagine. Do you really believe I'd be a hopeless lover?"

As she stopped she could see his eyes widening at her words. He was hooked, the same as Barry had been and she knew it. Hussein touched her lips and left the room, moments later he returned with a telephone.

He pushed a piece of paper into her hand and moved closer. "That's the international code to get connected. I've included Sirec's home address so they know where you'll be, I can do no more. You've got fifteen minutes, call whoever you want. When I return I'll expect you ready for me. I want the works, Karen, what you're asking could get me killed if Sirec finds out."

She leaned over and kissed him. "Like I said, you can do anything you want with me, take me in any position, but there is one more condition. Have you a condom? I'm not prepared to get pregnant on top of everything else."

He nodded pulling a packet of three from his pocket.

She gave a laugh. "Optimist, Hussein? Do you think you've the staying power for three then?" she mocked.

He grinned at her. "I have, but can you?" he teased.

Karen shrugged; the man was attractive in some ways, so she told him what he wanted to hear. "Oh yes, Hussein, you can believe it."

He dropped the packet on the dresser and left the room.

She sat for a few minutes unsure. Should she be doing this? What would they say to her? Would they disown her after seeing the photos? All these questions ran around in her head, but the alternative of being sold with perhaps little or no chance of escape, that terrified her. Then Karen suddenly made a decision, deciding if they put the phone down on her, at least she'd know for certain she was on her own. As it was there was still hope they'd still want her home, no matter how stupid she'd been. She began to push buttons, holding her breath as it began to ring.

"Hello, who's there?" a voice came on the phone. Karen's heart skipped a beat. "Daddy, it's me, Karen," she whispered as tears were beginning to run down her face.

The phone went quiet for a moment and Karen suddenly panicked that he'd hung up. "Daddy, it really is me, please say something, don't hang up," she stuttered.

"Karen, I'm sorry, darling, your voice has come as a shock, we thought you were dead. The car, it went over a cliff, nobody could have survived. Then the police came round a few days ago saying they'd had a call about you being on a boat, but we weren't to get our hopes up as they'd received a great many hoax calls about you and we were to play it down if the papers telephoned, until they'd made further enquiries."

Karen realised he was talking about Barry's call, which, as she feared, seemed to have fallen on deaf ears, but by her calling he would know she was alive and tell the police. "I wasn't in the car, Daddy. They took me on a ship; I've been raped and beaten, Daddy, now I'm to be sold as some sort of sex slave tomorrow. I don't want to be sold, I want to come home, please come and get me, I'm so scared."

Tears were streaming down her face, unable for a moment to speak; she could hear him calling her mother to come.

"Karen, you must get a hold of yourself, love. Now take a deep breath and tell me where you are. We'll be on the next flight out. You can be certain of that," he said with a voice of authority.

She pulled herself together and carefully read out the details on the paper. Then she gave him the name of the ship, including the names of everybody else she could think of.

"That's a good girl. Now please tell me again about what's happening tomorrow."

Again she told him everything she knew. Her father listened, stunned that Frank Whittle had done this to her. He was glad he was dead or he'd gladly have killed Frank himself.

By now her mother had arrived and grabbed the phone from him. "Karen, Karen, darling, is that really you?" she shouted, unable to control her emotions.

Karen took a deep breath, frightened of what her mum thought of her. "I'm sorry, Mummy, I was stupid to let that man trick me. I thought he loved me. Please believe me," Karen whispered.

"Tricked you, who tricked you?" she asked.

Suddenly it dawned on her Assam had lied, he'd never sent photos and never told her parents about Grant. It had all been a trick to make her believe she'd be disowned.

However, her mother didn't wait for a reply. "Why can't you come home, Karen?" her mother asked, unable to grasp what had happened to her daughter.

"They won't let me, Mum. You've got to come for me, tell them I'm still a child. Beg them to let me come home. I can't take much more," she began to cry, the emotion of talking to her family too much. She'd tried so hard to be strong, believing all the time her family thought her dead or a slut not worth bothering about, but this wasn't the case, they knew nothing of her affair. Now all she wanted was to go home. Then the bedroom door opened and Hussein stood watching her, pointing to his watch. She nodded slowly and he left the room.

"I've got to go now, Mum, people are waiting for me, this call has cost me dearly, believe me," she whispered. "Please come, don't let me down, you and Daddy are my last chance. I've nobody else."

Karen could hear her mother shouting for her to stay on, her father trying to assure her he'd come as she pressed the button and suddenly all that came back to her was the dial tone, then silence. She placed the telephone on the dresser and rinsed her face in the washbasin. She stood at the mirror brushing her long hair.

Hussein entered and came up behind her, gently slipping his hands round her body and grasping her breasts. "Are you ready now, Karen?"

She pushed his hands away, then turned slowly. He stood still, hardly daring to breath, expectancy for what was going to happen written all over his face. Karen took a deep breath, the doubt and lack of confidence in herself suddenly all gone. Her secret life with Grant still unknown and she owed this man nothing.

She shouted at a startled Hussein. "You bloody lot are all the same, wanting payment for everything. A bloody phone call, two bleeding quid at the most and I have to pay with my body." She pushed him to one side and made for the bed, falling back on it and staring straight at him. "Well come on then, what are you waiting for? I'm ready to make payment. If you're not man enough I'll even take my own knickers off," she screamed at him.

Hussein by now was in panic, the girl was hysterical and making it sound dirty and sordid.

"Well, Hussein, why are you still stood there? Perhaps I'll even like it if your dick's anything like your mouth. I'll tell you this though; you'd better kill me after, because if this Sirec is anything like everyone says he is, he'll not take too kindly to his girl being raped."

At that moment Rias stormed into the room. She looked at Karen and then Hussein. "What's going on, Hussein?" she demanded.

"That girl tricked me. I gave her the phone, the chance of freedom and she suddenly becomes hysterical."

Karen laughed at him. "Not quite the truth, Hussein. What was your condition, ten minutes on the phone in return for the rest of the night with my legs open? Wasn't that it? Well I've used the phone so I'm here on the bed ready to make the payment you demanded. But I won't lift a finger to help, or respond in any way. For me its rape, not love, you have no right to ask me to love you."

Hussein's mouth had dropped open, the girl was turning it all round, he wanted to kill her. But his sister cut in.

"That's enough!" she shouted. "Hussein, get out, you bring shame to this house. You bring home a girl, taken from her mother and father, bound for a life of slavery, maybe even death, and you want to add to this poor girl's misery. Can you not imagine what she's going through? You stood in front of me, less than two hours ago, and offered this child a night when she could lay down and sleep in safety. One night, Hussein, one night she had a chance to close her eyes believing no one would disturb her, but you couldn't even give her that, could you? I'm ashamed to even believe my brother could sink so low as to consider forcing a child to have sex with him, for a lousy phone call. What can she think of us?"

Hussein's face had changed, a look of shame spread quickly over it. He moved towards Karen, she shrunk back, pushing her act to the limit. He offered his hand. "I'm sorry, I don't know what came over me. My sister's right, I've shamed her and at the same time I've shamed myself."

Karen grasped his hand and squeezed it gently. Her manner had changed, she'd won and now a few chosen words would make this man squirm. "It was partly me," she whispered. "I so desperately wanted to talk to my daddy, hear my mum's voice, tell them I wasn't dead, and to just know they'd not abandoned me. I may never have the chance again, so what would you have done, if you'd been me?"

He leaned over and kissed her cheek. "Sleep well, Karen, believe me, nobody will disturb you again in this house."

With that he moved to the door. Rias gave Karen a brief smile, well aware how neatly Karen had planned a way out of her promise. Just as she was closing the door Karen called her back. "Rias, is there a church round here?"

"What sort, Karen?"

She shrugged. "I'm really Catholic but any would do. You see, I went to a convent school, and religion is very important in my life, so in the last few days I've tried to pray when I was on the ship and at Saeed's house, but it was difficult. I'm not very good on my own and I'd begun to believe God had turned his back on me. So I'd like to pray, just once in church, ask him for forgiveness and to give me strength for the weeks ahead... That's all."

Rias could see no harm in taking her to the church and reached over, grasping her hand, "You'll come with me in the morning, Karen, we'll light a candle. God won't abandon you, test your strength maybe, but abandon you, no."

She stayed for a short time, allowing Karen to cry and held her, then when she was sure Karen was alright again, left the room, pulling the door gently closed.

Karen rubbed her eyes and sat for a few minutes, thinking about tomorrow and if her father really would come and get her. Then she stood and went over to the mirror, combing her hair. She felt good now, glad Hussein was gone. In some ways she'd actually resigned herself to letting him make love to her. Perhaps, she thought, it would make her feel more of a woman after Saeed's mother had messed about with her body. However, after talking to her family, what Hussein was intending seemed dirty and sordid. What possessed her to stand up to him she wasn't sure, but it worked and she was proud of herself. No longer tired, she decided to start her simple workout, doing a number of press-ups at first then deciding to carry on until she could go on no more. Still very fit, something kept telling her to keep it up, convinced in her mind she'd need the strength one day. Then finally exhausted, Karen returned to her bed and soon fell asleep with the knowledge people at last knew she was still alive, and more importantly, where she was. She was confident her mum and dad would shout to the world about her plight

Chapter 10

Garry Stafford shuffled uneasily in the confined officers' mess of the submarine. He'd been brought aboard with eleven other S.A.S. members three days ago after a long, uneventful flight from their home base in the UK. Now, after lounging about with nothing to do but eat and sleep, a meeting had at last been called.

His Commander was talking quietly to a man he'd never seen before at the front. His mate, Mark King, was concentrating on rolling a cigarette; at twenty-two, six foot three and a body toned by his obsession with weights, Garry was a man girls dreamed about and he had plenty of admirers. He'd turned his back on that to fulfill his ambition and join the Special Services.

However, the life he'd assumed they'd lead, going from one hot spot to another hadn't, until now, materialised. To be fair though, it wasn't for lack of trying; they'd done lots of training for assault but all the ones he'd trained for had been settled by negotiation.

"Gentlemen, may I have your attention," his Commander called above the hum of conversation in the room.

The room fell silent, save for the constant rumbling of the engines.

"Thank you," he said quietly. "I'd like to hand you over now to Sir Giles Horton from the Home Office, Sir Giles."

Sir Giles stood and after thanking him, looked carefully round the room at each man in turn. "As you may be aware, the civil war in North Africa is showing no signs of abating. Our troops out there, although only peacekeepers, have come under fire more and more often and despite our vigilance, arms are being brought at an alarming rate into the area." He fell silent for a moment, at the same time opening a folder in front of him. "We believe, no, let me correct that diplomatic word, we know, that many of these weapons are surplus from the conflict in the northern territories of Israel. The main gun-runner of the area has never been busier and is reaping the benefits. Two such shippers have become known to us, so in an effort to slow this cargo we intend to take out their main supplier's warehousing as a warning to others who believe this conflict to be a lucrative opportunity."

He fell silent while he removed large bulky envelopes from his bag, many in the room taking the opportunity to cough, caused by the now smoky atmosphere and poor air movement. "I have your sealed orders here. There will be three groups, each with specific targets. Commander Farrow will lead and coordinate the operation firsthand. We will be following the events in the temporary Operations Room set up on the carrier, Hermes. Good luck and I'll hand the floor over to your Commander, who'll brief you operationally."

With that, Sir Giles left the room quickly. Commander Farrow passed the sealed orders round to the appropriate groups. "Open the orders, gentlemen. We go at zero-four-thirty."

"Err, both Mark and myself don't have any orders, Sir," Garry said, dreading the Commander might be leaving them behind.

"No, you have a special assignment which we'll talk about later, however, you're part of my group, so familiarise yourselves with my team's operation for now." Then he looked around the room. "You will notice we keep as one unit until we arrive at the village called Harable, only then splitting to your directed assignments. A sub will be off the coast in four days, or if delayed, six day's time. We must rendezvous back together to meet it, as the sub can only come once and can't return. Miss it and believe me, it's a long walk home."

No one said anything, just studied their orders while Commander Farrow read his, before continuing. "Your own operation is scheduled for three days. It's a long time, I know, but these warehouses are deep in the countryside, very well protected by mountainous terrain from the air, so I've allowed extra time for unforeseen problems, then no group has an excuse not to be back at the pickup point."

He looked around the room, the seriousness in his voice all too apparent. "This operation's essential for bringing stability to the area. We know the rebels are short of ammunition and heavy guns. Our ships in the bay and the lads in the air have extracted a heavy toll on their fixed gun emplacements. This has changed the tactics of these so-called armies to a guerrilla operation. Guerrilla tactics, gentlemen, as we all know, require light, modern weapons. A ship's to be loaded with six hundred tons of ammunition, ten thousand semi-automatic weapons and two hundred anti-tank systems on the fifth of this month for just such an operation. That's four days from now. Our Government and the lads on the front line don't want this consignment to even leave port. Once at sea, diplomatically, we couldn't take out the ship; we know from past experience these shipments are a combination of Red Cross and humanitarian items, so you can understand there would be serious repercussions if we blew any out of the water. This brings me to the only real option, and that's to destroy the weapons before they leave the warehouses. If we succeed, we'll severely dent the rebels' ability to mount any operations."

The meeting went on for some two hours, by which time they were all familiar with their own roles. Garry could now understand the recent training; everything directed in this training to fortified warehouses. Before Commander Farrow dismissed everyone, he looked at the two lads. "Stafford, King, can you two stay behind?"

They remained seated and Commander Farrow closed the door, moving to the front. He handed them sealed orders and at the same time pulled out a map and photos of a house set deep in an estate. "Sirec Saleam is the brains behind this operation. He's Mr. Big in the gun-runner business, and supplies regularly into the Far East. We don't know much about his background or what country's sewer he originated from, but we know his house. Or rather we know of one. He has safe houses all over the world."

Garry cut in. "What's this man got to do with us?" he asked Commander Farrow.

"For this operation: nothing. Oh, it'd be nice to put a bullet between his eyes, but Sirec's in Europe, so we've been told. It's what's in his house the government wants," he replied, pushing over a photograph.

The two men stared at it for some minutes. "She's a good-looking girl," Mark commented.

Then Garry suddenly recognised her. "Isn't that the girl who was abducted and drowned in Wales?" he asked.

Commander Farrow nodded. "So everybody thought. In reality she wasn't drowned, she was put on a ship, possibly transferred to a smaller boat, then taken overland to a village two hundred miles north of Beirut. From there she's been sold to Sirec. She, gentlemen, is Sirec's girl now. Our Government wants her. In fact it's rumoured the PM's election chances rest with the safe return of this girl. The papers have caused mayhem, demanding the Government gets her back."

Garry frowned. "So where do we come in then?"

"You go and get her, it's as simple as that. We have the house and the location and while governments are arguing over what should be done, the S.A.S. go and nick her back from under Sirec's nose."

Mark scowled. "I'm no nanny; what about the warehouse attack we've trained for?"

Commander Farrow dismissed his words, his reply to Mark scathing and with total authority. "These are new orders. It's a dangerous job I know, but it's what we're here for and, gentlemen, this is what we, the S.A.S., the finest strike force in the world, are all about. I'm not bothered if it's a criminal, a weapon dump or yes, even an eighteen year old kid down on her luck, it's just as important an operation in my book. Do you have a problem with that?"

"No, Sir..." they both shouted in unison.

"Then study your orders, gentlemen, and I want you both fully conversant with that document and ready to board landing dinghies at 04-30. Do I make myself clear?"

"Yes, Sir," they both shouted again.

Chapter 11

It was after this meeting with Commander Farrow, and an uneventful trip to the village of Harable, that Garry and Mark found themselves leaving the main group and joining a local informer who was to take them on to Hariz. This village was some sixty miles from where the target warehouses were located, and close to Sirec's villa. Commander Farrow had arranged to meet up, after collecting Karen, eighty miles due west and less than fifty miles from the submarine pickup point, in three days. With satellite communication, Garry had received updated photos taken that morning; the exact layout of the villa and the surrounding area was confirmed to him. He now needed time to survey the location, find a means of entry and exit from the villa and spend a day studying the movements of people inside; with particular attention to the times the guards changed or conducted their security checks.

The informer, Arif, a man in his sixties, muttered constantly to himself as he coaxed the aged car along the main road into Hariz. He spoke good English and although Garry was able to speak Arabic, communication in English was preferable.

"Transport, Arif, what have you arranged for us to leave the area?" Garry asked as he fiddled with his radio.

"I have arranged nothing. You must remember it was only late last night I was informed you were to go to Hariz. Anyway there will be no problem, my mother's brother lives there, it's very large with some three thousand inhabitants and I will have no problem in finding a car." He stopped talking for a moment as he grappled with the steering wheel, trying to prevent the car from ending up in a ditch, then continued. "Your Commander has already given me money to buy a vehicle. I will show you before we get to Hariz just where it will be left. We have to be very careful as cars that seem abandoned are soon procured by the locals trying to keep their own cars on the road. The last thing you want is transport without wheels or engine, yes?"

Garry laughed. "Yes, Arif, that would be a little difficult to say the least."

By the time they'd come within four miles of Hariz, it had turned nine o'clock in the morning. Many vehicles had passed them going both ways and they'd sunk low in their seats. Suddenly Arif veered off the road up a dirt track. They climbed for some two miles before the track narrowed so much it was hardly wide enough for a man, let alone a vehicle. Even the terrain had changed, with the flat arid landscape giving up to dense scrubland. He stopped, climbed out and stretched. The other two followed him.

"Sirec's villa is north west from here," Arif began. "Follow the track through the gorge and you will see it below you. This road, or track as you may call it, was once part of the route to Iriza, forty miles away. Since Sirec built his house, the original track has been closed with the new one diverted round Sirec's estate and is now a very good tarmac road. Sometimes you may get one or two poachers or herdsmen using this part but it is our winter now and the herdsmen keep the animals in the valley. They won't be coming up here for another month or so. Your car will be waiting here. It will be fully fuelled and the keys will be," he stopped and looked round before walking to a large rock and bending down, "under this small stone by the side of this rock. If anyone comes this way they'll think the occupants are out hunting, but you can be sure they will come back in a couple of days time just to see if they were wrong, and the car had been abandoned."

While Arif explained to Garry, Mark had pulled out all their equipment and was quickly strapping it together for carrying. Now completed, he waited quietly for Arif to finish. Finally, with arrangements made, they shook hands and the two soldiers moved up the track. Arif watched them go and turned the old car round, heading down towards Hariz.

"What's the plan then, Garry?" Mark asked, as they moved slowly through the dense scrub.

Garry shrugged. "Your bet's as good as mine. Nobody seems to know just how many people are living there or anything. What I'm banking on with Sirec not being there, is that the security will be lax. Besides, what's there to protect?"

Mark nodded his agreement. "Yeah, that's a point, with luck then we'll be in and out before they know what's hit them, after all, somebody looking for Sirec is hardly going to attack a house knowing he's in Europe."

"That's my thought too, anyway we'll spend the rest of the day watching and decide later," Garry replied.

Suddenly, without warning, they came to a sheer drop, the track itself turning sharp right. Looking down into the valley they could see a villa some hundred feet below. Painted white, it stood out in the surrounding starkness of the area. They dropped to their stomachs and peered over with powerful glasses. As in the aerial photos, but not clear until now, were two walls, an inner low wall and a high outer one. The outside wall was at least twelve feet high with only one entrance and what looked like guardhouses either side. The inner wall was about eight feet high, yet again, with only one entrance and another guardhouse. Inside the inner wall the area couldn't have been more different. Extensive lawns, gardens neatly laid out, terraces round the massive central villa and a swimming pool, kidney shaped, sparkling blue amongst a sea of tropical plants.

"Wow, this is some pad, eh, Mark?" Garry whispered.

"Yeah, the kids really landed on her feet; do you think she would still want rescuing?" Mark commented.

"You might be right but on the other hand she could be in deep trouble. Men like this could get anyone in the world. Why buy an eighteen year old just to shag. Unless his tastes are more bizarre and relies on young girls to feed his appetite," Garry replied.

They watched for nearly three hours at the comings and goings. They noted every truck, every car arriving or leaving, logged times of guards patrolling the outer perimeter and could locate at least six guards wandering around in the inner walled area. By the side of the pool they could make out somebody lying on a lounger, but until now were unable to see who it was because of a large umbrella. However, a bell had rung from the villa and this person stood up to go inside.

Garry watched his glasses at full magnification. "That's the kid. That's Karen," he said to Mark. "Boy, she's got a fantastic figure; no wonder this Sirec wants her."

Mark, busily preparing some food, grabbed his glasses and just caught her as she went inside. "Well at least she's there. So what's the plan now you've seen the place?"

Garry picked up a sandwich and took a large bite, Mark did the same.

"It seems to me," Garry observed between chews. "the only way in is through the entrance. Scaling that wall would be easy but did you notice the wires above? They had insulators on and that spells electrification. Even that's not too bad for us to get through, but how do we get a girl out that way? She looked from here a bit of a bimbo and those sort don't climb walls, always afraid they'll break a nail."

Mark leaned over and pulled a file from his bag. He read it for some time then looked up at Garry, who, although still chewing his sandwich, had gone back to surveying the villa.

"I wouldn't underestimate this girl, Garry. According to the report from central, the girl's quite an athlete. Often from the age of fourteen, she went with her father on those action weekends. You know the sort of thing, grown men using paint guns and playing soldiers. It also means she'll probably have the ability to read maps, use a compass and hopefully melt into the terrain to avoid capture. Many a time she'd sleep rough on the Saturday night with others in the group when it was a two-day exercise."

Garry cut in. "If I'd known those weekends included girls like her, I'd have been there myself. Can you imagine waking up with her at your side? Besides, stuff the games, I'd be out with her, clubbing it."

Mark laughed, he couldn't agree more, but he read on from Karen's profile and frowned. "You might have had a little trouble convincing her to go clubbing with you, Garry, if she didn't want to."

"Why's that?" Garry asked.

Mark laughed again. "Well her father also sent her to self-defence classes, kick-boxing and judo. By the sound of that lot he must have really wanted a lad, so turned her into some sort of tomboy. But she must have liked these things because she's gained a brown belt and was to take the black sometime this summer."

Garry grinned. "You could be right, Mark, but at least I can dream, can't I?"

They both settled down again, and as night fell the inner courtyard came alive with lights. Between the outer and inner walls, down-facing, hooded streetlights lit every point, leaving not a shadow all around the perimeter.

"Well, that confirms it; we go through the entrance. Nothing would get into that villa without somebody knowing. We knock out the front security and go straight in. With luck they'll not know what hit them," Mark said quietly.

Garry touched his shoulder. "Not quite, Mark, I've been watching the comings and goings of vehicles. The food trucks, especially the local ones, go straight through into the inner yard and turn to the back of the villa. I think with Sirec away, there's a little complacency among the guards, and they are either too lazy to check or, as I suggested before, not that interested because there's nobody going to come while Sirec's away."

Mark sat up and looked at Garry. "You could be right there. The idiots are more interested in lounging about rather than doing their jobs." Then he grabbed the paper he'd been reading from yesterday, opening it at the sports page. "Got it, I should have thought about it earlier," he said. "Tomorrow night's the semi-final with Argentina. What's the betting they'll all be watching it? That means drink and plenty of it. Many will be out for the count, the rest lax in their patrols. We get in during the day, hide until perhaps one or two in the morning, find the girl and, if her dad's right and she's really athletic, we'll be over the wall in minutes."

With that agreed, they settled for the night; each would do a four hour watch, then the other would take over through the night until daybreak.

Chapter 12

The following morning, before light, the two soldiers were again on the move. This time they skirted the track, making their way down to the road that led to Sirec's villa. By daylight they were at the side of the road in a position that would force vehicles, particularly lorries, to a virtual standstill to negotiate a ninety degree bend in the steep road.

It was three hours before a heavily laden lorry swung round the bend which was suitable for their plan. Waiting for it to pass, they burst out of the undergrowth to the edge of the road and ran behind, out of rear view mirror sight of both the driver and possible passenger. With ease they both leaped on the back, climbing quickly over the tailgate and dropping into the rear of the lorry. Around them were sacks of produce, in Garry's mind enough to feed many people. Bedding themselves deep in the sacks, they lay still, hardly daring to breathe. The lorry slowed at the gates and they could hear voices.

"You're late, that stuff should have been here yesterday. Sirec's due Saturday and today we've got ourselves a party," the gateman shouted.

"It's alright for you; this bleeding truck of Sirec's is shagged. I've been in Beriz for five hours while they changed the bleeding water pump this time. When he's back I'll be at him for a replacement. All this fucking money and we can't get a decent transport system," the driver retorted.

"Well you'd better get the stuff round the back. I'll radio ahead and get some help for unloading," the gateman replied.

With that, the truck moved inside and both soldiers sank lower as the lorry approached the inner wall. This time however, they didn't stop. A short time later they came to a halt and heard voices again.

"Want some help unloading?" a man's voice greeted the driver.

"You can start if you want. I've had four hours of bloody hard driving, so for me it's a drink and a sandwich before I'm unloading this lot," the driver said, as he climbed down the side of the truck and slammed the door.

"Suits me, my drink's getting cold on the table," the man who'd greeted the driver replied.

With the conversation finished, silence fell around the lorry. Garry sighed with relief as he had resigned himself to a shoot-out. But this seemed now to have evaporated by the driver's insistence that he went for a drink first. Looking carefully out, the area was deserted, and within seconds they were on the ground, both holding sub-machine-guns with ammunition packs on their backs. They moved quickly, entering the building at the first open entrance, and then going silently down a long passage. They could hear the sound of the driver's voice in a room to one side but they carried on past until they met a small flight of stairs. At the top they opened a door gingerly and peeped through. Out of the servant's area the decor changed; floors tiled, walls decorated. Clearly this was the servant's entrance to the main rooms of the villa.

Turning, they came back down the stairs and started to try each door. Eventually they found one that led into a wine cellar. Garry decided this would probably be the least used room. The wines were expensive and would only be used by Sirec and his guests. Moving deep inside, they turned into one of the many corridors between the racking and settled down. It would be a long wait until nightfall.

"So far, so good. We'll set explosives all around this cellar. It's central to the villa; possibly we're under the main rooms. When this blows, apart from denying Sirec thousands of pounds worth of drink, the destruction should be staggering," Garry whispered, as he opened his backpack.

Mark nodded and took out a number of charges. He moved off, quickly placing them out of sight, pushing in the detonators and pressing the radio controlled switches of each one; they were ready for remote detonation.

"When I go to find the girl it'll be your job to find the generator. This place must have one, there's no power cable to the complex so it's around somewhere. I suspect it's in the inner wall because of safety and security. Set the radio charges and then move on to communications. I saw an aerial as we got out of the lorry. It's further round the villa and we need to disable that too. The odds are they would have battery back up of some sort and cutting power would not stop them calling for help," Garry said, as Mark returned.

Mark began removing the rest of his detonators and setting the radio numbers.

"I've set the wine room for one, the generator for two and the radio mast to three. If you want a full detonation, the override is zero. That will send all codes from one to ten," Mark whispered, after spending time doing his adjustments.

Garry opened his pack and handed a bar of chocolate to Mark, then took one for himself. Grasping a bottle from a shelf and pulling the cork with an adaptor on his penknife, he grinned at Mark. "We may as well use the man's drink; after all, they won't exist in a few hours. He's hardly likely to know we've taken one. Take care though, only one between us, this stuff's quite potent and we'll need our wits for later."

Mark grinned back, before taking a long swig of the wine. "God, what I'd do for a pint of beer rather than this shit. I don't know how they drink it, the bloody stuff's foul."

Garry eventually took the bottle from Mark and put it to his mouth. It tasted alright, agreeing with Mark though, a pint would be far more appreciated.

***

They had chosen well; it was close to one o'clock in the morning, and not a soul had come into the cellar. It was time to move and find Karen. Both of the soldiers had radio control buttons for the detonators. Mark was to detonate only if Garry hadn't by eight. They were to keep radio silence until Mark had set the explosives for the generator and aerial systems. Then he would send three call bleeps to indicate setting them, and that he was clear. They would then both meet in the car parking area on the other side of the villa. They'd seen a number of cars there all day, and surmised they were probably spare or belonged to people living in the villa. Either way, with at least four or five means of transport to get out of the villa in the confusion of the explosions, escape would be simple.

The two men checked each other's gear. Both were dressed in black from head to foot; ammunition belts round their waist and radio headsets with earphones and mouth mikes and they were ready to go. Finally, shaking hands and wishing each other well, Mark left first. He slipped quietly out of the same door they'd used to enter the villa, then turned in the opposite direction they'd come in aboard the lorry, and worked his way slowly round. On more than one occasion he ducked out of sight as a security guard wandered by. He watched them carefully; the men were amateurs, obviously relaxed and confident that their outer wall comrades would give any warning of intrusion. Often they'd be in pairs talking loudly, warning him of their approach. He'd no difficulty avoiding these men.

Soon he heard the distinct sound of a thumping generator. It was set some way back from the villa in its own cleared area. The door was wide open with light blazing out. Mark approached with caution and peeped inside. Someone was bending over the generator trying to oil something. Mark shrank back into the protection of the shrubs and watched. Eventually, whatever was the problem, the man had finished and came out from the room, closing the door after him. Mark noticed he'd left the lights on. This was a problem for Mark, as to open the door would send a shaft of light streaming out. He moved round the building and scrambled among thick growth until he was at the back. Pushing the undergrowth back, he found three thick cables coming out from the building and down into the ground. He attached the explosives tightly around the cables and pushed in the radio detonator. No matter what, the explosion would blow out the back of the building, and the resulting damage to these cables would almost certainly cut the power to the villa and perimeter lights.

Working his way back, he took his field glasses from his bag and studied the roof of the villa. The radio links and satellite dish were at the rear of the building and in the corner. He decided it had been placed there more for aesthetic reasons rather than security. In that position, which was good for him, the array of aerials couldn't be seen at the front or pool side of the villa. Climbing the side of the building was no problem. The different levels and architecture gave many footholds and wide ledges to get up to the next height. Within minutes he was settled close to the radio aerials, quickly placing the explosives at the base of each aerial, including the satellite dish. This would also destroy the cable links, making communication virtually impossible until repairs were made. He also pulled a long thin trip wire across the length of the roof. It would serve to perhaps make life that little bit more difficult if a radio-man came up, to affect repairs. With both tasks completed, he pressed the radio call button three times and then started to make his way down from the roof.

Meanwhile Garry had given Mark forty minutes and

then moved himself. Fitted with night vision glasses, he crept up the stairs and into the main part of the villa. Only the outside and porch lights were on and the villa was quiet. He quickly checked each of the downstairs rooms, machine-gun at the ready, fitted with silencer and set for single shot rather than multiple. Content that the rooms were empty, he went slowly up the stairs onto a wide balcony. There were many doors off this balcony, equally spaced along the hallway. Garry was disappointed; the place was so large that going through every room would be long and tedious.

"Alpha one, to alpha two, come in, over," he whispered into the mike.

"Alpha two receiving, over."

"I need help, there are too many rooms to search, I'm upstairs on the landing, over."

"I'll be with you in a few minutes, over."

Garry acknowledged then began the search, starting at the first room. With care he opened the door. The room was empty. Then he went into the next, which again was empty. In the third room he hesitated. Two people were in bed, one was partially covered in blankets, the other, a man, had one arm hanging off the side. Garry went closer, at the same time keeping the laser sight beam of the gun on the man's body. He moved to the other side and glanced down at the other person. It was a woman, but not Karen. Garry moved out of the room and pulled the door shut. He then took a spray can from his pocket and sprayed a mark on the door. Then he heard a noise from downstairs. Falling to the floor, he waited, gun directed at the top edge of the stairs, laser beam off. Mark appeared at the top of the stairs.

"Over here," Garry whispered.

Mark came over and nodded a greeting. "So what have you found?"

"First two were empty, the next is occupied, man and woman sleeping. We'll look in one more room, if there's no joy we go and get those two sleeping, and force it out of them," Garry said quietly.

They went to the next bedroom, opening the door silently. The gun swept the room, laser beam following. The room was empty.

"This is hopeless, let's go and wake the sleeping beauties," Mark sighed.

They entered the bedroom the two people were sleeping in. Mark closed the curtains securely. Then he moved to the side of the woman, Garry to the man. They glanced at each other and Garry poked the man in the ribs with the point of the gun. Mark did the same to the woman. The man stirred, opened his eyes and stared straight into the barrel of Garry's gun.

"Move a muscle and you're dead; if you understand, nod," he said quietly.

The man's eyes, wide with terror, nodded. Mark did the same to the woman. She was on the verge of screaming but, with the gun tip touching her mouth, she thought better of it.

"You understand English? Nod if you do," Mark asked quietly.

The woman nodded.

"You know where the English girl sleeps? Nod if you do."

Again she nodded.

"Show me; but before you get up, remember this gun will be at your head. One noise or try to run, in fact anything that you try to do without me telling you, and you're dead. Do you understand?"

She nodded again.

"Then get up and take me to her."

The woman, naked, climbed out of the bed. She tried to get a robe but Mark touched the side of her head gently with the tip of the gun. "Take me to the girl, don't touch a thing or you're dead."

The woman did as he asked after glancing at her partner watching her, Garry's gun at his head. They went down the passageway, up a flight of stairs and along another with a number of doors leading off. The woman stopped at one of the doors.

"She's in here?" Mark asked.

"Yes, but the door's locked. I've not got the key," she replied.

"Who has?"

"Security, they were told to keep her locked up at night until Sirec returns tomorrow," she said quietly.

"On your knees, head between your legs, quickly," Mark ordered.

The woman did as he asked and Mark moved to the door. A quick check revealed the lock was flimsy and inadequate. With one push of his shoulder it burst open. Mark stood for a moment and waited. Not a sound came from the rest of the house.

"Inside," he demanded. The woman stood and did as he asked. Mark followed.

Somebody was asleep in the bed, their head hidden under the blankets. Even the small noise from the door hadn't disturbed them.

"Wake her and tell her not to say a word but to get dressed in jeans and something warm. Then you kneel again on the floor, head down between your legs."

Karen opened her eyes as the woman shook her gently.

"Please don't say a word, just get up and dress. You're to wear jeans, t-shirt and a warm jumper. Not a dress, you understand?"

Karen nodded and climbed out of bed. Then she saw Mark stood some distance away, gun trained on the woman. Now she understood and quickly dressed into what she'd been told to wear, before slipping on trainers. She then grabbed a brush from the dressing table, underclothes, shorts and top from inside a drawer, before stuffing them all in a carrier bag. Mark hadn't said a word; the woman was still on the floor, unable to see what was going on. Mark touched her with the tip of the gun.

"We return to your room now," he said quietly.

They all went back to the room. Garry was still stood over the man. Mark told the woman to get back into bed and cover her face. Garry told the man also to do this and then urged Karen out of the room with Mark. Seconds later, she heard two low thuds and Garry joined them.

"British S.A.S., Karen, we've come to take you home. Not a word until we speak to you, silence is imperative. Keep close and do exactly as we say."

She gave them a weak smile and they all returned back down the stairs, through the servant's area and out into the courtyard. Then they moved swiftly towards the front car park. Mark grasped Karen's arm and pushed her down to the ground. Garry moved from car to car until he found one that was open. Climbing inside he pulled a small gadget from his pocket and slipped a section into the car lock. Seconds later a snap came and the lock fell to pieces. Turning the broken lock inside, the car's ignition came on. He then waved them over. With three of them in the car, he pulled the small remote detonator from his pocket and selected zero. A press and seconds later, the explosions rocked the villa. All the lights failed with flames shooting from a number of windows blown out by the blast. Within minutes the whole place was ablaze.

Not waiting any longer, he started the car and they moved slowly at first, before gathering speed straight through the first gate and crashing through the lowered barrier of the security at the entrance. Two security men stood there, staring at the flames coming from the villa, at first not sure what to do about the car approaching them until it was too late. Mark turned and faced Karen.

"I'm Mark, this is Garry. We are, like I said, British S.A.S and I hope you're Karen Marshall?"

Karen grinned. "Yes I am, and thank you for coming for me. I must say your departure for a clandestine group was pretty spectacular."

Garry shrugged. "We did that for a laugh really. To tell you the truth, we had it wired in case something went wrong. I don't like the sound of this Sirec or his ponced up villa, so what the hell, give him a bit of rebuilding to do, I say. Anyway while they're trying to bring that lot under control, we'll be far away."

Mark cut in. "You know, Garry, this girl's as cool as a cucumber. Not only did she dress, she even packed. I must say, under fire, she'd be some girl."

Karen hit him in fun. "I know this place, believe me in the daytime it's like an oven, then at night its bloody cold. I was just being practical that's all," she retorted.

"Practical?" Mark said. "She brought a bloody hairbrush as well."

They all fell silent and Garry swung the car round and up the steep track. This car would be known and he needed to change it for the one Arif was leaving. They got to the end of the track but there was no car.

Garry slammed his hands on the steering wheel. "The cheating bastard! If I see him again I'll put a bullet into his head." With that he swung the car round and they sped off down towards the main road. They travelled on for some miles before the car started to cough and splutter and finally came to a halt.

"Fuck, the bloody fuel's run out. Right, let's get it off the road and then we walk," Garry said quickly.

They all piled out and pushed the car off the road and down a small bank. It seemed well hidden so they moved off. At first following the road, then across country. Mark was reading the map, setting their route by a satellite navigation unit he was constantly watching. By now dawn was beginning to break and Mark called a halt. Settling down in a small clearing, away from any casual passer-by, he handed out dried biscuits. "We're here for the day now, so get some sleep if you want. I'll plan our next move."

Karen did as he asked, using her clothes bag as a pillow. She was shattered and needed to rest.

***

It wasn't until after nine that she opened her eyes. Mark was asleep; Garry was sat looking at her.

"I can watch now if you want to sleep, I've done it before," she said quietly so as not to wake Mark.

He nodded and leaned back, soon he too was sleeping. Karen looked at the gun by Mark then picked it up, fiddling with the mechanism. She found how to release the ammunition clip and by the time the two were awake, she'd managed to pull the gun virtually apart.

Mark looked at the pieces on the ground and grinned. "Go on then, get it back together if you can," he teased.

Karen frowned at it and tried her best but nothing would fit, so he took it from her. For the next hour or so to pass the time, he went through it stage by stage until she could do it blindfolded.

'You learn quickly, Karen, if you want a job we'll have a word with the Commander and you're in," Garry mocked.

She smiled softly and grabbed the completed gun. "I don't just want to know how to take it apart, I want to know how it works. What's this switch for and how do you control it?" she asked quietly.

Mark looked at Garry then towards Karen. "Why? You've got us to protect you. Anyway you'll be home in a couple of days."

She stood and looked across the barren landscape. Then turned and faced them. "I've no intention of being caught and going back in that hell-hole. I've been raped, beaten and spent half my time naked in front of leering men. I'm grateful for your help, more than you'll ever imagine, but Sirec's no wimp, he'll follow; perhaps try to get me back. After all, I cost forty thousand dollars. That's a lot of money."

Garry had listened to her and cut in before she could carry on. "That is a lot of money, Karen. Have you met this guy?"

She shook her head. "No, Sirec was due tomorrow, I think. I've been waiting for him for a week now. His villa though was really cool and I at last got meals I could actually eat and enjoy. Before going there I've been living on mostly bread and cheese with some sort of thick soup or on the ship, bacon butties. God I hate them. Then as soon as I came to Sirec's, I was taken to a large store where they fitted me out with casual clothes, some evening wear and decidedly sexy underwear. I was getting worried how kinky this guy was with what I was expected to wear. Mind you, in some ways I was enjoying it, you know, dressing for dinner, swimming in the pool all day, and then I got speaking to the cook. She was French and we hit it off. She told me to try and get out; many girls had been there before me, they disappeared within a few weeks and it was rumoured they'd been killed. He's a room that is kept locked where he would take the girls. Never once had she seen one in his bed in the mornings, so whatever his perversion, it was in that room, not his bed."

"So how did you expect to get out then?" Mark asked.

She shrugged. "I'd managed to call my dad and hoped he'd get the Government to intervene before what happened to the previous girls happened to me. If that didn't happen, I'd no real idea. Besides trying to get in with the cook, she may, if we'd become closer, have helped me escape, but I don't know." Then she stretched, pushing her hair back with both hands before looking across at them watching, her eyes no longer sparkling, but cold and hard. "Anyway if the worst came to the worst and my life had been in danger, I'd have killed him."

Garry laughed. "And just how would you achieve that, Karen?" he mocked.

Her features never altered, her eyes cold and uncaring. "Two years I've trained in self-defence and kick-boxing. I'm also close to black belt. The average man wouldn't know what hit him with those types of skills. I've also kept myself very fit. I can do forty press-ups without a problem. Okay, I've not got big obvious arm muscles but have no doubt in my training, it's a tiny step to go a little further and break a man's neck, especially if he's trying to screw me at the time and his guard's down."

No one replied and Garry pulled three tins of meat from his pack, handing them out. "I'm not sure you understand how difficult it is to kill a person, Karen, in close combat," he eventually said, between bites of the tinned meat. "But, short of the belief you could kill someone by using this black belt training of yours, why is it you want to know how to use the gun?"

She looked at him for a moment. "The point is, say you two got killed or we got split up? I'm not going back to be screwed every night by whoever, that's for certain, so what are my options? Fight my way out? Not really practical, besides, I'd not get far and it wouldn't bear thinking about if I was captured. So the only option I'd have then, is to turn the gun on myself."

"And you think it's that easy to kill, Karen?" Mark asked.

"I don't know, but if I'd had a weapon over the last few days, after what I've already been through, I wouldn't have hesitated. Does that answer your question?"

Garry shrugged. "What the hell, we've hours to kill, so to speak. If you want to know how to use the bloody thing, Karen, I've no objection. How about you, Mark?"

"So long as she doesn't turn the gun on us in error," he replied dryly.

She laughed and Garry pulled an array of weapons from his bag.

"Right, Karen, listen and learn. The machine-gun you've taken to pieces is your real weapon. It can fire a hundred rounds a minute. That's enough to cut a man in half at ten feet. It can also single shoot. In that mode you've got real control, little or no kickback, and you can use the silencer. Deadly accurate with the laser sight and you've also got an optional laser beam. You know the sort they use in presentations to point something out? At hand height it's difficult to know where the gun is pointing, but with the laser on you can watch the beam and know exactly where it's aimed."

She listened intently, trying the options herself, and within an hour was able to control it without any problems. The handgun was a different matter; totally inaccurate, without lots of practise. She decided that would be the gun she could turn on herself. Even she couldn't miss her head with the barrel touching her throat. The day passed quickly and the two soldiers were enjoying her company. Karen knew how to play up to lads, what to say, how to talk to them as if she was interested in them alone, and they both fell for it. She'd even changed earlier into shorts with her t-shirt. Garry in particular couldn't take his eyes off her.

***

As the sun set, they looked again at the map.

"We need a car, how about we go into this town called

Hashal and see what's available," Garry finally said after studying the map.

"Hashal is where Saeed lives. If we could find his house we'd have transport for certain," Karen commented.

Garry frowned. "It's a bit of a long shot, Karen. Do you know the way?"

She shrugged. "I went to a church on Saturday; it was less than quarter of a mile from Saeed's. If we can find the church then I'll find his house," she replied confidently.

"So you think this Saeed would help out then?" Mark asked.

She laughed. "Of course he'd help. Saeed has a definite soft spot for me, I can promise you that," she lied.

With this agreed, they waited for dusk, then set off across the fields towards Hashal. Mark had estimated about three miles, which was nothing. The soldiers hid the weapons in their bags so as not to alarm anybody they might meet. As they entered the town they kept to the side streets and followed the main road to the centre.

Karen suddenly grasped Garry's arm. "That's the church, I'm certain. If we follow the main road for a few hundred yards, turn left and second right, Saeed's house is at the bottom."

The two lads were impressed but Karen shrugged it off. After all, she told them, two years running round woods with her dad, playing one group against another, was good training for observation.

By the time they'd arrived at the house it was completely dark. Mark handed Karen the bag with his equipment inside to look after, and moved off. Armed only with his handgun, for concealment, he intended to look for possible alternative transport if she couldn't get Saeed's car, besides keeping a watchful eye on anybody approaching the street.

She stood for some time staring at the house, remembering the abuse of her body by Saeed's mother. Then she thought back to the night when she was supposed to have been auctioned. Knowing she'd been sold and only waiting for her new owner to collect her, she'd become alarmed when Saeed came into her room, unfastened the ankle iron and threw some knickers at her, telling her to remove her clothes and put them on. Karen tried to object, as Hussein had said, she'd already been sold to a man called Sirec, so why should she do this? He ignored her objections, pulling his baseball bat out from under his jacket and threatening to beat her if she didn't do what he'd asked. Still she'd hesitated; however, his next words had terrified her.

"Put the bloody knickers on. We want entertainment down there so you dance on the stage for my friends," he'd demanded, "or it's the brothel. I'll just have time to get you there before their late clients arrive. As for your buyer, I've a dozen girls more his type, ready to replace you."

Terrified he'd do what he'd threatened and desperately needing to go to Sirec's house, as that was the address she'd given her dad, she'd removed her clothes and slipped the knickers on quickly. They were g-string type, see-through and she felt decidedly embarrassed as he marched her down the stairs through into the big room. There were only four men sat around and already music was playing. Saeed demanded she climbed onto the stage and dance for them.

She'd done the best she could in making a show, but the men sat round the stage were leaning forward, touching her legs and pushing her off balance, laughing amongst themselves as she nearly stumbled. Then one stood and started tugging at her knickers, before succeeding and pulling them down to her feet. As she'd knelt down to pull them back up, everyone was shouting that she was a hopeless dancer and take her off. Saeed stood and took her hand, helping her down from the stage. Karen was thankful it was over and she could get away from these men. But Saeed had other ideas, rather than take her back to her room, he sat back down again on his chair, forcing her to bend over his knees. Then he began slapping her bottom, telling her as she couldn't dance, she needed to be punished and he'd have to find something else she might be good for. They were all laughing at her mock punishment, when one dropped his trousers in front of her, waving his manhood in her face. She panicked and began screaming hysterically, but a blow with something to the back of the head stunned her into silence. While in this daze, she was lifted bodily off Saeed's knee and stretched out on a table with a cushion placed under her buttocks, lifting her bottom high. Then her arms were pulled above her head and her wrists tied to the table legs with cord. Her legs hanging over the edge on the other side of the table were pulled wide apart by others, each ankle securely tied the same as her wrists to a table leg. One man had leaned over the table, his breath a mixture of stale tobacco and heavy garlic. He began kissing her and playing with her breasts. Karen had wanted to throw up, but in this position she was afraid she'd choke on her own vomit. However, worse was to come as, like on the ship, the men were unfastening their trouser belts, demanding they should be first. But Saeed dismissed their demands, claiming she was his property and he was to be first. Before taking her, he began rubbing something greasy between her legs which allowed him to enter her with ease. Then while he pounded her body, he had tried to warrant his intrusion by saying something about how they couldn't let her go without a good send-off. After all, it was her eighteenth birthday, and didn't girls come of age in England then?

Eventually when they'd all finished with her, someone released the bonds. She was exhausted, internally sore, with a throbbing headache from the blow to her head. She was dragged off the table, then two of them half carried her to the toilet to clean herself up. After throwing up in the pan she'd tried to clean herself, using the sink and toilet paper, still shivering in shock, when Saeed had come in, handing her the usual knickers and shirt.

He'd leaned back on the wall, watching her dress. "You're leaving tomorrow," he'd begun. "If you know what's good for you, you'll say nothing of tonight. Sirec, your new owner, wouldn't want a girl who'd been, shall we say, well used."

"Gang raped you mean?" she'd cut in.

He grinned. "Whatever, Karen, but hear this. Tell him what happened tonight and he'll not want you in his bed. You'll be handed to his men to have fun with. When they've had enough of you, the next stop would be the brothel, so he can earn his money back. Say nothing and this man will look after you; you'll have an easy life satisfying just one, rather than many. It's up to you, I will have been paid."

She'd said nothing.

"I'm waiting for your answer," he'd demanded.

"What's there to say? I have no choice; it didn't happen," she'd answered.

He nodded and urged her out of the toilet, taking her back upstairs to her room. She'd laid on the bed, tears trickling down her face. At least she was leaving for somewhere else. This time, she'd hoped it would be only one man, something perhaps she could cope with.

***

Brought out of her thoughts when Garry touched her arm, he pointed to a car arriving. A man climbed out, followed by three others. She recognised them instantly as her abusers. Her heart stopped, fear again welling up inside, but she knew what she had to do. They were laughing as they entered the house through the small door in the wall. Karen was thinking fast, the last thing she wanted was Garry tagging along.

"I'll go and see him; you stay here till I return. Saeed will be shocked but he'll help, I know he will," she said quietly. Garry looked at her strangely. "No, Karen, it's too dangerous, we go together," he replied.

She brushed his objections aside. "Don't be daft, he'd panic. Just give me fifteen minutes. There's only one entrance to this place so even if he wanted to, he couldn't get me out without you seeing."

"But he might hurt you," Garry persisted.

Karen shook her head. "No, Garry. I slept with Saeed every night, I'd no option. He'd bought me and demanded I kept him happy. He wanted to keep me, I wanted it as well. He was kind and thoughtful and Sirec was an unknown, but Sirec had already paid and what Sirec wants, he gets round here."

Her lies were calculated to allow her inside alone. She'd noticed his more than passing interest in her and while it might shake him about Saeed and herself, she had to say it.

"That's sick, Karen; you were only seventeen for God's sake."

Ignoring his objections, she replaced the t-shirt she was wearing with the shirt from her bag and knotted the ends, exposing her midriff. Then she looked him in the face. "Get a life, Garry; this is the real world out here. Age means nothing, apart from it being nicer to screw a young girl than a fat slob. What are you going to do, kill him? For what, taking my virginity? Believe me, Garry, Saeed didn't take it, there have been others before him, since I was taken. So what's the options, pinch the car and when he finds it gone he calls the police? Alternatively I'll get the key with his blessing, and we're on our way home?"

Garry knew she was right; even now the police would be looking for them after torching the villa. "Well, if you're sure, Karen. Fifteen minutes and I'm coming in. These men are not to be messed with; you're playing a dangerous game."

She gave a forced laugh, leaned over and kissed his cheek. "I'll only be ten at the most, then send the cavalry in if you want."

Garry reluctantly agreed and walked to the small door with her, Karen pushed it open still carrying Mark's bag, and went through. Garry glanced around before moving to the other side of the small avenue, then stood in the shadows watching the door. He wasn't sure if she could pull it off, but without transport and with a good distance to travel, they were in deep trouble.

Meanwhile Karen had shut the door behind her and slid the bolt. Placing Mark's bag on the ground, she pulled the zipper open. Removing the gun, she checked the magazine was fully home and locked, she then fitted the silencer before slipping the safety catch off and walked determinedly to the front door.

To anybody, the door would seem locked, but Karen had watched Saeed from the lounge, and there was a knack, a simple lift and push. Entering the house, she could hear the men laughing and joking in the main room. The room they'd raped her in. The room many girls, like her, were sold into a life of hell, a life of despair. She moved quickly to the door, kicking it open, stepping inside and edging slightly round the wall and away from the door. She'd decided if someone came into the room, with the position she was in now, she'd see them. The four men who'd arrived in the car were sat around a table, playing cards. Saeed was stood leaning against the fireplace, drinking from a flagon. He looked round to see who had come into the room and stared transfixed for a moment.

Then his face broke into a grin. "Why it's Karen, what a nice surprise. I like the get-up, kid, you look particularly sexy in those shorts and top. Mind you I was certain you'd gone to Sirec, he couldn't have thrown you out and sent you back already, could he?"

Karen didn't reply but stood motionless, watching him.

He placed the flagon he was holding on the side-table and put one hand to his mouth with an exaggerated action, as if he'd realised something. "I know what it is, Karen, you've missed our little leaving party so much; decided one man for you at a time isn't enough, so you've come back for a re-run?" Saeed said, with a hint of mocking in his voice.

She smiled softly. "Think a lot of that very small pimple between your legs? I suppose the only time you use it is to rape somebody, any other time the woman wouldn't be able to do anything for laughing."

His face changed, and he slammed the table with his hand. "You little shit! I'll show you what a man can do to a..."

He fell silent. Karen raised the gun slowly, stopping only when the beam of the laser sight was resting on his chest. Her features had changed, her face expressionless, and her eyes cold. Then she spoke again, this time her voice was harsh and demanding. "Okay, you've had your fun, let's get down to business. This, if you've not noticed, is a gun. No ordinary gun, it's capable of cutting you in half with the sheer firepower. In simple terms, Saeed, see the little red light on your chest? If I squeeze this trigger, ever so lightly, it's goodbye Saeed."

He glared at her but didn't move. "You've made your point, what do you want?"

"I want my money," she replied quietly.

"Money? What money?" he hissed.

"The money Sirec paid for me. It's mine and I want it," she demanded.

He started to laugh and, grasping the flagon again, took a long drink. Wiping his arm over his mouth, he gave a snigger. "I think you've got it wrong somehow, Karen. You're sold, I get the money. It's not you're sold, you get the money. So why don't you drop the gun, then your pants. I think you perhaps need a good spanking to remind you of your position," Saeed scathingly replied.

When she replied to his scorn, it was with sadness in her voice. "I trusted you, believed you were a man of his word and at least had some respect for me," she began. "Oh, I knew you were only in it for the money, but I didn't cause you any trouble and never objected to your mother messing about with my body, even though I felt decidedly embarrassed with you sat there watching. I've had time to think at Sirec's house, and realised I wasn't affected by the oils, as I thought, but that you were actually giving me drugs to keep me subdued. You were not concerned if I had any allergies, or how they might have affected me. Everything you've done was as if I was a piece of shit under your foot. I wasn't even a human anymore, as far as I can see, I was just something to make you money."

She fell silent for a moment collecting her thoughts; no one in the room uttered a word, in some ways trying to assess the state of mind of this girl stood in front of them holding a gun. Except Saeed, who sat there indifferently and took the opportunity of her silence to take another drink.

"That Saturday night was different," she suddenly carried on. "When I got on that stage knowing I was sold, I thought it was a little harmless entertainment at my expense. After all, everyone I've met, even my so-called boyfriend, seemed to relish pulling me down or embarrassing me, indifferent to my feelings or thoughts. Whatever you say about brothels, I can't believe they'd have treated me the way you lot did? To take me like that, stretched out on a table and tied down, makes you all the worst kind of rapists, besides real sick bastards, if that's the only way you can get your kicks?" Tears were trickling down her face while she spoke, her voice shaking as she continued. "I could hardly walk when you'd finished with me. Even the next day it was still dribbling down my legs. I've needed the last week, waiting for my so-called new owner to take over from where you lot left off, just for the pain to go. But what could I do? I was chained up and drugged, accepting what was being done to me with the constant threat, if I objected, of a beating or ending up in a brothel as an alternative..." Then the tone of her voice changed to one of aggression. "Now it's different; I can say no, because I'm in a position to fight back. So I'll ask just once more. Give me the money, Saeed, or I'll blow your brains out," she demanded.

Saeed's face still had a look of amusement from her first demand for money, however, to add insult to injury, he began to clap. "Nice little speech, Karen, what do you want me to do, say I'm sorry? It doesn't work that way. I paid good money and owned you. That means I could do what I wanted with you. Besides, you were lucky I'd a few more girls available, otherwise you'd have been amusing me and my friends every night. Anyway, you're worth nothing and you get nothing. Go back to Sirec, kid, while you're still alive."

She shook her head slowly. "No one owns any person in this world. Oh, I agree you can hold someone against their will, even exchange this person with another for money if you want; but claim you own them, who do you think you are? God?"

He shrugged. "Argue it how you like, but I fed and housed you. In my book you were owned."

Karen grinned. "God yes, you're right, I forgot you actually fed me. But I seem to remember it was mostly with stale bread, cheese… lots of cheese, some revolting stuff you called stew and not forgetting the drugged drinks. Tell you what, Saeed, how about I pay you back for what I thought of your hospitality?" The gun fired and Saeed was sent spinning to the ground, clutching his shattered left leg.

"I'll kill you for that," he shouted at her.

"That was not what you should be saying, you should be

thanking me, after all, I was only paying you for my food, Saeed," Karen replied with a grin on her face.

The gun fired again and Saeed's other leg was shattered at the foot. He screamed in agony.

Karen laughed. "Oops! Sorry did that hurt, my finger touched the trigger? Maybe if you paid me my money I'd stop fiddling?"

"Give her the fucking money, Saeed. Your stupid remarks will get us all killed," one man shouted at him and then the others shouted too, afraid the girl would turn the gun on them.

Saeed, in considerable pain, pointed to a large vase on the sideboard. "It's in there."

One rushed to the vase, knocking it to the floor and shattering it into fragments. Then he pulled a thick wad of money from the remains before holding it up.

"Throw it over here," she called.

He did as she asked and Karen grinned at Saeed. "I'm not bringing very good luck for you, am I, Saeed? What with losing at cards, spending money on me and now losing the payment... I hope my performance on this table was worth all the money you've paid out or lost?" she ribbed.

Saeed dragged himself across the floor and leaned on a chair. "You're dead, girl," he hissed.

Karen smiled at him. "I suppose you would like to kill me, Saeed? You know your mother read my palm the night you made me do that lap dance. Did she tell you? You see she was very scared and said I should never have come to this country. Do you know why that was?"

Saeed at that moment, in agony with his legs, really didn't want to answer this girl's questions, so he just shrugged. "She's a stupid old woman. Always claims she could read palms. So what load of rubbish did she tell you? Long life perhaps, maybe lots of kids? Mind you after Saturday night, mine probably!"

Karen shook her head. "Sorry to disappoint you, Saeed. I'm not pregnant; you just pulled my period forward, except, if I had been, I'd have relished the abortion to watch a little Saeed swilled down the sewer. Probably the same place your mother found you?"

Saeed scowled. "Well now you've got your money, piss off. You'll not be free long enough to spend any of it. Then, little girl, you'll not be going back to Sirec, I have better places for the likes of you; five men a session will be nothing to what you can expect before I finally kill you."

"Yes, Saeed, with a sick mind like yours, I suppose you would spend lots of time dreaming up such a place… until I was re-captured and you could actually send me. But if you think I'm going to give you that opportunity, you're more stupid than I thought." She hesitated for a moment, before continuing, her voice shaking slightly. "Tonight's shown me just what sort of people you really are, even in front of a gun you want to pull me down and threaten, because you consider I'm still that piece of shit under your foot. So you've made my mind up. If I leave here without you paying for your crimes, I'd let down every child who has passed through these doors. Children who, like me, had a family, but you took that and their dignity away, selling them into a life which could only be described as a living hell…" Karen fell silent while she brought together her final words to the men in the room. Words she'd dreamed of hearing in a court, if she'd ever managed to escape and tell the authorities what they'd been doing with children. But of course, those thoughts were to keep her spirits up when she was down, now this was reality. The men in the room, on their part, stared transfixed at this girl, trying to understand what she was about to say.

She looked at each one of them, her eyes cold and her face expressionless. "You see, only I'm present as the witness for the prosecution, the others you've sold over the years, like I was, are still with their buyers or dead. There is of course no judge or jury, so I'll be them as well. Have you anything to say before I consider the verdict?"

"You're insane; who do you think you are, standing there as some prima donna, talking like that?" Saeed asked with venom in his voice.

"My name's Karen Marshall," she screamed at him. "A name from a life you demanded I forget; Assam believing he only had to grind my valuables into the dirt and I'd forget. Well I won't and never will. So I ask you the same question. Who do you think you are? God...?"

"I'm not God, but perhaps you think you are, Karen, standing there with a gun?" he replied quietly.

She shook her head slowly. "I suppose you may believe I think I'm God, but I don't, although I do have a problem. If I took you to the local police, they're so corrupt, like you, a few pounds or whatever your currency is, will get you released and me? That doesn't bear thinking about. So yes, see me as God if you want? After all, you're all on trial."

The room fell silent as the minutes ticked by and then Karen sighed. "It would seem by the silence, none of you can think of anything in your defence? In that case, the jury finds you, Saeed, guilty of people trading and the rest of you guilty of gang rape, which, I suspect, is your usual type of entertainment if Saeed's comment earlier is to be believed? The only punishment fitting to your crimes is a sentence of death and this gun will be your executioner."

Her last words spurred the men into blind panic, but before any could scramble far from their seats, the gun came to life and four men lay dead or dying.

Saeed's face had a look of terror. He'd never once believed she had the nerve to kill; now everything had changed. He started begging for his life, offering her anything she wanted; but Karen remained indifferent to his pleadings, as if she was in some sort of trance. All she could think of were his mocking words as he and his friends took her on the table and Jane standing at the edge of Assam's ship before her throat was cut on his say-so. There was no need for that. The girl was a mother and now a child would have to grow up without a mother's love. Then there was Debbie, a stupid girl perhaps, but he conned her into thinking she was going home. However, more importantly were the faceless ones who'd come before, they too were entitled to retribution. Finally she'd had enough of his whimpering. If he'd been holding the gun he'd have been laughing, probably making lurid remarks or forcing her to stand once again naked in front of him, before being forced over the table and strapped. She shook her head slowly, at the same time gently squeezing the trigger. Saeed was thrown back by the impact of the bullets entering his body, and then the room fell silent.

Bending down and picking up the bundle of money, she walked out of the door. In some ways Karen felt sorry for Saeed's mother, but she was as bad as him, allowing children to be abused. She should have called the authorities, anything, to stop the trade in human misery. However, she'd been content to turn a blind eye and allow her son to make money. Now she would have to live the rest of her life knowing her prediction of death was more than just a prediction... it was reality and she'd lost her son. On her own part, Karen was content. Her promise to herself that every person who'd abused her would pay the price had begun. With Saeed's money, she was in a position to go after the others who'd helped bring her to this country, and they too would pay for their crime.

Taking the car keys from the side-table in the hall, Karen pulled the front door shut, replaced the gun in the bag and sauntered back to the two waiting soldiers. Smiling at them, she offered the keys to Garry.

"Saeed was glad to help. Told me it was Sirec's problem

if he'd let me escape, he'd been paid. Told me to leave the car in a car park and give him a call. They're playing cards in there and I think he's winning, so he didn't really want to be disturbed."

Garry looked at her strangely but said nothing. What hold did she have over this man who gave her the keys?

Chapter 13

During the time Karen and the two soldiers had been hiding out the day after her rescue, a large black limousine roared past the security stationed at the entrance to Sirec's villa without stopping. Eventually it was forced to stop some sixty feet from the inner wall because the area was littered with fire tenders and police vehicles. The man who climbed out was expensively dressed, a little over six foot, well built with black hair tied back into a small ponytail. His features were Latin, his face olive brown. As he walked towards the entrance in the second wall, a man ran out to meet him.

Small, fat and covered in dirt, the man stopped short, gasping. "Sirec, we didn't expect you till late tonight."

Sirec looked at the man's dirty face. "It would seem not, Jordan, but when I'm told my villa has been destroyed it concentrates the mind somewhat. Perhaps I should see for myself, while you try to think up a good explanation as to what happened?"

Sirec walked on through the entrance with Jordon virtually running at his side to keep up, terrified at what Sirec was about to see. Jordan had hoped to have had time to tidy things up before he'd come.

"We don't know, Sirec," he began, "one moment it was quiet, then around two o'clock in the morning all hell broke loose. Security told me there have been at least two explosions. One in the power room followed by one below the radio masts. That, I'm afraid, was the killer, it took out the gas pipe from the storage tanks. They exploded and..."

He stopped in mid-sentence as Sirec could now see the extent of the devastation. The once superb villa was just a smouldering ruin. Not a roof was left, the walls partially destroyed, and contents of the villa scattered everywhere, shattered into pieces.

Sirec spun round and grabbed Jordan by the throat. "My villa... I should kill you and all the bloody security on last night. Why should I not do that, Jordan?"

Jordan was sweating, his mouth opening and shutting like a fish, at first without a sound coming out before realising he must answer. "But what more could I do, Sirec? The alarms on the perimeter weren't activated. The security insists no one came through, we can't understand who's done it unless it was an inside job. And the only person it could have been was the new girl I collected from Saeed last week."

Sirec looked at him for a moment, inside he was boiling. Then he grabbed Jordan's shoulders, his face inches from him. "Are you suggesting an eighteen year old kid brought in a suitcase of explosives, which I presume you might have noticed her carrying when you collected her, besides being trained in demolition tactics, and did this? If you are then you're more stupid than I thought. This is the work of military, a classic operation. First destroy the power and communication and you have panic. Then I ask myself why, why had they come? They'd more than likely know I wasn't here, so why, Jordan, why?" he screamed.

"To get something?" Jordan muttered.

Sirec pushed Jordan away. "Yes, Jordan, to get something." Sirec kicked a table lying shattered on its side while he stared at the villa. Then he turned to Jordan. "Has the safe been opened?"

Jordan shook his head.

"Any signs of a search? Like forced doors or open drawers?"

Again he shook his head.

"The girl, the girl you collected from Saeed. Where is she?"

Jordan shrugged. "Gone, I think," he said indifferently.

"You think, you bloody think!" Sirec screamed at him once again. "She's either fried to a crisp in there or she's done a runner, or..." Sirec went quiet for a second, then removed a cigarette from a gold case, and lit it, deep in thought. "The firemen, have they recovered any bodies?" he asked quietly.

"Two; they were the buyers from Parma due to meet you later today, but the strange thing was they'd been shot," Jordan replied.

Sirec sighed. "Why do I employ you, Jordan? Even your little pea brain might have realised; two people shot, an English girl missing. My bet is, mercenaries paid for by her family. They placed explosives around the house in case of problems, found the girl's bedroom, maybe with the help of our guests, maybe not, shot the guests so they didn't raise the alarm, and blew the bloody place to pieces either for the hell of it or more likely to make their escape. Do you think that sums the whole bloody mess up in one go?"

Jordan nodded without uttering a word.

By now another man had joined them; Sirec turned and pulled this man aside. "Halif, send out the word. I'll pay a reward of a hundred thousand for anyone who finds the men who did this. Another twenty for the girl, alive mind you. Then get over to Saeed's and find out how in hell they knew she was at the villa and most of all, take our payment back. As far as I'm concerned she never arrived here so he's blown it. That'll give him an incentive to find her."

Halif frowned. "The men, I understand a bounty for them, Sirec. But the kid? She's one of many, what's so important?"

Sirec grasped his arm, propelling him towards his waiting car. Now out of earshot and lowering his voice so no others could hear, Sirec frowned. "It's not the girl, Halif, she's nothing, but our reputation's everything. Allow one to get out and there'll be others. Our little sideline would be at risk, that I'm not prepared to chance. Mind you, I've a feeling somehow that if we find this girl, we find the people who did this."

Halif nodded his understanding and turned to leave. At that moment Sirec's mobile telephone began to ring. He pressed the buttons and listened. However, as he listened Halif became nervous. Never had he seen Sirec so angry.

Eventually he switched the telephone off before slamming his hands on the roof of the car in anger. "It's bad, Halif, these people have hit the warehouses. I'm being told its total destruction." He fell silent a moment, deep in thought, then spun round, facing Halif.

"Raise the bounty for their capture to half a million. Let our friends know in the different factions, I want these people no matter what the cost. With that sort of money at stake there'll be nowhere to hide. Our eyes and ears will be in every village and on every street.

By the time Halif had arrived at Saeed's, it was well after dark as his driver turned into the narrow street. Another car missed them by inches when it roared out. Halif glanced behind and made the last two numbers of the plate. He wasn't sure but it might be important. His car stopped outside Saeed's and Halif quickly walked through the courtyard and banged hard on the front door. Four times he banged before he heard shuffling and complaints from inside and the door opened slowly. Saeed's mother stood there in her nightclothes.

"You bang enough to wake the dead. I suppose you want that lazy son of mine. They're in the main lounge, when they start with cards the house can collapse around them, nothing will bring them out."

Halif pushed past her without a word, striding quickly across the hall into the main lounge as she followed slowly. When she arrived he was standing looking around at the destruction. "I think perhaps you should be calling for an ambulance, there's been some sort of accident," he said softly.

The old woman stood for a moment transfixed at the carnage, then seeing her son she let out a blood curdling scream before going into hysterics, running over, cradling Saeed in her arms, moaning softly. Just at that moment Saeed opened his eyes, raising his hand, touching her face. Her eyes opened wide, first convinced he was dead, now realising he wasn't.

"Please, Sir, call for help. My son's alive, please I beg you," she pleaded.

Halif raised his telephone and spoke quickly.

Saeed pulled his mother close. "It was Karen; she came as you foresaw."

The mother shook her head vigorously. "You're mistaken, my son, Karen is with Sirec, she will not return. No girl escapes Sirec."

"No… No, she was here. How, I don't know, but it was Karen," he whispered, now very weak.

She looked up a Halif. "My son's saying this is the work of the girl we sent for Sirec, but that cannot be."

Halif frowned. "The girl's missing. He could be right, old woman. Tell me, does your son have a car?"

She nodded. "It is an old BMW, grey with a black roof," she replied.

Halif began making his way to the door. Then he stopped and turned. "I wish your son well. If this girl is the killer then when she's brought back and when Sirec's finished with her, it is he who will decide her future."

Then he made to leave the room but the mother called after him. Halif returned reluctantly, already convinced the car that had nearly collided with theirs earlier was Saeed's BMW.

"What is it you want, old woman?"

She held a blooded hand up in the air, pointing at it with

her other hand. "I read her palm. That girl brings only death and destruction; she has revenge in her heart. Saeed sees me as a silly old woman. That maybe so, but ignore this warning at your peril. I beg you, Sir; do not bring that girl back into this house."

Halif smiled softly. "I believe you, old woman. The death and destruction is already with us. It is time our honour, your son and his friends, be avenged. The girl will be caught within the hour. She will be punished no matter what her destiny holds."

Saeed's mother remained silent. Halif left and she looked down at her son when she heard the front door close. Saeed was looking up at her, weak but stable.

"You wouldn't listen to your mother, my son. That man also... will not heed my words. Karen walks with the 'Angel of Death' at her side. I have no knowledge as to why she came to our shores but until she leaves them, death will always be a part of her life. You see... in her hand, I saw the unmistakable sign of death, but I did not see Karen's death."

Chapter 14

Karen sat quietly in the back of the car. She'd changed into her jeans and jumper. Mark was driving; Garry was busy trying to contact Commander Farrow but all he got was static.

Mark glanced across at Garry. "I think we've got company. That car behind has been with us for the last mile or so. When I sped up so did they, and now as I've slowed, they've slowed."

Garry frowned, removing the machine-gun from Mark's bag before checking the magazine. He seemed confused and snapped out the ammunition clip and studied it carefully. "Did you use this gun in the villa?" he asked, at a level that Karen couldn't hear.

Mark shook his head. "No, you used yours. Why do you ask?"

"The clip's nearly a third empty," Garry replied.

Mark glanced in the rear view mirror; Karen had bunched her clothes up and made a pillow. She seemed asleep.

"Check the silencer; see if it's been used," Mark whispered, dreading Garry's reply.

Garry placed his nose to the silencer and glanced across at him. "This has been used as well," he whispered, now beginning to realise why she'd been so insistent she went alone. Her remarks about Saeed and herself had clearly been contrived to make him think they were more than just friends, but it would seem they were not even that.

"I'm a bloody fool, Mark. She said Saeed would help if she went in to see him alone. She even made me believe they were really good friends and he'd give her the key. He fucking did, but not before she put a bullet in him."

Mark's eyes narrowed. "You mean to say Karen's used it? No, I can't believe that! It would take an awful lot of guts to shoot somebody. Anyway she wouldn't know...," then he suddenly hit his forehead with his hand, realisation spreading across his face. "We both fucking showed her didn't we, spent half the bleeding day telling her how it operated?"

Garry touched his arm. "Not a word, but from now on, keep the guns away from her. God knows what she's done back there, but if she has killed someone we're in the shit and that car behind could be radio on ahead. I thought it was funny they'd not tried to stop us."

"So what do we do now?"

"We get off this road, force them to follow and make an ambush. I'm not prepared to be caught, especially after what that bitch might have done."

Garry picked the map up and studied the road. "My guess is they would have set up an ambush about five miles further along this road. Apart from a few sidetracks there's no way off for a mile. After that there are plenty of options. Watch out for a track on the right in about two miles. It cuts across towards the coast before changing to just a foot-track out. We'll dump the car, then make our way across country and pick up the road about ten miles further on."

Mark never replied but began to slow slightly so as not to miss the track. In the meantime, Garry had prepared the guns. He'd no illusions that they would have to fight but was still not entirely convinced Karen had killed Saeed.

As they approached the junction, Mark slowed quickly and turned hard into it.

Karen woke and looked around. "Are we there then?" she asked sleepily.

Garry turned and grinned. "Sorry, kid, we've had to take a small detour. I'm afraid we may have to walk a little. Are you up to it?"

She just shrugged and collected her things then glanced

back at him. "If you don't mind, I'm not a kid. I've a name and I expect you to use it," she said curtly.

Mark laughed. "Oh, stuck up, are we?" he mocked.

Karen glared at him. "No, I'm not stuck up, but it's not a lot to expect to be called by my name, rather than 'kid'."

Mark was getting fed up with this girl's 'holier-than-thou' approach. "We'd also expect someone we're helping not to take the law into their own hands," he said scathingly.

"And what do you mean by that?" she demanded.

The car jerked to a stop and he spun round, looking her directly in the face. "What I mean, Karen, is how did you really get these keys. Did you let him give you a quick shag when you went into Saeed's house, or did you blow his balls off with my gun?"

Karen opened the door and began to climb out, glancing back inside and pulling her bag out. She stopped and looked at the two lads sat there watching her. "You make me sick. It was me who got you the keys; you two would still be pissing about trying to pinch a car. So how I got them is my business, not yours."

Mark reached across the seat and grabbed her arm before she could pull it away. "No, Karen, it's not your business, it's ours. We've put our lives on the line for you. We're entitled to know just what you've let us into. I know my gun's been fired. What Garry and I need to know now, is just what went on in that house?"

She snatched her arm away from his grip, climbed out, then stood at the side of the car. Both lads also got out.

"We're waiting, Karen," Garry said.

Karen shrugged indifferently. "So I killed the bastards, what of it?" she said without remorse.

Before any of them could answer, the car that had been following suddenly appeared from around the bend. It was approaching fast; two men hanging out of the doors on either side were holding machine-guns.

"Shit, let's get out of here," Mark shouted.

They all ran for their lives, stumbling over boulders and into scrub. The two men were firing their guns, bullets spattering around the three of them. With Garry leading, then Karen and Mark lagging behind, they stumbled on. Moments later, Mark screamed in pain and fell forward. Garry stopped, knelt to the ground and trained his gun in the direction of the pursuers. Karen had also fallen to the ground and she crawled back to Mark. She touched his shoulder and felt the wetness of blood; Mark didn't move. Pulling the gun from his hand, she lay flat on her tummy and waited. There was not long to wait. Three men came crashing through in the same direction they'd run seconds earlier. These men must have been convinced that the people they were pursuing were still running, but that wasn't the case and seconds later both Karen and Garry fired virtually at point-blank range. The men had no chance to escape or dive for cover. They were all dead before they hit the ground.

Silence came suddenly after the guns and Garry whispered to her. "Don't move. There could be more."

She did as he asked and after a few minutes of inactivity, Garry moved over to her side. "I'm going to take a look, you stay here with Mark. I'll be back soon."

She'd no chance to object or even to tell him she thought Mark was dead. But she did as he asked and waited, her gun ready for action. Within minutes there came a single shot, then somebody was coming towards her.

"It's me, Garry, don't shoot," he shouted.

She stood and watched him approach. "How's, Mark?" he asked as he came closer.

She shook her head. "I think he's dead. There's an awful lot of blood and he won't move," she said quietly.

Garry knelt down and lifted Mark's arm, holding his wrist for a moment, trying to find a pulse. Then he looked up at her. "So are you satisfied now? Getting your pound of flesh were we? Just how many more are going to die for you, Karen, before you're satisfied?"

She looked back at him, tears in her eyes. "That's not fair. I never asked you to come. I didn't shoot Mark."

Garry looked back at his friend and started to turn him over before removing the dog tags, going quickly through his pockets. "That may be so, Karen, but we had it under control until you let loose in that house."

She glared at him. "Oh yes? I'm not stupid you know. I do know the sound of a muffled gun shot."

He looked up at her. "What are you saying?"

"What I'm saying, Mr. Bloody Perfect, is that it was you who killed the two people in the villa. Do you not think that's more of a reason for these people following us, rather than Saeed's death?"

Garry stood there, saying nothing at first, then he handed her Mark's bag. "Okay, from now this argument stops, till we're safe. Then you can explain the pros and cons to my Commander. I don't think, no I know, you'll not get very far with him."

She snatched the bag and followed him back down the path. A man lay alongside the other car. Garry pulled him away. "We'll take this car; they probably know your man friend's car by now."

Karen allowed it to pass over her; Saeed was dead and in her mind, that was all that mattered.

Without another word they climbed inside and Garry turned the car round, before driving slowly up the track to the main road. They'd travelled for some time before Karen stretched then pointed at a roadside cafe. "Let's stop and eat, I'm starving," she suggested.

Garry couldn't see any reason why they shouldn't, so he pulled the car off the road and drove across the small car park before stopping in the shadows of some trees. "I'll do the talking, we eat, then move on," he said softly.

Karen nodded and they went inside. A few people were sat about; nobody, after a cursory glance at the strangers, took any more interest. Garry, with some grasp of the language, managed to order chicken and rice for both of them. Whilst waiting for the food, he was looking at a notice in the corner offering accommodation for the night. It was getting on for midnight and what better place to hide out than in a hotel bedroom?

He wandered up to the bar and talked for some time before returning. "We're going to stay here for the night. The owner has some discreet cabins behind. I've pretended we are on our way to get married and he's very understanding as your parents don't know yet. It's cost double and we'll have to share a room but he'll keep his mouth shut."

Karen let him finish before replying. "So long as you don't think tonight's our wedding night, I don't mind."

He stared at her, not believing what he'd heard. "You think a lot of your bloody self, don't you? Believe me, Karen, if you were the last person on earth, what you're suggesting would be miles from my thoughts."

She grinned at him. "Come off it, Garry. Since I put my shorts on this morning you've hardly taken your eyes off me, so don't come the innocent."

Not wanting to be drawn, he realised how astute this girl was. Each time he tried to pull her down, she'd respond quickly, leaving him lost for words. Soon after the meal they followed the owner through the back door and into a small cabin. There was a large room, furnished with a double bed, settee, table and chairs. Through another door was a small bathroom. The man grinned at them, handing the key to Garry, before leaving and closing the door after him. Garry took a handgun and went into the bathroom, urging Karen to follow him. He taped it under the toilet cistern and looked up at her watching him "This is insurance, Karen, just in case."

Back in the main room he sat at the table and opened a document. Just then a knock came to the door. Karen opened it and the owner stood there with a tray. On it was a bottle and two glasses. She thanked him in French and he gave her a wink. Karen smiled back at him, embarrassed at what this man might be thinking. Closing the door, she came to the table and filled both glasses.

"I need to go through a few things with you, Karen, just in case we get separated, or there's an accident like Mark's. You need to know how to get back to our group."

For the next hour he gave her everything she needed. By the time they'd finished, the bottle was empty and it was close to two in the morning.

Karen stood, and then stretched. "I'll use the bathroom first if you don't mind?"

Garry nodded and began packing the bags. When she came out she sat on the side of the bed combing her hair.

"I was wondering about the sleeping arrangements," he said, hesitating at the bathroom door.

She looked across at him for a minute. "Garry, let's get a few things clear, shall we? You can sleep with me, on the settee, the floor, wherever you think best, I don't care. You see, I'm no longer embarrassed about being practically naked around men; that was knocked out of me in no uncertain terms. Not that it means I like it, I don't, but I'm realistic enough to realise we both need a good night's sleep and the bed's the obvious choice. All I ask is that you don't look on it as an opportunity for sex. Contrary to what you might think, I'm a one guy girl."

With that she removed her jumper, slipped her jeans off, and then climbed into bed. Garry turned and went into the bathroom. He liked this girl in some ways but was unable to forget it was her actions that had caused the death of his friend. To his way of thinking, she wasn't to be trusted and he intended to keep his distance. Returning to the room, he climbed into bed alongside her. The perfume she was wearing, while you couldn't help but notice it in the car, was overwhelming now.

"You stink," he said.

Karen turned over and looked at him in the dim light. "In what way?"

"That perfume you're always wearing, it's very strong."

She sighed. "Oh that, it's not really perfume, more a body oil. I'm covered in the bloody stuff. Saeed's mother rubbed it in everyday and the oiling to my body even continued at Sirec's house. Saeed told me they used it to soften my skin and give it a sheen. Whether it does or not, I don't know, what I do know is, it always made me feel sleepy. Does it really smell that bad? I'll go and have another shower to see if it will wash more off, if you want?"

Garry dismissed her offer. "No it's alright, I'll get used to it. It's just that I've never been this close to you before and didn't realise, that's all," he replied.

Their eyes met for a moment before she looked away. "Okay, if you're sure? Anyway, I'm going to sleep, goodnight." With that she turned away and lay there wide awake. She listened as his breathing changed and knew at least he'd have some sleep. How long she lay awake she wasn't sure, but the pain, probably caused by a bad period which had been nagging at her all day, was becoming worse. Eventually Karen couldn't stand it any longer and slipped out of bed, quickly making her way to the bathroom. She walked around a little then sat on the closed toilet seat. The movement was making the pain ease and she began to feel a little better. Then, just as she was going to return to the bedroom, the door into the cabin burst open. Through the gap she could see two armed men. Her first instinct was to scream, but she didn't. Coolly, she went to the toilet and pulled the gun out and pushed it into the back of her knickers, pulling the t-shirt over to hide it. She could hear them shouting at Garry to get up, so she decided to go into the room. Opening the door, they both spun round to look at her. Karen was rubbing her eyes as if she was sleepy.

"Who are you, what do you want?" she asked.

"Don't move," one shouted at her. Then he looked down again at Garry. "You, get up, you're both coming with us."

Karen cut in quickly. "Do you mind if I get my jeans on at least, I'm freezing?" she asked.

The man glanced round, saw her jeans and jumper on the floor and picked them up. After checking the pockets carefully, he threw them across at her. "Be quick about it."

Karen did as he asked and transferred the gun into her front pocket, covering the bulge with her jumper. She was confident they wouldn't search her again; after all, she'd come out of the bathroom wearing only knickers and a t-shirt.

Outside they were both hustled into the back of a Land Rover and one of the men positioned himself opposite. Across his lap he'd a machine-gun. The other man made his way to the main bar and disappeared inside.

Karen slipped her hand into Garry's and moved it onto her leg until he could feel the gun. She glanced across at the man, he was watching the bar so she moved slightly, allowing Garry to slip the gun from her pocket.

Suddenly, Garry shouted at the man, startling him. This gave him precious seconds of confusion while the man tried to grasp why he'd shouted. In these seconds, Garry raised the handgun and shot him between the eyes. He died instantly, then Garry moved fast. Grabbing the man's machine-gun, he jumped from the Land Rover and ran towards the bar, throwing himself to the ground as the other man came out, carrying two cans of beer. This was his downfall, unable to get to his gun, Garry had him in a clear line of sight. This man was dead before he hit the ground. Garry ran to the front of the Land Rover.

"Get the bags, I'll start this thing," he ordered. She did as he asked and soon the Land Rover was roaring down the road away from the carnage.

"So why were you in the bathroom?" he asked.

"I had a pain, I was going to have a hot shower but it eased and I was just coming back to bed," she replied.

"I'm glad you didn't have the shower, besides it took some guts to bring that gun out, Karen," he shouted above the noise of the engine.

She leaned over and kissed his cheek. "That wasn't guts, Garry, that was self-preservation."

He grinned. "All the same, I'd hate to be on the receiving end of one of your self-preservation stints."

She laughed and leaned back on the hard seat. With less than thirty miles to go, they were home and dry.

As they'd left the bar, the owner had watched the fight and now he was busy dialling. The person on the other side of the phone listened carefully then slammed the phone down. Moments later three Land Rovers were heading down towards the road Garry and Karen were travelling on. The occupants knew they could intercept these two killers within a few miles. This time they wouldn't get away.

Twenty minutes had elapsed and Karen was looking back behind them when she saw the approaching vehicles. "I think we've got company, Garry. It looks like this vehicle, only painted brown and green," she shouted.

He glanced in the rear view mirror. She was right and they were approaching fast. "I don't suppose you can drive with all your talents can you?" he shouted.

"No, sorry," she shouted back.

"Then you'll have to climb into the back, keep below the rear tailgate, and try to hit them with my gun," he shouted.

She did as he asked, climbing among boxes, pushing

them to the front to give herself somewhere to hide. One box burst open and a number of round steel balls fell out. "What are these?" she shouted.

"Pass one over," he called back.

She leaned forward and handed him one. Garry's eyes lit up. "They're grenades. Pull the pin out from the top, count to five and throw. They explode."

Karen sighed to herself. She'd seen movies, she wasn't daft. All she wanted to know was what they were; she'd have looked very stupid throwing out something she thought was a grenade when in reality it was a large bullet for a gun or something. Now settled behind the tailgate, she peeped over. The Land Rovers were very close and she switched the safety off the machine-gun, setting it for maximum output of bullets. Lifting the gun over the back, she closed her eyes and pulled the trigger. Seconds later she stopped and peered out. One vehicle was missing but the two that were left, were closer than ever. At that moment one started to fire at them. She could hear the bullets hitting the tailgate, others were flying over the top of her. Karen had never been so frightened. She pulled out two of the grenades and was just going to remove the pin when the Land Rover veered to the left, then the right, throwing her about in the back.

"For God's sake, I nearly dropped the bloody grenades then. Can't you be more careful?" she shouted.

Garry didn't reply, so she grasped the two grenades and pulled the pins. Counting slowly she suddenly panicked, how fast is a second? Was she too slow? With no real answer she threw them over the back and waited for an explosion, but nothing happened. Not dissuaded, she grabbed two more. Again guns were firing, bullets hitting the vehicle with ever increasing regularity. This time she didn't panic; she counted slowly and carefully to five, then threw out of the back.

The front driver of the approaching vehicle saw the two grenades fly out from behind the tailgate, so he screamed at the gunner to concentrate fire in that direction. However, although he tried to avoid them, they passed under his vehicle, one exploding directly under, the other seconds later, forcing the driver behind to swerve. Both vehicles left the road, smashing into stones at the side before being propelled across to the other side, spinning over in mid-air and skidding upside down along the road before coming to a halt. Karen peeped over, her eyes lighting up.

"Stop! Stop! We've got them all," she shouted.

Their vehicle came to a halt and Karen climbed out of the back, pulling open Garry's door. Then she stared dumfounded. He was covered in blood, only managing to turn his head towards her, the pain he was suffering all too apparent in his face. "Sorry, Karen, you did well, love, but it's not finished yet. You'll have to go and check they are all dead, if not you'll have to kill them."

Her eyes widened in horror. "I can't kill in cold blood, you'll have to do that," she demanded.

He reached his hand out and touched her arm. "I can't, Karen, it hurts pretty badly. Please go and see if anyone's alive, we could still be in great danger."

She said nothing, just grabbed the machine-gun and walked back up the road. The sight of mangled people, some partially dismembered, made her retch. Not daring to get too close, she fired the gun at each and every one of them, indifferent as to whether they were alive or dead. Then she returned to Garry.

"Don't ever ask me to do that again, it made me sick!"

He opened his eyes. "Are you sure they are all dead?" he asked.

"They're dead as far as I'm concerned. I'm not going back to check, if that's what you mean," she retorted.

Garry smiled at her words. He was asking a lot but what he was about to say now would really shake her. "You'll have to go on alone; I can't come with you, Karen."

She stared in disbelief at him. "You've got to come! I can't go on alone."

He offered his hand. "You must. The Commander's only four or five miles away. You can make it, believe me."

She stood, not wanting to move. "But if I help, we'll get there somehow. I know I can't drive but it's not too far to walk," she persisted.

Garry was beginning to panic; the longer she hung around, the more likely it was someone would come down the road. "For God's sake, Karen, just go, will you? If you're caught, do you know what they'll do to you? Me, I'll either die or they'll put me in hospital. I've a feeling if they find you here, I'm dead, but if you're missing they'll at least want to question me and I'll have a chance to survive."

She stood for a moment, then made her decision, walking to the back of the vehicle. Pulling out a belt of ammunition she put it over one shoulder and diagonally across her chest. Finding a belt with a holster for a handgun, she fastened it around her waist. Taking what was left of the grenades, she clipped them to the belt. Then she swung a machine-gun over one shoulder and a rifle over the other. Moving to the passenger side of the vehicle, she took the bag containing her clothes and money, picked up the handgun lying on the seat before slipping it quickly into the holster on her belt, then walked back round to Garry. "Due north, you said, for half a mile, then north east for four and I'm to use the radio to contact the Commander," Karen said.

He looked her up and down, surprised at the array of weapons she carried. "You're going home, Karen, not to war," he commented.

She sighed. "I need to protect myself, anyway due north, is that the way I go?" she persisted.

"Yes."

Leaning over, Karen kissed him on the lips. "Good luck, Garry, I'm sorry it's got to end this way but I did my best."

He grasped her hand. "Here, you'll need a watch and a compass," he said pushing both into her hand. "Look after yourself, Karen. You deserve to go home; I've never met a girl as brave as you."

She smiled. "You and Mark did it all really; I've just been a nuisance. Although it is nice of you to say so," she replied softly.

He squeezed her hand. "Karen, will you go out with me when I get home? I'd like to get to know you a lot better, without all this hanging over us."

She grinned. "I might, if when we meet again and you ask me nicely. After all, I'm between boyfriends at the moment and you do have an advantage."

"I do... what's that?" he asked.

She laughed, trying to make light in a serious situation. "You've slept with me and at least I know you don't snore. I'd hate to sleep with a man for the rest of my life who snores."

He began to laugh. "So we're not just talking a date here, Karen, but something a little more permanent perhaps?"

She suddenly looked very shy. "I told you, I'm a one man girl. Let's see how it goes, shall we?"

"I'll hold you to that, Karen, besides we've got to meet again."

"Why do you say that?" she asked.

He grinned. "I want my watch back."

"Oh! Yes of course. I'll look after it then until you come to collect, shall I?"

"You do that. But now it's time you were gone, good luck, love."

He closed his eyes and Karen took one last look before walking away. She knew he was, without some immediate help, close to death. He'd helped her and it did no harm to flirt a little. After all, she'd probably never see him again.

Turning off the road after half a mile, she made her way

across the fields following the compass as Garry had shown her. She was full of confidence she could defend herself, with the handgun for her own suicide, if things weren't going her way. As it was getting lighter she decided to lie low for the rest of the day. She was less than a mile from the meeting place. Garry had told her the Commander would only move at night, so even if they were there already, she'd have plenty of time to get there before night fall and they moved on. She dropped off the narrow path and moved further into a field. It was full of a cereal crop standing some three feet high. Well inside, she settled down, completely hidden from any person passing along the path. It was getting hot and she rifled through the bag, finding a half eaten piece of chocolate and two biscuits. Karen felt better after the food but the day was warming up, so, removing the jumper and changing into shorts, she rolled the jeans and jumper up, using them as a pillow then lay down and was soon asleep.

Karen awoke with a start! What it was that woke her she wasn't sure, but sitting up she could just about peep above the cereal crop. She could see nothing and after gathering her clothes and pushing them into the bag and taking a last look round, she began making her way towards the far end of the field. At that moment at the bottom of the field, directly in line to where she was heading, a man climbed over the fence. He didn't seem to see her at first but when he did he started waving his arms and shouting at the top of his voice. Then he began running towards her.

Karen panicked, not knowing what to do, certain in her own mind this man posed a threat and she'd no intention of allowing him too close. She dropped the bag and swung the machine-gun round. Switching to single shot, she raised the gun, looking carefully through the sight for the telltale red spot of the laser. Karen didn't want to kill him, only dissuade him from coming close, so she squeezed the trigger gently, allowing the bullet to whistle close to his head. The gun jerked a little as it fired, then she waited. Still he came. Still he waved his arms, shouting at her. His language seemed strange and the gestures towards her frightening.

She sighed and this time raised the gun, squeezing gently again. The man seemed to stop in mid-air then disappeared from view. Karen lowered the gun, her heart pounding. Grabbing her bag, she began to run. Then, seconds later, she stumbled, rolled and fell headlong into a ditch. She lay there for a moment before standing gingerly, the front of her caked in mud from head to toe. A slow realisation came to her. Had the man been warning her of the hidden ditch? Had she shot him for nothing? She would never know.

Dragging herself out and following the edge of the ditch, she found a crossing some distance down. Once across Karen was undecided if she should go and look for the man. She'd aimed to stop him, not to kill him, but wasn't used to the gun's recoil and couldn't be sure how accurate she'd been. Finally, deciding against finding him, she picked her way slowly to the edge of the field. Another ditch ran along this boundary this time with water running, not mud. Quickly pulling her muddy clothes off, then using the t-shirt as a cloth, she wiped herself down before dressing in jeans and jumper. Then, after rinsing the shorts and t-shirt, she stuffed them in the bag. Studying the compass, she moved on, crossing two more fields, diverting round a building that looked occupied and finally stopping close to where the Commander and his men should be.

Starving and desperately wanting a drink, Karen settled down among some shrubs, chewing at the remaining biscuit, her thoughts going back to Garry, wondering if he'd been taken to hospital. She hoped they'd take him; after all, he was only defending her and didn't deserve to die. She looked at Garry's watch he'd given her for the twentieth time, soon they should be here and she'd hear the call. However, before that, she decided she should take time to study the area, make sure she was in a position to see who came and perhaps have a chance to escape, in case it was a trap.

Chapter 15

Commander Farrow watched the warehouses explode with satisfaction. They'd initially had a difficult time getting close but Farrow had not been discouraged. He'd already decided in his own mind that, with such a high value of goods and the warehouse at capacity, the owners would double the guards. This was, he found, precisely what had happened. He'd spent some time studying the surrounding area before finding a way to create a diversion. The fire he'd started on parched scrubland had the desired effect. With a helpful hand from nature, drifting dense smoke soon engulfed the warehouse. Many guards scattered, unable to breathe without choking, leaving only a few security staff. Then it had been relatively easy to breach the perimeter fencing and set the charges. His major task now was to join up with the other two groups and return to the pickup point as soon as possible.

Hitchen was making notes after having radio communication from the other groups, when Farrow asked for an update.

"We've had contact with Group Two, Sir. They've encountered heavy resistance in the area and managed only partial destruction of the target. Since the explosion, local army militia has been mobilised. They are waiting new orders from you as to what you want them to do. We've also had one contact from Group Three. They've collected successfully and are at this moment returning at speed to the meeting point."

Farrow looked at his maps, Group Two was nearly fifty miles due south. If they'd only been partially successful, he would need an assessment of the damage before deciding if it warranted a return to destroy completely. This possibility had been envisaged as the initial planned pickup time could be delayed a further three days if necessary.

"Get Group Two back on the radio," he said to Hitchen.

Within five minutes Farrow was talking to the officer in charge. "Are you saying we should join up and try again, or is the destruction enough?" Farrow asked.

"We still have one warehouse intact, Sir. The cable to the charges failed. Activity's very high at the moment but we're holding position. We've a feeling they might begin movement within forty-eight hours. Trucks have been queuing down the road waiting for the all clear from the fire teams for some hours now. We estimate twenty to thirty trucks are already in the queue."

Farrow made notes then switched the radio mike to transmit. "I can't see any other option. We'll delay pickup for three days. I'll join you with all haste after meeting up with Group Three."

The link broke and Farrow called Control. They agreed with his assessment, telling him they'd inform the submarine to reschedule for three days' time.

Farrow called the team together, explaining the new orders. Then, glancing at his watch, he told them to pack. Within ten minutes they were on the move. Two hours later they had arrived, a short distance from the meeting place with Group Three. Farrow moved closer to Chapman, his Second in Command. "Set up a perimeter surveillance operation, just in case. I'll go with Cook and Hitchen to meet Group Three."

Chapman nodded his understanding, taking two other soldiers. Farrow moved quickly to the arranged meeting place, then raised his radio. "Group Three, come in," he listened on the free channel of his radio.

"This is Three; I am receiving you, over," came a girl's voice.

Farrow stared for a second at the radio, why would a girl be calling, he wondered? He moved closer to Hitchen, his voice low. "We may have a problem. Fall back in defensive position with Cook. I'll acknowledge the call and ask them to come in. Also inform Chapman we may need back up."

Hitchen moved off without a sound. Farrow gave him thirty seconds then raised the radio to his mouth. "Group Three, show yourself. This is Leader One, all is clear, over."

Nothing happened, so Farrow called again. This time there was a response. "You came with two others. You're already in my sights; I need to be sure you are who you claim. Tell your men to stand at your side, place your weapons on the ground, then back away three feet, over."

Farrow glanced round but he could see no one. Then he looked down to switch the radio over again and saw the telltale red laser spot steady on his chest. Now he knew the direction but was unable to move for fear of the person firing. Farrow raised his radio again. "Hitchen, Cook, cancel the last order and join me, over."

They did as he commanded and soon they stood alongside him. "Delay two minutes, Chapman's on his way. He'll be in position soon," Hitchen muttered under his breath.

Farrow didn't acknowledge but asked the two of them to place their weapons on the ground and, like him, step away. Then he raised his radio again. "Group Three, you can come in now, we've done as you've asked, over."

Farrow strained his eyes into the gloom, expecting the person to appear from the direction he'd decided they must be, after catching site of the laser beam.

"Don't turn round. If you're who you claim you are, there's a password known to Garry and Mark. Can you give it now?" a voice came from behind them.

Farrow gave a hint of a smile; the lads had done well, one at the front and the other behind, without giving their positions away. "The sun is shining late tonight," Farrow recited.

He waited and then heard the click of a safety going on. "Thank you. I've lowered my gun now, you may turn round," Karen said quietly.

Turning round, Farrow found himself looking at a girl. He'd seen photos but they did nothing for her. The girl stood watching him was taller and far more attractive than he'd imagined. "I presume I'm talking to Karen Marshall? The name's Farrow, Commander Farrow. Perhaps, Karen, you could tell me where Mark and Garry are hiding? I would also very much like to know why you're carrying such an arsenal of weapons?" he asked.

She remained still, just looking at the three of them. "Mark died in my arms yesterday. We were being chased by three people in a car. There was a gunfight and Mark was at the rear, protecting. He never knew what hit him and didn't regain consciousness," she stopped and pulled out two dog tags. "These are his, Garry asked me to bring them."

Farrow took them from her hand. "And Garry, where's he?"

Karen shook her head. "I don't really know. This morning we were overcome by two men dressed in army uniforms. Garry seemed to think they were mercenaries but I'm not sure. Anyway Garry, after a fight, shot them and we took their Land Rover. We thought after that we were home and dry but three more Land Rovers began chasing us. It was very frightening. I was hidden behind the tailgate but at least it gave me some protection. I got one with the machine-gun, two others with grenades. Garry was driving, bullets were flying everywhere and he was hit. It was a bad injury; he lost a lot of blood and couldn't move so he told me to leave him. He was afraid if I stayed they'd kill us both. Alone, he thought he'd have a chance. I suppose he was right to think they'd probably take him to hospital rather than kill him there."

Farrow moved to her side and grasped her arm gently. "That was a very good report, Karen. It couldn't have been easy for a young girl to go through such an ordeal; we'll look after you from now."

She gave a weak smile. Garry had said the same, now she'd only believe it when they arrived on English soil. "You've not got any water and something to eat, have you?" she asked. "I've had nothing since yesterday and I'm starving. I've had to avoid places I might have found food, in case I was seen."

He called Hitchen, who instantly produced a large sandwich and a can of beer. She thanked him, before sitting on the grass to eat. For the first time she felt safe.

Farrow sat down alongside her. "Are you up for a walk tonight? We need to team up with another group. Its forty miles but we'll soon find transport; in the meantime we'll walk. The main road's about five miles across country, if we stay on this side of the hill it's a sixty mile drive on pretty bad roads."

"I don't mind, whatever you've got planned I'll fall in with," she replied, then carried on eating.

At that moment Chapman appeared. "We watched her go around you, Sir. I decided not to act because we couldn't see the others."

Karen grinned. "I knew you were there, you know, I'd seen you all arrive and split up, besides, I could have taken you out easily."

Chapman looked indignant. He'd taken a sudden dislike to this girl. "Cocky little kid, aren't you? What makes you so sure you'd have got the better of us?"

Karen finished the beer, then stood up. Her features had changed, her voice hard. She looked him directly in the eyes. "Don't ever call me 'kid'. The people who thought me just a kid are now dead. My name is, Karen, Karen

Marshall." She fell silent for a moment, Chapman was becoming red in the face at this girl's words but she'd not finished with him yet. She swung the machine-gun round and patted it gently, her voice scathing. "As for your so-called attempt to back your Commander, my laser sight was on you before you'd even settled in that hedge over there. I've been here ages and checked every possible place someone could hide. If the Commander hadn't given me the correct password, I could have taken you out very easily and if you are wondering how this little kid could have done that? I'll remind you; I spent two and half years in this sort of operation nearly every weekend. You may say that's just fun and not reality but I'll tell you this; those people were ex-marines with some very keen amateurs. They all took the games very seriously and yes, I was young, but they treated me as one of the team and I often slept alongside them out in the woods. Okay, our guns were paint splatters but that made it even worse; you had to be very close to get a kill, and your sort of carefree approach, before hiding, would have made them laugh."

Commander Farrow listened carefully to her words, he'd thought it strange she hadn't been quivering in a corner or crying in hysterics when they'd found her. That would have been more than acceptable under the circumstances, but now he understood. Her precautions had been good, checking the area, like he would have done. She was well armed, hand grenades in the correct place and she had approached from behind very successfully. Then to even know where the back up was, this confirmed the reports he'd read of this girl, that she was very capable for someone so young. Now he needed to diffuse the situation and bring his team together. He stood and came between them, placing a hand on each of their shoulders. "I think Karen's, owed an apology, Chapman. She's been through a lot and I agree with Karen, she's not a kid and we shouldn't talk to her in that way. In fact I'd go as far as to say she's a very resourceful young lady and we should congratulate her. It's now up to us and especially you, Chapman, to show her that we, too, are a professional team, besides being well able to keep her safe and reunite her quickly with her family. Now I want you two to shake hands and from now on, even you, Karen, treat each other with respect."

Chapman stood for a moment, then broke into a smile, offering his hand. "I'm sorry, Karen; it was the wrong choice of words. Commander Farrow is right, you're a resourceful girl and, I might say, a very attractive young lady, welcome to the S.A.S."

She smiled back and took his hand, grimacing at the strength in his grip, but not complaining. The others also came to her, shaking her hand and giving their names. Within five minutes they were ready to move off, Farrow happy in some ways that feelings had been vented on both sides. All of them now knew Karen's potential and while they would still protect the girl, they would also have confidence that she wouldn't break into hysterics at any moment.

Chapter 16

Sirec entered the hospital and was quickly shown to a private room. Saeed was inside, propped up with pillows in bed, pain written all over his face.

"You don't look too well, Saeed."

"Neither would you if you'd been shot as many times as me," Saeed replied with some indignation.

Sirec didn't comment on him being shot, but followed a different tact. "Perhaps you can tell me about the Friday night before Karen left you?"

Saeed frowned. "Friday, Sirec, what's that Friday got to do with anything?"

"A great deal, my friend, were you not playing cards?"

"I always play cards on a Friday."

"I hear you lost the game? You also lost my girl for a night as well."

Saeed frowned. "I didn't lose her, Sirec, I used her as collateral till the banks opened. She was well looked after, never at risk of escape and brought back the following morning."

"Oh yes, Saeed, she was very well looked after," Sirec replied as he leaned over him and squeezed his injured leg.

Saeed screamed with the pain.

"So bloody well, in fact," Sirec shouted, "they let her ring home and tell everyone where she was, who she was going to and I suppose everything else she could remember about her abduction. Now my villa's destroyed and you, my friend, unfortunately, are still alive."

Saeed's mouth dropped open. "I never knew that, Sirec, you must believe me? But you can be sure I'll kill him and the whole of his bloody household for letting her get to a phone."

Sirec didn't respond, but walked to the window, looking out. "You told Halif that the girl shot you," he said, without turning.

"Yes and she took my money. She's another who will pay for it. I've lost a leg, my other foot's shattered and I might even lose that, besides having to wear a bag to piss into for the rest of my life. When I get out of this bed, I'll find that kid and wrench her heart out her chest while she still lives. Show it to her, beating in my hand, before nicking it slightly with my knife. Death will be slow as I force her to watch the life-giving blood pump from her body," Saeed said with satisfaction.

Sirec smiled to himself, this was a very bitter man. "You intend to do a great deal of killing, my friend, but you forget in your desire for vengeance that the girl belongs to me, unless of course you have my money, plus, shall we say, another forty thousand as compensation? Otherwise I decide her fate; it's not in your hands."

Saeed looked at him strangely. "What's she to you? The kid would only have been one of twelve you will have had already this year. I suppose she'd have ended up like the others by the end of the month? It's my right to kill her; she's brought shame on my family."

Sirec still didn't turn, just gazed out. "No, Saeed, you brought the shame on your family, not the girl, but you can be sure I'll be very interested in talking to her and finding out just why she came back to kill you. Whatever you did must have been very bad to display so much anger to make a young girl want to kill? However, I digress; she interests me. That kid's got guts. She's clever and not afraid to fight. It's time I started looking for a more permanent relationship. I think she could be that woman."

Saeed had begun to feel very scared. If Sirec found out what he'd done to Karen on the last night, there was every chance he'd exact revenge for not following his instructions.

He always insisted the girls he took were to be prepared, treated well and never touched. Somehow he must find and kill Karen before she talked.

"You're not thinking right, Sirec. Lie down with that girl and you'd be lucky to wake in the morning. I watched her; she never batted an eye after gunning down four people. I've also heard that at least seven others have died. No, Sirec, take my advice; if you want a nice girl, I'll find one, she would even be a virgin if you want, but Karen! Forget her, let me sort that girl out."

Sirec spun round, walking back to the bed, and Saeed shrunk back, terrified Sirec would grab his injured leg again, but he didn't, he just sat down on the chair alongside.

"But that's the point, Saeed. I live with death everyday, it excites me, I relish the danger. Now I can think of nothing else but her. It'll be my intellect, my charm, against a girl who'll be hell bent on destroying me. Think of it, if I succeed in taming this girl, convincing her I really want her for herself, then the way she came to me would be of little consequence. I'd have a girl for life instead of a stream of simpletons. I want her back, no matter what the cost."

Saeed listened to Sirec's ramblings. The man was insane, but Sirec could be talking money again and that interested him. He was already down on the deal with what he'd paid to Assam, besides losing Sirec's money. Then there would be the cost of this hospital, so any extra payments he could extract from him would be welcome. But of course, whatever money Sirec paid to try to bring her back would be a waste on Sirec's part. Karen would be dead before she could have a meeting with him. However, much he wanted Sirec's money, he was confused as to what Sirec wanted of him.

"What do you want me to do, Sirec? I'm stuck in this bed for the next month at least, and thanks to her, crippled for life," he asked.

Sirec was now composed and moved again to the window. "This Assam, he knows her well?"

"He was with her for a number of weeks and spent time preparing her for her new life. If you want to know about her as a person, he's the man to talk to."

"You still have your contacts in England, yes?" Sirec asked without comment to Saeed's previous answer.

"Of course."

"Then this is what I want you to do. Call England; get your people there to stay close to the parents. I need to know if they hear anything before it becomes public knowledge. Tell them to pretend to be a freelance reporter; offer a big payment for an exclusive story. Most people are greedy and will fall for that. If the rumours I'm hearing are true and it's not mercenaries hired by the family but the British S.A.S. who pulled her out, because of their involvement, there's a very high risk they might just slip the net which is already closing around them in this country. You will also contact Assam. I want everything he's got on her sent to me. I also want him to set a course for Cyprus, not enter their waters, but wait for instructions."

Saeed frowned. "Why Cyprus?"

Sirec pulled a cigarette out and then lit it slowly before replying. "I'll soon have conformation if this was a military operation and if it was, their nearest UK military land base is Cyprus. From there they could fly her home. The military have transport planes leaving all the time to the UK. We have many contacts in Cyprus, and it's possible that we may be able to snatch her back. Assam could provide the means of getting her back to this country. But if we miss her in Cyprus then you will use your resources in England to take her again. I'll arrange for her to leave the country then."

With those words, Sirec left the room. Saeed lay there in deep thought. H hoped the S.A.S. was leading the operation, if they were there would be no chance of getting near her in

Cyprus. However, once she's returned to England, that would be a very different story. He'd only need to wait a short time and soon, when she and her family were convinced she was safe, she'd fall back into a normal life and then he could easily snatch her back. Not for Sirec of course, but himself. She owed a heavy debt for killing his friends and crippling him. She would pay for it in many ways before he finally killed her. A grin of satisfaction came over his face as he picked his mobile telephone up from the side-table and began calling contacts.

Halif was stood outside Saeed's room waiting for Sirec. "The man who was with her, is now fully awake and able to talk. Do you want to see him?"

"I do, I certainly do," Sirec replied with enthusiasm.

Entering the room Garry was in, Sirec walked over to the bed. "You're feeling better?" he asked politely.

"Yes, thank you. Where am I?" Garry asked.

"You're in a private hospital at my expense. You were lucky my people picked you up before the military did. They don't take too kindly to people wandering about their country, destroying military warehouses and killing innocent civilians. At the very least they'd have tortured you, even put you up in front of the cameras for propaganda reasons. I've saved you from that."

Garry, still doped from the painkillers, frowned, confused. "So what's in it for you that I should get this star treatment? I'm broke, spend all my money on having a good time and can't repay you?"

Sirec sat down alongside him. "First things first; I must know if you are a mercenary or British S.A.S.?"

"I'm a British serving soldier, that's all I can tell you."

Sirec nodded with understanding, he'd suspected S.A.S. involvement as the overall operation was typical of them. However, until now, he couldn't be sure if the attack on the villa had been a separate operation by mercenaries.

"I suppose your orders were to collect Karen?"

"I can't tell you my orders."

"I could of course force you to answer, but it is of no consequence. We know she didn't die in the fire so it must be assumed, even if it wasn't planned, you did actually take her with you?"

"I can confirm that."

"Thank you; was she with you for some time?"

"She was with us for only two days, but why the interest?"

"I have a great deal of interest in Karen because she belongs to me."

Garry laughed, but cut it short as pain shot through his body. "I'm not sure that Karen or the British Government would see it that way. She's got the impression that she was abducted and sold in some sort of auction. Perhaps you'd better explain to Karen herself how you come to the conclusion that you own her? In our country we call it kidnap and you go to prison for it."

Sirec shrugged. "That's incidental, she will understand when we meet as to ownership, but I digress. I'd like you to tell me a little about her."

"Why?" Garry asked.

"Well, you took her back before we could meet. I've a little time to spare and you're going nowhere for the moment, so why not talk?"

Garry could see the man's point, but failed to understand just what he'd want to know about her. "You know she's only just eighteen and a bit young for you?"

"Of course I knew her age; however, you must understand what you call young is not regarded as young in these parts," Sirec corrected, "but I stop you, please go on."

"Okay. She's tall, very slim with blue eyes and long dark brown hair and as far as I'm concerned, decidedly attractive."

Sirec held his hand up. "Yes, yes. I know all that, I've a

number of photos; what I want to know about is her personality. Is she, as everybody seems to keep saying, competent, bright and interesting to be with?"

Garry couldn't believe what he was hearing; this man had an infatuation for Karen, seemingly desperate to have someone talk about her. It worried him, a man like that would follow her all over the world. She'd never be safe unless he thought her dead. But there was no harm that he could see, in playing along. After all, she must be still free and safely with the Commander, otherwise he'd not be asking these questions.

"The time Mark and I were with Karen, we found her very intelligent and certainly a bright girl," Garry continued, "she is also very resourceful and fully committed, no matter what it takes, to going home."

"But she'd listen to reason and realise her home is with me, wouldn't she?" Sirec cut in.

Garry shrugged. "I suppose, anybody would listen to an argument, but unless you had some bloody good reasons, I can't see you convincing her to come back with you. That's if I'm reading what you're thinking correctly? A man she called Saeed found to his cost, that to mess about with her is not to be advised."

Sirec nodded his head up and down. "I suppose she didn't tell you just what this man Saeed had actually done to make her want to kill him?"

"No, we didn't have time to get that out of her. Stupidly we let Karen enter his house alone. She said she knew him intimately and he'd do anything for her. We needed a car and he had one. Besides which, she knew the house and how to get in so we didn't disbelieve her. I now believe he treated her very badly and she went in there with the sole intention of killing him."

Sirec stood and walked to the window. "Thank you for your honesty; I also believe that. But now I need to know something that's important, both for your life and that of Karen's. What were your plans after the operation, in how you intended to leave this country?"

Garry shifted his position. "What day is this?" he asked.

"Thursday the twentieth, why?"

"Then they've already left. The pickup was last night, I'm afraid you're too late, Sirec, the girl's going home."

Sirec stood silently for a short time, then turned and made to leave the room.

Garry called after him. "What will happen to me?"

Sirec glanced back. "I should kill you, after all, your people have destroyed my warehouses. You, lad, have destroyed my home and taken my girl, but I don't kill cripples. You will serve to be a reminder for others who might want to walk in your footsteps as to the futility of it all."

Garry eyes widened at Sirec's words. "What are you on about?" Garry whispered, hardly daring to know the answer.

Sirec gave a sickly grin. "They didn't tell you then?"

"Tell me what?" Garry demanded.

"A bullet had lodged in your spine. They tried to get it out but it was messy. These people aren't that good, so in trying to save your life, which was the priority you understand, they managed to sever your spinal cord. I'm afraid you'll never leave that bed. Your life in the S.A.S. is finished, so, I suspect, is your sex life. That's if any girl would want you? We will in due course inform the British Consul, and they, I presume, will want to fly you home."

Garry lay there, stunned at his words.

Sirec stood watching him. "It was all a waste of time; you've paid dearly, have you not?" Sirec said softly.

"What are you saying, what was a waste of time?" Garry asked.

"To collect my Karen, of course; you see she'll be returned to me no matter what. There's no place in the world she can hide. Unlike you, I know people, some easily bought, others more difficult, but in the end everyone has a price. Someone will tell me where she is. Then Karen will be brought back. So you see, Garry, I'll call you, Garry, if you don't mind? You've been crippled for nothing; even the weapons your friends blew up have already been replaced."

With that, Sirec left the room. Garry could hear him laughing outside with somebody else. He felt very down and depressed with Sirec's words. Karen had made an impact on him and for the last hours he had thought of nothing else. Her promised date when they met up again, now dashed by these bungling idiots. A girl like her wouldn't want to go out with a cripple, of that he was sure.

Chapter 17

Three hours had elapsed since Karen had teamed up with the Commander. They'd had an uneventful forced march across country, before climbing aboard a canvas covered truck procured by two of the soldiers sent in advance of the main group. Now they were heading south to assist Group Two, who were still trying to come up with a means to destroy the final warehouse.

Initially Farrow had tried, unsuccessfully, to take all Karen's weapons off her. She'd been adamant that they were hers and she intended to stick with at least one of them, 'for her own personal protection' she claimed, until she was 'definitely on the way home'.

Farrow considered, after trying to reason with her for some time, that it was perhaps pointless trying any longer. He'd no intention of placing her on the front line and where she was going to be waiting for them would offer no chance to utilise any of her weapons. So as not to raise tensions any higher, he agreed she should keep the laser guided machine-gun, its ammunition and the grenades on the ammunition belt. The rifle, which she'd procured from the Land Rover, was in bad condition and could explode if she used it, so he insisted she gave that up. Karen, looking at the rifle with Farrow's help, understood and finally agreed to this, but didn't volunteer to Farrow that she had a handgun, having moved it from the holster and into her jeans.

The truck eventually turned off the main highway and they travelled for about two miles before coming to a halt. The men scrambled out and began to cover the vehicle with branches and other items they could find around for concealment. Then they grouped together round Farrow. "Chapman and two of your group remain here with Karen and defend this position. The rest of you will come with me," Farrow ordered.

Chapman said nothing, just saluted and pointed to two men for the task. In some ways he was disappointed, having to 'nanny' this girl, but he was also realistic. Even if Karen hadn't been here, the truck would still need defending, so he resigned himself to the task and watched quietly as Farrow moved away.

Karen sat quietly on the tailgate of the truck, sorting her few clothes out from the bag. Morning was beginning to break and she'd decided to change into her shorts.

Chapman was a short distance away cleaning his finger nails with a penknife. He glanced up at her. "Are you good at cooking?" he asked.

She looked up from what she was doing. "Cooking what?"

He patted his rifle, grinning broadly. "I could get us a rabbit."

Karen scrunched her nose. "What, a live one?" she asked hesitantly.

He began to laugh. "Well it's not going to come frozen from a bloody supermarket. I'll skin it if you're that squeamish."

She shuddered. "I wouldn't know what to do with it. Anyway it's hardly likely to be much good on its own; we'd need vegetables and things like that. Can't you settle for a biscuit?"

Chapman called over to one of the others. "Did you hear that, Franco, Karen wants us to get vegetables and all the trimmings. This is a girl that's slept with men, drinking and farting all night and she's never lived off the land."

The other men burst into laughter, making Karen feel decidedly ill at ease.

"It's not that funny and I didn't sleep with them. I was often with my dad and never allowed to drink, I was too young," she said, trying to defend her position. "Besides, I'm not a bloody cook anyway."

Chapman had finished messing with his nails and threw the penknife hard into the ground a few times. "You're not really good at anything are you, apart from pretending to be grown up and showing off like last night at my expense. I would have put you over my knee like I do with my kids at home when they get out of line if Farrow hadn't been there. He's weak and stupid; even lets you keep the weapons. What for? You've probably not got the guts to fire a gun anyway."

Karen looked at him for a short time. She didn't like this man or the others for that matter, but she was stuck with them, whether she liked it or not. It was possible, as with Garry, she could be in a situation where she needed their help. With this sort of attitude towards her they'd probably just dump her. Jumping down from the tailgate, she removed her jeans and replaced them with her shorts, finally taking off her jumper. Four weeks back she'd have been hiding shyly behind the truck rather than stand in front of men in her knickers, now she didn't even give it a second thought.

"You don't think much of me, do you?" she asked Chapman.

He shrugged. "Why should I, you're a cocky little bitch. And I'll tell you this, strutting around in shorts and t-shirt will have no affect on me; like I said, I've kids and a wife I love?"

Karen grinned. "I don't strut around, thank you, besides I'm not really bothered if I have an effect on you or not. I'm not that desperate I want sex from a man who's older than my dad. All I ask is you don't try to knock me down all the time."

"Yes, love," he replied in a patronising way, "just go and sit in the sun like a good little girl and leave the soldiering to us."

Karen sighed, she stood facing him. "Right that's it;

you've done a lot of big talking so I'm going to give you an opportunity to show how good you are. Why don't you come at me with that knife of yours?"

He laughed at her. "What, this penknife?"

She frowned. "No... The knife on your belt."

"Don't be childish, I'd kill you," he retorted.

"I don't mean kill me, just get me in a position where it's at my throat and you could kill me. If you can do it twice, I'll apologise and you can even put me over your knee, like you keep threatening, if you want? But if I take it off you, or throw you to the ground twice, I win and you apologise. What do you say?"

Chapman never moved, but the other two had been listening and began ribbing him.

"Go on, Chapman; show this cocky little girl what the S.A.S. can do," Franco urged.

Still Chapman kept muttering under his breath about how he didn't fight girls.

Franco persisted. "She's putting you on, Chapman; the reality is, she's kinky and wants to go over your knee. Mind you, if you keep saying no, she'll win by default. So I'll tell you what, here's ten quid, the winner takes all. How about you, Hawkins, have you got a tenner as well, it'll make it more interesting?"

Hawkins pulled two five pound notes from his jacket and threw them on top of Franco's money, grinning. Then he looked at Chapman. "Go for it, Chapman," he ribbed, "you don't often get a pretty girl wanting to fight you.. Show her a thing or two before giving her a good spanking."

Chapman stood, pulled his jacket off, removing the gun belt, and drew the knife from its sheath. "You're sure about this, Karen, fighting with knives can get you injured very easily?" he warned.

Karen stepped back. "Listen, we've got to sort our differences out one way or the other. I'm just a girl who's had a few self-defence classes. I'd like to try them out in a relatively real situation, that's all. Besides, it'll pass the time and I might end up with egg on my face and a sore bum, but I'll take that chance."

Franco cut in. "Treat her gently, Chapman, but it sounds like she's already resigned to the punishment."

Karen glanced at Franco. "I'm not intending to lose, but if I do, I'll not renege on the deal," she replied curtly.

Chapman suddenly stepped back and lowered his body, holding the knife out in his right hand. "Okay, you've asked for it, girl. Defend yourself."

She turned and faced him, keeping her legs slightly apart, her eyes concentrating on the hand with the knife. Chapman suddenly lunged forward. Karen moved like lightning to her right. Chapman had seen her action, and his arm holding the knife followed, crossing his own body. Within a second Karen, having hoped for this, literally flew back to the left, at the same time lunging forward and grasping his wrist with the knife and wrenching it up, kicking his legs from under him, and throwing Chapman completely off balance. He fell to the ground with a thud. She stepped back and stood there.

"The first point to me," she said quietly.

Franco and Hawkins watched with more than a passing interest now. Never had they seen a girl move so fast and disarm a man so easily. Franco moved close to Hawkins, his voice low. "This kid's a judo expert. Chapman was really taken by surprise then, next time he won't let her get him so easily."

Hawkins nodded knowingly, not replying.

By now Chapman had got up and was brushing the dust off himself. "Lucky break that, Karen. You've not told me the complete truth, have you? A girl going to self-defence classes doesn't move at that speed."

She laughed. "Then it's up to you to find out my

capabilities, isn't it?"

He just grinned slightly and nodded his head. 'Yes, you little minx,' he said to himself, 'I'll show you this time."

They were now back in the same position, facing each other, Karen again watching the hand with the knife, Chapman weighing up her position. Then suddenly he went for her, dropping the knife arm, before bringing his other up to grasp her right arm. Karen saw it coming and side stepped the other way, lunging herself at him, grasping his neck and trying to get her leg round his. But Chapman was too strong and literally lifted her in the air, throwing her away like a rag doll.

Karen rolled in a ball and sprang up before he could follow her down. She ended up behind him and in seconds, high kicked him squarely in the centre of his back. Chapman lunged forward, narrowly avoiding falling flat on his face. He spun round to face her but she was ready again and high kicked him hard in the chest before retreating.

Chapman shook himself. "You've done a little kick-boxing as well then. You're full of surprises, I must say."

Ignoring his comments, she positioned herself again, ready for his attack. This time he went for her, turned slightly, then hit her with all his body strength. For Karen it was like hitting a brick wall, she'd no chance and was sent reeling away from him, completely off balance. This time he followed and in seconds spun her round and had the knife to her throat.

"One to me, Karen?" he whispered, and then pushed her away.

However, as he turned, she lunged for him again, grabbing his neck with her arm and kicking his legs from under him. Chapman fell heavily to the ground, Karen followed.

"Two out of three to me, I win?" she said breathlessly.

"No, that's cheating, I wasn't even ready," he protested.

She rolled away and sat up. "I know, but to tell you the truth, you're too strong. I confused you at the beginning because you didn't know what to expect but now... I give up, you win. You can take your prize if you want, I probably deserve it for being so stupid," she said quietly.

Chapman stood and offered his hand. "Come on, Karen, don't knock yourself. I accept your win, I was only joking when I said you'd cheated. In any fight I shouldn't have turned my back, but for all that you're a plucky girl with the guts to admit defeat, and yes, if you'd carried on, my superior strength would have defeated you in the end. Think about it, you must be six stone lighter than me, that's a hell of a lot of weight for anyone to give away."

She gave him a weak smile, accepting his hand to pull her up, before dusting the dirt off her clothes. Chapman opened his bag and handed her a can of beer. The two others joined them and Hawkins patted her on the back. "So how did you learn that sort of fighting then?"

She gave a shrug. "I've done self-defence, kick-boxing and in judo; I'm a brown belt, I was supposed to go for my black this summer. Anyway, I think I bit off more that I could chew. I really didn't think strength mattered, my instructor always taught me it didn't, but he was wrong. Chapman lifted me as if I was nothing, I think I realised then if I carried on I'd lose and probably get hurt."

Chapman finished his drink and crushed the can in his hand. "Don't be so down on yourself, Karen, you really were good. I underestimated you and that's a real advantage in a fight. Many men would have done the same, not expecting skilled retaliation."

She glanced at him between gulps of the beer. "So what are you saying?" she asked.

"What I'm saying, Karen, is in a straight fight I'd have struggled to win, in fact, I'd go as far as to say you'd have won, or you'd have injured me enough to escape. As it was, even with your skills, forewarned is forearmed and the second time, once I knew, it was sheer brute strength that saw me through."

She offered her hand to him. "So we're friends then, you're not going to keep having a go at me?"

"Yes, I take back everything I said about you and I won't want to smack your bottom. Besides, I'm a father, it's not something I should do to a young lady, win or lose," Chapman replied, grasping her hand and shaking it hard.

Then he had an idea. "Tell you what, we've got all day and probably tomorrow. If you're up to it, and I think you are, we'll show you some of our training tricks. With your background you'll have no problems in disarming any man, no matter what his weight is, after we finish with you."

Karen looked a little dubious. "Okay," she replied nervously, "so long as you don't hurt me too much. I'm not a wimp but I like to think I'm feminine and not some tomboy. Besides, I do want to be able to walk home."

Chapman patted her back. "That's a girl. Don't be so worried; we'll try to make sure you don't get hurt. If you do, you won't feel a thing, it'll be over in a flash."

"What will?" she asked.

He suddenly looked very serious. "Why death, if the knife slips, Karen, what else?"

"You're joking aren't you?" she gasped.

All the men burst into laughter, then Chapman pulled his knife from the sheath before handing it to her. "Right, first lesson, how to hold a knife."

By late afternoon they'd all had enough in the heat. Karen was laying out in the sun, the men checking and cleaning their guns. No word of Farrow's progress had reached them and Chapman was becoming more concerned.

"They should have called by now. Send a call signal, Franco," Chapman said quietly.

Franco leaned over to the radio and listened for some

time, then pressed the automatic call signal generator. With no response he called again. This time the radio broke into life.

"Group One to Group Two, come in please, over."

All the men sat up, listening intently.

"This is Group Two, receiving strength four, over."

"Where have you been, we've called six times in the last hour, over?" Farrow asked.

"We have been trying to raise you as well, it may be atmospherics. Have you completed over?"

"Yes, but met heavy resistance. We've casualties, require the use of transport, over," Farrow replied.

Chapman grabbed the mike. "Have you co-ordinates, over?"

Farrow gave coded co-ordinates and Franco busied himself decoding then finding the location on the map. "Got it, it's a good fifteen miles south; three of its cross-country. I don't think, looking at the terrain on the map, the truck could get much closer than a couple of miles from where they are," Franco eventually said.

Chapman raised his mike. "I'll send co-ordinates of a possible pickup. We estimate two hours. If you're not there we'll come and help you, over."

"Okay, over and out."

Chapman glanced round, resting his eyes on Karen. "Sorry, it wasn't intended that you should be near any danger. You could stay here and we'll pick you up on the way back, if you want?" Chapman asked.

She shrugged. "Can't be helped so let's go, I'm not staying here on my own, that's for certain."

As they approached the pickup point, Chapman kept scanning the area with his binoculars. He saw nothing.

"Farrow's not here so we'll have to find him. If we leave the truck well away from the road it might not be noticed. Franco, you stay with it. Karen, you too," Chapman ordered.

Karen glared at him. "I'm coming with you, you said I could before and if somebody's injured, I could help."

Franco cut in, not really wanting Karen to stay in her current state of mind. "She's probably right, Chapman, they may want help with the injured and anyway, I'd rather stay alone. It's easier to look after the truck without worrying about somebody else in case of trouble."

Chapman nodded his agreement and soon they were on their way, Chapman leading, Karen and Hawkins some twenty yards behind. The terrain was flat at first; no houses in sight, not that Chapman had expected many. This was an area used by military and illegal traders over the years to cross the border into Israel. However, as they moved forward, the area became hilly, giving many places to hide.

Chapman raised his radio and pressed the call button, sending the automatic call signal. Immediately he got a response, and after a quick conversation they turned east and pressed forward as fast as they could. In less than fifteen minutes they'd teamed up with Farrow.

"Good to see you, Chapman, how far is the truck?" Farrow asked, shaking him by the hand.

Chapman removed the map and pointed to a position about two miles away. "We came on the direct route, Sir. It'll be difficult with the injured to go back that way, but if we go northeast and follow this ravine, after a mile it should be a great deal easier."

Farrow agreed and they packed up. As they walked, Farrow talked quietly to Chapman. "The military were involved and they'd formed a circle round the area, closing in slowly. We'd done the job and were getting out. It was a case of fight or be captured. So we chose a weak area of the circle, caused by the terrain, making the soldiers split further apart. I'm afraid we sustained injuries, it's bad, Chapman."

Chapman listened, not making any comment. This shouldn't have happened and it was up to Farrow, not himself, to explain when they arrived home. They'd travelled only half a mile when one of the injured had deteriorated to the point where Farrow decided to stop and allow their medic to check the injuries. Karen took the opportunity to move away from the group and find somewhere to go to the toilet. She'd not dared to ask earlier because of the problems with the injured, now she was desperate. Farrow was watching the medic when he heard a distant throbbing.

"'Copter, 'copter, down everyone!" he shouted.

He'd hardly stopped talking when a helicopter appeared from the valley below, rising quickly in front of them. A powerful loudspeaker attached to the underside of the helicopter was blaring out. "Drop your weapons and stand away from them. You're surrounded. There's no escape," the voice shouted at them curtly.

Farrow swore to himself but with injured men he could see no advantage in them trying to fight their way out. "Do as he asks, men, I'm not prepared to lose anybody else," he commanded.

They all did as he'd ordered, then watched helplessly as the helicopter came to land thirty yards away. Three men jumped out, running towards them, guns outstretched.

"There's only three, Sir, we'd take them easily," Hitchen hissed under his breath.

"I said don't move, that's an order," Farrow replied quickly.

While this had been going on Karen was walking back, completely oblivious to the fact that the soldiers had been captured, when a hand grabbed her, pulled her down and a man placed his hand over her mouth to stop her screaming. "Keep very silent, Karen, we've got company," Chapman told her, his voice low, at the same time removing his hand.

She did as he asked and the two of them crawled forward to peep over some rocks. The position placed them both on the other side of the helicopter. She could see the three men standing a short distance from Farrow. One was waving his hands about trying to tell Farrow something. Chapman touched her arm. "If we take the machine-gun position mounted on the helicopter, Karen, we might be able to free the team. Are you with me?"

"Of course, what do you want me to do?"

"The gunner's got his back to us, and with the helicopter ticking over like that, he'll not hear me coming until it's too late. I want you to go for the pilot and stop him using his radio to call for help, can you do that?"

"I'll try, you don't want me to shoot him, do you?"

"No, just keep your gun trained on him till I come and help you."

They were just going to go when she grabbed his arm, "Chapman, will you promise me one thing?"

"What's that, Karen?"

"If this doesn't work, I can't be taken alive, no matter what. You lot may be okay, but for me I'd go back to a life that doesn't bear thinking about. I want you to promise that will not happen."

He looked at her, saying nothing.

"Please, Chapman, I beg you, don't let them take me. If you won't promise me, I'd have to pull the ring of one of these grenades which could injure others around me."

He nodded. "If that's what you want, Karen, I'll not let them take you. Now we must move before other troops arrive."

Both of them crawled forward. With the huge open sides they'd no difficulty in climbing aboard. Chapman went for the soldier stood behind the mounted machine-gun, Karen turned into the cabin.

"Don't turn round, there's a gun at your head. Cut the engine," she demanded.

The pilot said nothing but leaned forward and pulled a lever. The engine slowly died.

"It is done," the pilot said in perfect English.

Moments later, Chapman was at her side. He squeezed her arm and nodded. "Good girl," he whispered then turned to the pilot. "Call them on the loud speaker, tell them the 'copter is taken and to lay down their arms."

He shrugged then shouted a few words into the mike. Then he turned to Chapman. "I told them but it's pointless. You see within a few minutes this place will be crawling with soldiers. You and your comrades have no chance," he said indifferently.

Karen looked out of the window. "They don't seem to be doing anything," she said quietly.

"Tell them again," Chapman shouted, "this time be more authoritative."

Once again the pilot demanded they drop their weapons, this time Karen could see the men doing as he asked and moving away from Farrow and the others.

"That's better. Now out of the helicopter and join them," he demanded.

The pilot unclipped his belt and slid out of the seat, stepping down from the small cabin into the rear of the helicopter. Karen had backed away and was watching, her gun following the pilot's movements.

He glared at her. "You're just a kid, what are the British sending these days?"

She smiled. "That may be, but already some of your kinsfolk have found when somebody's holding a gun, age or sex have little importance, they still die."

He shrugged, then turned and jumped down onto the ground before moving over to the soldiers already taken prisoner by Farrow, who'd by now realised what was happening.

He walked over to Chapman. "Good work, Chapman."

"It wasn't just me, Sir, Karen took the pilot herself."

Before he could say anything, Karen cut in. "The pilot

said others were on their way. Can anybody fly this thing?"

Farrow turned and called to one of his men. "Get this 'copter going, we need to get out fast. Karen said others are on their way," he called.

The pilot of the helicopter stared at her for a moment, then looked at Farrow. "She's Karen Marshall?"

"She is, what of it?" Farrow replied.

"But that's Sirec's girl. The whole country's looking for her. He's offered half a million for her return," he stuttered.

Karen laughed at him. "Half a million, you say? Pity you've not been able to collect then. If your friends had protected the helicopter better, we'd have had no chance."

By now the helicopter was roaring, Farrow called Karen and the two others guarding the pilot and soldiers. They moved quickly, sitting on the open side of the helicopter, their guns still directed at the prisoners. Within seconds the helicopter rose into the air.

Farrow patted Karen's back. "I didn't have time to congratulate you, Karen. You never cease to amaze me with your capabilities."

She felt proud at his words and moved to the back of the hold, settling down close to Hawkins.

Hawkins grinned and offered her a biscuit. "One for the book that, Karen," he said, between crunching noisily.

"Why?" she asked.

"Well, Farrow's never given us any compliments," he complained.

It was time for Karen to laugh. "Why should he, it's your job?"

Hawkins didn't have time to respond as at that moment they began to descend. Karen could see Franco by the side of the lorry, waving at them. As the helicopter touched the ground, he too climbed aboard, then it instantly lifted again. Hawkins, able to speak the local language, had been monitoring the radio traffic and called back to Farrow.

"They are onto us, Sir. Possibly the pilot has told someone; they've ordered the helicopter to be brought down at any cost."

Farrow indicated his understanding. "Keep us posted if you hear anymore about us..." he shouted back.

Karen, having finished the biscuit, was passing the time cleaning her gun and checking how much ammunition she still had. It was at that moment she saw a flash from the ground, others too had seen it and the helicopter banked sharply, the engines protesting as the pilot started to throw it about. Moments later there was an explosion and the whole machine shuddered.

"That was close," Farrow shouted to the pilot.

"We've another two incoming, Sir. I think they mean business," Chapman shouted back.

Hawkins moved closer to her side. "There are more missiles on their way, Karen. We'll have to brace for impact," Hawkins shouted above the roar of the engines.

She looked confused, not knowing what to do.

He grasped her shoulders, pulling her head close to his chest. "Keep your hands hard over your ears, love," he shouted, gripping her tightly.

She did as he asked and held her breath, waiting for the impact. 'Surely this time we'll all be killed?' Karen thought to herself.

There was no more time to worry as another explosion came, sending the helicopter spinning. Then the third missile hit, Karen had never been so scared. The whole aircraft was thrown about like a toy, metal screaming as it was ripped apart. She could also hear men shouting at each other, Hawkins held her tight, not allowing her to see what was happening. Suddenly there was a thud that shook the helicopter to the core; this was followed by two more, then silence.

"Out! Out! Out!" someone was shouting. "We're down."

Karen felt strong hands grasp her, dragging her out of the helicopter. "Run, kid, run for your life, she's going to blow," Chapman was shouting in her ear.

Karen didn't need any more urging, she just ran, or rather stumbled, over a soft field away from the helicopter. There was no mistaking the smell of fuel, even her clothes stank of it but she kept running. Suddenly, there was an explosion behind, throwing her to the ground, then another came, before silence. She lay there stunned, as if something had punched her hard in the back.

Then someone was at her side. "Come on, Karen, it's time to get out of here."

Looking up, Chapman was stood looking down at her. "Where's Hawkins?" she asked.

Chapman shook his head. "Sorry, love, he didn't get out. Killed instantly when we hit the ground, he'd not braced himself properly, I'm afraid."

Tears came to her eyes. The man had saved her life, holding her close, ignoring his own safety.

"Come on, Karen, we can do nothing, we've got to go. This place will be swarming with soldiers soon," he said, grasping her hand.

She stood silently looking around. There were bodies everywhere, none seemed to be moving. Chapman didn't let her dwell, propelling her away fast.

Chapter 18

When Sirec arrived at the crash site he was met by a man in army uniform.

The man shook his hand. "My name's Khan, I presume you are Sirec? Perhaps we should talk in my command vehicle," he suggested.

Sirec nodded and followed him to a large van with steps leading up to a door at the rear. Inside was a small glass-enclosed office with three people sat in front of telecommunications equipment, including television monitors. Beyond that was a meeting area with a large table and chairs. Khan offered Sirec a glass of whisky and they both took a seat at the table.

"Is Karen among the dead?" Sirec asked directly.

Khan shook his head. "No, Sirec, there was no girl among them. We do know, however, she was aboard. The pilot who was forced out, before the S.A.S. took over the 'copter, told us of a tall girl with darkish hair and blue eyes, answering to the name of Karen."

Sirec lit a cigarette. "So where is she? Surely, with half the bloody army in this area, you must have covered every inch by now?"

"We have and she's not turned up. We do have prisoners. We also, by the headcount, reckon there are two others either with her or on their own," Khan answered quietly.

Sirec stood and began pacing the little room. "I don't believe this. How can she avoid us so well? How did your people let her and the others escape? According to first reports they had them cornered and were holding them till you lot arrived?"

Khan shrugged. "Tell me about it. I understand it was

the girl who captured the pilot with another S.A.S. officer taking the gunner. Apparently, with a gun at his head, the officer forced him to order his comrades to let the British go. Where she was when they initially landed and took the soldiers is anybody's guess, but she wasn't with the main group."

Sirec sighed. "Okay, let's see the prisoners. Perhaps we can find the pick-up point at least, before she and the others get there?"

They left the command truck and made their way across to another large lorry, inside were small cells. As Khan climbed the steps he glanced back at Sirec. "We have the Commander. The other two prisoners are on their way to hospital, they are pretty badly injured."

Sirec nodded, telling Khan to wait while he talked to him and then he went inside. He pulled a small stool from an empty cell and sat down opposite Farrow. "My name's Sirec, perhaps your people have talked of me?"

"Commander Farrow, Special Services," he replied.

Sirec offered him a cigarette and lit another for himself. "Bad business this, Farrow. You know you've cost me plenty. Not monetary loss you understand, but my reputation."

"Your reputation, why do you say that, after all, this is just a business risk for you?"

"I agree with you, Farrow, business risk with the warehouses yes, but you went too far and destroyed my home which was protected by guards who now I've got to punish, besides which, you also took my girl."

Farrow sighed. "Come off it, Sirec, the house and equipment were built with blood so both are at risk, but the girl? She was never your girl; the kid was abducted, brought to this country and auctioned like slaves in the past. No, Sirec, complain all you want about property but don't complain to me about the girl. She's a British subject and entitled to be protected, as far as possible, by the British Government."

Sirec said nothing for some time, just drawing gently on the cigarette. Eventually he looked back at Farrow. "So how did you find Karen's company? Was she, as everybody is telling me, tough, mature and sexy or was she immature, crying all the time and wanting to go home?" Sirec asked quietly as if he'd never heard Farrow's comment about Karen's abduction.

The Commander narrowed his eyes, not understanding the man in front of him. He'd expected a grilling for the location of the pick-up, but Sirec seemed to have no interest in that. However, if it meant giving the others and Karen more time to escape, he'd play along.

"You've never met her then?" Farrow asked.

Sirec shook his head. "No, that's why I'd like you to tell me about her."

Farrow drew on his cigarette as if thinking. "Karen's no fool; she's clever, resourceful and yes, tough, providing you keep in mind she's still very young."

"Tell me more," Sirec cut in.

He could see the interest in Sirec's face, before it was just indifferent, now he showed genuine interest. Had he perhaps some sort of infatuation for the girl? "What would you like to know about her?" Farrow asked.

"She was sexy, wasn't she?" Sirec persisted.

Farrow grinned. "She had a natural femininity about her and the younger soldiers in my command seemed to like that. I would have thought, after what she's been through, being sexy would, I believe, be the last thing on her mind. After all, she's had a bad time, caused in the main by you."

Sirec scowled. "It's not my fault what happened before she came to my house. Once there, Karen was treated with the utmost courtesy. I even had her taken shopping for new clothes and anything else she needed. So I find it offensive to say I've given her a bad time."

Unable to believe what he was hearing, Farrow was now convinced Sirec really did have an infatuation for Karen. "So you're telling me it wasn't you that had her sent over from England then?" Farrow asked.

Sirec shook his head. "No, I certainly didn't. I first heard about her from a contact who deals in girls. You see, in this war-torn country there's a shortage of eligible young girls. Many have been killed, not intentionally you understand, but by constant bombing and fighting. Children have taken the brunt of it, mothers have fled, others have died. So the upshot of it all is a steady stream of girls coming in from Asia, unwanted by poverty stricken parents. These girls are cheap and end up in brothels. European girls are rare, often forced here like Karen, but I'm digressing. When I first heard about Karen she was already on her way. Somebody in England, after a dispute, had paid for her passage. She'd been offered for sale and I received her photo. Unfortunately my European trip made it impossible for me to intercept her when she arrived. So I sent somebody to purchase her on my behalf."

Farrow shifted his position, trying to be indifferent to his questions. "So the Towkey isn't anything to do with you then?"

"The Towkey's owned by the Captain, I believe," Sirec began, "he, shall we say, is a man of dubious morals. Cargo, whatever it's made up of, has a price for transport. He's also a businessman and saw a value in Karen, making contact with my staff directly. The problem was a local buyer had already been contracted and the Captain couldn't, or wouldn't, do a deal without including him as well. It's understandable, as the Captain would have other girls for sale in the future and this agent would be able to place them." Sirec suddenly stopped and looked directly into Farrow's eyes. "Whatever you think of my morals in buying her, Farrow, you can be sure my intervention in this girl's life saved her from what could have been a fate worse than death for a girl like her."

Farrow could understand this. "I don't disbelieve you, Sirec, and perhaps with you she'd have had a life as close to normality as could be, for a caged animal, but I think it's time to let her go home. Besides, I'm not sure if you could take her alive."

Sirec seemed confused. "Why's that?" he asked.

Farrow shrugged indifferently. "Like I said, Karen's tough, very mature for her age. I never once saw her cry. It was her help that got us the helicopter. That girl captured the pilot and then helped to force the others to give their weapons up."

Sirec grinned. "And you think I don't want a girl like that? She's my sort of girl, Farrow, can't you see that? But your comments interest me, why is it you don't think we can take her alive?"

Farrow stubbed the finished cigarette on the floor and looked up at Sirec, watching him. "Quite simply, Sirec, the girl wants to go home. Convinced if she's caught, you'll kill or force her into prostitution, she wouldn't take that believe me. Karen even suggested that if there was no way out, she'd turn a gun on herself. But even if she couldn't get at her gun, she's carrying two grenades, if she pulls the pins, that's it." He fell silent for a moment, then continued. "I believe she's got the courage to do that, I suspect it's something you wouldn't want to happen? I've a feeling you're still convinced she should be back with you," Farrow said, choosing his words carefully.

Sirec stood and banged the side of the cage with his fist; Farrow could see the determination in his face.

"Karen's mine and I want her back. I will give orders to take care with her. There's a lot of money at stake for her capture. People know she's worth nothing dead. Even more than that, their own lives are worth nothing if she is dead," Sirec retorted.

"Perhaps, Sirec, but does she want you?"

Sirec seemed suddenly to compose himself. "We shall see, Commander, but thank you for your observations. However, you and I have a more pressing point. I need to know how your people and Karen intended to leave this country?"

Farrow shook his head. "I don't know, Sirec. You see we missed the pick-up point by one day. Then the lucky break with the helicopter gave us the chance to get us over the border into Israel. From there, we'd be taken to a war ship standing off your coast. How the survivors of the crash and Karen are going to do that now is anybody's guess. They will contact control who'll arrange with them a new pick-up point."

"So you believe they'll still head for the border?" Sirec asked.

Farrow shrugged. "They could come in with attack 'copters undercover of dark, arrange a new sea rendezvous or direct them to the nearest border. Your guess is as good as mine," Farrow lied.

Sirec rubbed his chin thoughtfully. "I don't think it's your only option, Farrow. The helicopter, I agree, wasn't in the equation, so you'd have had to have an alternative. That's got to be where they're heading. I'm not one for torture or violence but I must have the location. You have five minutes to think about it. Tell us what we want to know and you may go home. The alternative's a quick injection and you'll sing like a bird. Unfortunately, the side effects are not good. The drug is, shall we say, still under development, all our tests up to now have resulted in brain damage. It is not something to relish, Commander, believe me."

With those chilling words, Sirec left the vehicle and walked slowly back to the command station.

Khan ran to meet him. "We may have her, Sirec," he said breathlessly.

Sirec's eyes lit up. "Where? Tell me, man, where is she?" he demanded.

Khan stopped him. "We've not actually got her yet, Sirec, but we have the ones she was with, so Karen can't be that far away. I've close to three hundred troops closing in, each one wanting the reward, so it's only a matter of time now," Khan blurted out before Sirec could finish.

Sirec just gave a growl under his breath and went quickly inside the command vehicle with Khan, listening to the radio traffic from the troops in the area. "Take care, Khan," Sirec began, "the girl's carrying grenades as well as a gun, but she's not to be harmed. She's convinced she's bound for the brothels before she is killed. The girl won't accept that and Farrow says she'll attempt to take her own life. If you allow that to happen, Khan, I will blame you. I'll also be very annoyed and perhaps take it out on those who run this operation. Do we understand each other?"

Khan nodded, understanding too well that Sirec's threats were not to be taken lightly. "I'm on my way, Sirec, I will take personal charge. Karen will not be harmed and she'll not be able to harm herself."

Sirec lit another cigarette and glanced at Khan. "Send your team to interrogate Farrow. I want the pick-up point in case your people miss her. This kid's turning out to be very good at melting in with the surroundings; I want insurance."

Chapter 19

Karen collapsed to the ground exhausted; they'd been running for some time before Chapman called a halt, so he and another soldier she knew as Stefan, could survey the area.

"There's a heavy convoy coming up from the south. They're heading towards the helicopter crash site," Chapman said softly. He watched for a short while, then made a decision. "We'll head north-easterly for about a couple of hours to circle away from the troops. I know it's a risk and we should travel at night, but we're too vulnerable in this position. Are you up to going on yet, Karen?"

She nodded. "Yes, but I'm glad I'm not in the S.A.S. permanently. I'm completely knackered with one of your operations while you two just keep going."

Chapman grinned; he needed to boost this girl's confidence, well aware she was close to the end of her endurance, but not admitting it. "You're doing well, love, when we take raw recruits on training exercises they wouldn't be still going like you are, believe me. Anyway, let's go, plenty of time later for resting."

Grabbing their equipment they were on the move again. The terrain was rocky, affording a large amount of protection, but as they progressed it was becoming more obvious that soon they'd be in open countryside with no places to hide. Just to the edge of this area they stopped and settled down.

Chapman pulled out a tin of corned beef and three cans of beer. "This will have to see us through; it's the last except for a small block of chocolate. We also have to make contingency plans. Each one of us must know how to get to the pick-up point, besides knowing the password and call signals."

"Why me, I'll be with you, won't I?" Karen asked, alarmed at his words.

Chapman knew she'd ask this. "We've still a fair distance to go, Karen, I can't guarantee we'll all be together or somebody isn't injured. So if we were to split up, or anything else happens, at least everyone will have a chance to get home."

They spent some time studying maps and sorting routes. With one GPS between them and only the soldiers with maps, Chapman had pulled out a note pad and began making drawings from the maps so they were easy to understand. It was a slow process as one had to be on watch all the time, however, it allowed the rest of the day to pass quickly and as dusk fell they were on the move.

Five miles followed of fast route marching before Chapman called a halt, taking time out to study the terrain before them. He glanced across at Karen. She was repacking her bag after slipping a jumper on. "Come and join us, Karen," Chapman called.

She came over and sat at his side.

"There's a large line of soldiers fanned out in front and to the side of us. They seem determined not to allow as much as a small animal to get past. I think within the hour we'll have nowhere to go."

Karen glanced at him, concern on her face. "So you're saying we're trapped?"

"It's going to be difficult to avoid them, so yes, we're trapped."

"And we can't fight our way out?"

He shook his head. "We can't fight an army, Karen, we'd be killed for certain. Alternatively, if we're captured then we'd have a chance of being kicked out of the country. Now the world knows about your plight, they'd struggle to keep you here as well."

Torn between hoping beyond hope that he was right, Karen deep down knew differently. She'd killed Saeed and his friends, so her fate was sealed. Besides which, the bounty on her head told her somebody wanted her back desperately. Tears were forming in her eyes, her voice low and hesitant. "They'd never let me go, probably not even admit they had me. You must keep the promise you made to me at the helicopter, Chapman. When it's absolutely definite and there's no escape, you mustn't let me be captured alive..." she hesitated. "You must put a gun to my head."

"You're serious about this, Karen, was it really that bad, love?"

She looked at him in the dim light. "I've been beaten, gang raped twice, spent more time naked than dressed, often paraded around. I was forced to learn some sort of lap dance, ending up naked as usual and then expected to offer myself. I've even had someone's balls forced into my mouth and made to chew them. If I was your daughter sitting here and you knew she was returning to that sort of life, what would you do?"

Chapman, for the first time, began to realise what this young girl had already been through and the sort of life facing her. She was right; he couldn't let her go back to what, for her, was a life of hell. He grasped her hand tightly. "I understand, Karen, so yes when the time comes, love, I won't let you be captured alive."

Nothing more was said, Karen now knew unless some miracle happened, which was hardly likely, she'd only an hour to live. Her only consolation was that the authorities were aware of Assam's involvement; she'd killed Saeed, so perhaps a few girls would remain safe in their homes because of her actions.

"Right, let's move and see if we can avoid capture, shall we? Chapman said, with some confidence in his voice.

They set off once more. In reality it was a token move,

all of them knowing they'd soon be captured. Chapman again stopped them before surveying the landscape in front. It was hopeless, not only were the soldiers behind, but they were now in front; there was no way out, but a plan was forming in his mind. "Right, seriously we've no chance, if we stay together that is."

"What do you mean?" Karen asked.

He moved over and sat down at her side. "You should go on alone, Karen. Stefan and I will head them off. Even if we're caught, like I said, it probably only means them kicking us out of the country. They have no other option as we would be an embarrassment. For you, it's slightly different. They're after you and this time, like you believe, I don't think this Sirec will let you go so easily."

She sighed; typical, when the going gets rough they abandon her to save their own skins. "So I just sit here while you two move on, hoping they'll follow you?"

"Not quite, Karen, we'll break out into the open and use torches so we can be seen. With luck they'll turn to follow and give you a route through."

She sat for a short time saying nothing. At least he had some sort of plan and if there weren't so many soldiers coming their way it might possibly work, but she held out no hope of that. She looked across at him, "It wouldn't work, would it? I want the truth, Chapman."

"It's a long shot, Karen, and if you really want the truth, we'd have a very slim chance of pulling it off."

Tears were beginning to form. "Then this is the end of the road for me, I suppose?" She tried to give a forced smile. "Well at least I gave them a run for their money, didn't I?"

Chapman touched her hand. "You did, love, and you were very good to get this far."

Looking down, she clenched her hands together, hardly able to speak. "Will it hurt a lot?"

"No, love, I promise it won't hurt," Chapman lied.

"Then you'd better get it over with then. I'd just like time to tidy myself up, become a little more feminine again and say my prayers... Then, just do it."

No one said anything when Karen stood and began to remove her belt and weapons. Never in all her life had she been so scared and even now she was trying to delay the inevitable, by taking time combing her hair.

It was Stefan who broke the silence. "It's only an idea, but we could bury her, Chapman."

Both of them looked at him.

"How do you mean?" Chapman asked.

He grinned. "Well, I've been thinking and now believe it'd work. The search is fanned out and moving forward. When I was stationed in Vietnam, the enemy would bury themselves, breathing through a straw and just waiting until we passed; then the bastards would suddenly jump out, guns blazing, from behind. Get caught in that sort of ambush and believe me, you're in the shit."

"So you're suggesting we bury Karen, give her a breathing straw, and she waits until the soldiers pass before setting off to the pickup point. It'd work?"

"It might, except we don't take any chances that she shows herself too early, particularly when the soldiers were still around. We leave the radio earphone stuck in her ear and we tell her when it's clear to go."

"But how would we know?" Chapman asked, now more than interested in Stefan's suggestion.

Stefan pointed to the hills to the side. "We get the soldiers closing front and rear of us to turn and head for the hills by giving our position away. It would mean we get caught but that's going to happen anyway, so we bed down at the start of the hills and watch the searchers pass through where we're sitting now. When they are well clear, we just call Karen and then leg it ourselves up the hills so they are not sure how many there are of us, giving her more distance behind the soldiers."

"What do you think, Karen? If it doesn't work you will have to put the gun to your own head, but at least it gives you a chance to survive and even go home? It's your decision, love."

Karen said nothing for a moment as she was still in a daze, she didn't want to carry on any longer. She was tired of running and desperately scared of being left alone. She looked down at her bag then sighed, "It was a good idea, Stefan, but I'd only be delaying the inevitable, I really can't cope with anymore. Besides, if I did go on, how do I find the pick-up point? I've only got notes, no real map or anything. I don't even know the language and have no food; they'll pick me up in hours even if I tried. I think I'd rather just get it over with."

Chapman stood and grasped her hand, squeezing it gently, knowing how much he was asking of her, but far better than the other option which he didn't want to take. "Don't knock yourself, Karen. If anybody could get home, it would be you. The route's very straightforward and you have your notes. I'll also give you my map; you're a good map reader so you'll have no trouble on that side. Anyway, I remember a girl coming up behind trained S.A.S. without them knowing a thing, so using conscripts to look for you will be completely useless if you keep to those tactics. But don't worry; we'll divert them by miles. You'll have a clear way through, believe me."

She looked at him, still unsure. "I suppose putting it like that, once they pass here, there's a chance I might just get through?"

"You'll easily get through, Karen," Stefan urged.

All of them fell silent, each with their own thoughts, then Karen sighed. "Okay I'll give it a go; I still have my hand grenades, so even if the gun doesn't work they'd never take me alive," she replied somewhat nervously.

Chapman gave her a thump on the back. "That's the spirit, love. You'll get there, I've no doubts about that," he urged, then reached down to his ankle and unfastened his knife holder, handing it to her with the knife. "You fought well yesterday, Karen, like a true S.A.S. soldier. It's not much, but I'd like you to have it. You never know, it might save your life one day."

She threw her arms round him and held him tightly for a moment, before kissing him on the cheek. "When we meet back in England, would you take me out for dinner and to a nightclub? I've never been to a nightclub and I am eighteen now?" she asked.

He laughed, glancing at Stefan. "Karen, we'll do more than that. We'll lay on a real S.A.S. party and believe me, you might get very drunk, but you'll love every minute, what do you say, Stefan?"

He agreed wholeheartedly and gave her a hug as well.

"Carry on, Karen, the way you have so far and believe me you will get home, love," he whispered in her ear.

She thanked him for his confidence in her and kissed him on the check as she'd done with Chapman, then it was time for them to go.

After a final farewell, they carefully buried her with only a small pipe in her mouth sticking out of the ground to breathe through, and an earphone in her ear connected to the radio. As a further precaution, her other hand rested on top of a grenade, one finger in the loop of the pin. Karen felt better with that suggestion, because, to turn the gun on herself if she was discovered, might be very difficult and they could grab the gun off her. This way five seconds would be too short a time for them to stop her committing suicide. Finally, after reiterating the instructions to stay buried until she heard one of their voices over the radio, Karen was suddenly alone. With nothing to do but wait, she began to pray, at the same time thanking God for this chance to live.

It wasn't long before she could hear the sounds of people calling each other, trucks rumbling and the steady thud of a helicopter. At one stage she believed they must have been only feet away and she gripped the ring of the grenade that much harder. However, Chapman's attention to detail on her hiding place must, she thought, be brilliant because soon the voices and noise receded until she could hear nothing else.

***

It was another forty minutes after she'd last heard voices before the radio earphone came to life inside her ear. "This is Chapman calling the all clear. Good luck, over and out." Then the radio went dead.

Karen pushed the small rocks and soil off her and stood cautiously, before scanning the horizon with glasses given to her by Stefan. She could see in the distance, soldiers spread out across the hills, but moving away. Behind her, the way Chapman had told her to go, there was nothing. Not waiting any longer, she set off and travelled around ten miles, avoiding any buildings with lights, before deciding to take a rest.

The food situation was critical with less than a quarter bar of chocolate and no water. It was important, she decided, to try to find some sort of nutriment. This time, instead of avoiding occupied buildings, she moved closer to one, entering a small courtyard with care. The only light was in the house, so she moved quickly to the barn. Inside it was littered with straw and farm implements. Gazing round in the semi-darkness, lit only by the full moon, Karen saw what she'd come for. Moving quickly she reached under a hen settled in the straw and pulled out an egg. The hen, because of the dark, was in some sort of trance and only gave a few clucks. Repeating this a number of times with others, eventually she'd three eggs. Carefully placing two in her bag and piercing the other at both ends, she began sucking. It tasted good, so settling down in the straw she lay back. An hour's rest would be sufficient and then she'd move on before the occupants knew anyone had been there at all.

Her mind drifted back to the time on the ship, then Assam and finally this man called Sirec. Everything seemed more of a blur than actual reality, in some ways she even felt flattered so many people wanted her. The money in her bag was more than she'd ever seen in her life but it had been hard won. Her experience of men, after Grant, seemed she was good for only one thing; their sexual gratification. Saeed had learned the errors of having this opinion, the men on the ship, Towkey, would also learn it if it took every penny she had in the bag; they too would die. With these thoughts Karen fell into a troubled sleep. Every few minutes coming alert as animals in the barn moved around restlessly, and then she froze. The rustling had become louder and something was crawling over her legs. She backed off, pairs of eyes everywhere in the barn seemed to be staring at her, then the realisation of just what they were. Rats! There seemed hundreds of them! Karen screamed involuntarily, stumbling out from the barn, and retching for what seemed some time at the thought of them crawling over her. However, her noisy exit from the barn had also disturbed someone inside the house. Dogs had begun to bark, followed quickly by a man emerging from the house carrying a shotgun.

With nowhere to go Karen stood her ground, swinging her own machine-gun round and clicking the safety catch off. Spreading her legs slightly so the gun would not knock her off balance if she fired, she waited and watched. By now the man had switched a powerful torch on and began sweeping the farmyard. In seconds the beam rested on her and she raised the gun switching on the laser sight. It settled on the man's chest.

His light seemed to rest on her face for a second before dropping quickly down. She stood very still, waiting for him to react. The man, on his part, was stunned, seeing the machine-gun pointing at him, and backed away. Not, however, before placing his own gun and torch on the ground and turning quickly to run back inside the house, slamming the door shut. Karen smiled to herself, he was sensible, his weapon no match for hers. She walked over to the gun and torch, removing the cartridges from the gun and throwing them across the yard before stuffing the torch in her bag. Realising these people may be very poor and the loss of the torch a serious blow to them, she placed a twenty dollar note under the gun. Then she moved quickly out of the courtyard and started to cut across country, soon leaving the farm far behind.

By daybreak she'd made good progress and felt very pleased with herself. Looking for somewhere to hide was foremost in her mind and eventually she settled for an olive grove, affording some sort of hiding place, a hundred meters from the track she'd been following. Removing her belt, she slipped the handgun from its holster and placed it, with the safety off, a little to one side of her. Then she pushed loose leaves and small rocks over to completely hide it from view. Chapman had shown her this and she also remembered Garry hiding the gun under the washbasin, warning her always to have a back up plan, in case of capture. He'd been right of course, without his forethought they'd have been in custody now. She couldn't see the real value of doing this in the middle of nowhere. However, it gave her something to do and perhaps, if she admitted it, a little more confidence. As the day wore on, she heard a number of vehicles pass on the road, but nothing else. Eventually she closed her eyes, and was soon asleep.

Chapter 20

Sirec was sitting, drinking by the side of a pool. The hotel he was staying in had seen better times, before civil war, but now it was the only one left, still operational, in the area.

Halif walked over to him, followed by a man dressed in the clothes of a farmer. "Sirec, I think you should listen to this man's story," Halif said when he was at Sirec's side.

Sirec looked at the man for a moment then back to Halif. "What does he want?"

"He's met Karen."

With that Sirec sat bolt upright, his interest now directed at this man alone. "You've met Karen? When was this?" he demanded.

The man, obviously nervous in front of Sirec, just nodded.

"Speak, man," Sirec shouted.

"She came to my farm last night, Sir," he blurted out.

Sirec's eyes narrowed. "Why should she do that?"

"I'm not sure, but she'd been in the barn. I heard a noise and went out to see. She was just stood there in the yard, her gun following my every movement." The man fell silent, waiting for Sirec to say something.

"How many were with her?"

The man frowned. "There was no one with her, Sir."

"So what did you do then?" Sirec eventually asked.

He shrugged. "What could I do? I dropped my gun and ran. She was holding something like the man's gun over there," he said, pointing at one of Sirec's guards. "My shotgun's no match for that."

"Did the girl speak?" Sirec asked.

"No, Sir, but she did take my torch and left twenty American dollars as if in payment for it.

"Sirec leaned back deep in thought. "Why should she want a torch?" he asked himself. Then he glanced over to Halif. "Bring a map will you?"

Soon a map arrived and Sirec asked the man to point out his farm. Then he drew a line straight through from where the helicopter had came down. "She's following a direct route to the pick-up point, Halif. We have her now."

Halif looked at the map, then at Sirec. "You want me to go?"

Sirec shook his head. "No, call Khan and get him and his men there. I'd like you to go and see Assam. I still have a feeling this girl might elude us; if that happens, Assam holds the key to her return."

The farmer, who'd stood quietly, cut in when Sirec fell silent. "May I go now?"

Sirec nodded. "You did well to come. See he gets paid for his trouble, Halif."

The man thanked him and made to leave, then he stopped and turned. "The girl's very well armed, Sir, she stood there without any sign of fear. Take care approaching her. I saw grenades on her belt, and spare ammunition, besides a handgun holster."

Sirec smiled. "We know, but I thank you again for your warning."

As the man finally left, Sirec leaned back, deep in thought. It had now become a cat and mouse game, a very dangerous one. His Karen was all he expected of her, the next few hours would show just how good she really was, and for this, she had his respect.

Halif finally returned and Sirec looked up at him."What's your opinion, Halif?"

"On what?" he asked.

"Karen, of course."

Halif shrugged. "She's got guts, I'll give her that. As to whether you could keep her caged, even if we got her back, I very much doubt. Personally I'd let her go home, Saeed's mother has been right up to now. That girl's bad luck and has only brought death."

Sirec shrugged indifferently. "The ramblings of an old woman, Halif. The girl's been lucky, being brought out by the S.A.S. Now it would seem something's gone wrong, and she's on her own. When she's brought in, the world will never know what her real fate was. Then I'll have my fun taming this girl."

Halif said nothing; Sirec seemed to have gone into some sort of trance, so he left him alone. At least Karen had given Sirec an interest away from the devastation of the warehouses and villa; he was like an animal stalking its prey. However, it was a one-sided game, pitching hundreds of searchers against a young girl. Not really a game between a hunter and the hunted, and once caught, he'd tire of her in weeks the same as every other girl Saeed had brought. But tame her, he doubted it, she was not the sort of girl to fall into this lifestyle like the others.

Chapter 21

Karen froze; something cold was touching her face. A voice was shouting at her to wake up. She opened her eyes. Two soldiers were stood over her; one had the tip of his gun inches from her face. The other stood back, watching.

"Don't move, just push the gun away and take the belt off," the one holding the gun demanded in broken English.

Karen did as he asked, throwing the belt to one side along with her machine-gun. She could kick herself for being captured so easily. She'd been tired, and with lack of food, had been unable to keep her eyes open and she'd soon fallen asleep. This was the result.

Studying her captors, who both looked like conscripts with little idea as to how to handle a prisoner, she tried to devise a plan. In her understanding, they should have lain her face down on the ground and searched her, perhaps even tied her hands. Then again, no soldier would move his gun off the quarry while he talked to his partner. When this soldier turned to talk, his gun followed. For all these simple errors she was thanking them, and it would seem with this sort of complacency on their part, she had a chance to escape.

"Salem, go and wait at the road," the one holding the gun said in his own language. "The truck to pick us up will be here in less than two hours. We've got ourselves a lot of money; I'm sure this is the girl Sirec's looking for."

Salem frowned. "Why me, can't we all go together?"

His partner moved closer to him. "There's a chance other soldiers will pass, if they know we've captured her they, too, will want some of the reward. So we wait for the captain, he's a man of honour. He will see we get our money."

Salem nodded in understanding. "You're very clever, Hamish. You are also right, others will take over, claiming they helped in the capture, and then we may even lose the reward. I will do as you ask, but remember, she's not to be touched or harmed. Sirec has issued that warning many times."

"I will watch her, that is all. When we have the money, many women will be flocking at our feet," Hamish said quietly.

With that agreed, Salem made his way to the road leaving Karen alone with Hamish. Hamish settled down a short distance away, his gun resting across his legs. Karen moved to one side slightly to see his reaction, but Hamish didn't seem to care. All he could think about was the money, more money than he had ever dreamed about, all because Salem wanted to go to the toilet; otherwise they'd have never seen her.

Karen's hand started to rummage under the loose shale, trying to locate the handgun. She couldn't understand why it wasn't there, she was sure this was the place. Glancing back nonchalantly, she looked at the ground once more, then realised her error. Her gun was at least two feet behind where she was sat, closer to the base of the olive tree. How she was going to get there without him objecting, she'd no idea.

Looking back at him, she smiled to herself, a simple but effective idea was forming, would he fall for it? "The sun, it's too hot. Can I move please?" she asked slowly.

He frowned, not understanding.

She pointed to the sun, brushed her hand across her forehead and pointed to the shade under the tree. His eyes lit up in understanding, and waved her towards the tree. She thanked him and moved back the two feet. Her left hand was soon resting on the gun. Unable to believe this man's stupidity, she watched him carefully, keeping her hand still when he glanced at her. However that wasn't much, now he'd started to rummage in his backpack, eventually pulling out a can and opening it noisily. Then, tilting his head back, he started to down the drink. Karen took this opportunity and snatched the gun from the ground, quickly checking the safety.

"Hey you!" she called, at the same time standing up.

He stopped drinking and looked across at her stood there. The gun held in two hands, steady as a rock, pointed directly at him. With his full attention she nodded towards his gun, gesturing him to move away from it. Karen could see the terror in his face; she was now convinced she had two conscripts and not soldiers. Hamish did as she asked, very aware of the warning given by his captain about how dangerous she could be. How she'd got the gun he'd no idea, but he'd every intention of staying alive, no matter what.

Karen moved quickly, exchanging her gun for the sub-machine-gun, at the same time making him lie face down with his hands on the back of his head. She searched his bag, looking for something to tie him up with, but there was nothing. Then she moved closer to him until the gun touched his head.

"Call your friend," she demanded.

He looked up at her, not understanding. She pointed to the road, then at him, before she pointed back at the road, moving her fingers backwards and forwards.

His face lit up and nodded. "I understand," he spluttered. Then he called Salem. Twice he called until Salem responded, sprinting up from the road to see what he wanted.

Karen had moved back and watched his progress; even this man's gun was slung over his shoulder, indifferent to any potential danger. When he finally arrived out of breath, Salem weighed the situation up, immediately going for his gun.

Without hesitation, Karen sent a warning shot to his side. "I shoot to kill next time, now throw your gun away," she demanded.

Salem could understand English to a degree and did as she asked. Then a grin broke over his face. "So what are you going to do now? Within twenty minutes many soldiers will be here. Perhaps it would be better if you threw your own gun down and accepted the inevitable."

"No talking, you join your friend and lie face down," she shouted at him.

"And if I don't?"

Karen shrugged indifferently. "Then you and your friend die. I have no time to argue," she replied softly.

Salem looked at her for a moment. 'Yes,' he thought, 'you would kill. Some day you will pay for this.' Without another word he moved over to Hamish and lay down at his side.

"You have a weapon?" he whispered.

"A knife in my boot, that's all," Hamish whispered back.

Salem glanced across at Karen. "She's not watching us but is searching the bags, can you get it?" Salem asked.

Hamish never said anything, just moved his hand down very slowly towards his leg, and the knife. Karen still didn't notice this action, confident that with the distance between them and her that she could kill them before they could pose any threat. Hamish grasped the knife and pulled it slowly from the sheath, passing it across to Salem.

"You've only one chance, Salem, don't make an error," Hamish urged.

Salem smirked. "She's as good as dead."

Karen saw Salem suddenly stand and raise his right hand, the knife flashing in the sun. She swung the gun and fired the moment the knife left Salem's hand. He was flung back with the impact; Hamish panicked and scrambled up, wanting to run, but was also caught in the deadly fire, dying before he'd even hit the ground.

However, this happened in less than a second, just as the knife sank deep into Karen's side. She screamed in pain, dropping the gun and grasping the knife, pulling it painfully from her body. Blood was streaming out and she felt suddenly dizzy and lightheaded. She grabbed her shorts from the bag, and screwed them up before pushing them tightly against her side, trying to stop the bleeding. She was acutely aware that she must get away quickly, even though the pain was clouding her judgment. Glancing at the two men lying there, she could see only one was still moving. But she ignored him; both were injured too badly to follow, of that she was sure. Karen readied herself to move off, taking her personal items out of her bag and using one of the soldier's rucksacks instead. Aware it was a risk moving in the daytime, she could see no other option. How they'd found her so far off the road, she wasn't sure, but it had served to make her aware there was no real place to hide.

The going was hard and slow, having to avoid the road, adding perhaps three miles to the journey. As dusk came she'd travelled less than five miles. Now desperately worried, with the pick-up the next night, at this rate she'd not make it. The injury was just about bearable, the bleeding all but stopped. Karen felt weak from the loss of blood, apart from being close to starving.

It was then, as she was negotiating a small ravine, that the helicopter suddenly appeared from behind her, its light sweeping backwards and forwards over the ground. Breaking into a panicked run, she slipped and fell headlong down the ravine. Seconds later she hit her head on a rock, passing out instantly.

***

Coming round sometime later, it was still dark; she felt

disorientated, her head throbbed, her body not responding to what she wanted it to do. The helicopter was nowhere to be seen, so she assumed by falling into the ravine, they hadn't seen her. The pain in her side was intense, blood was everywhere. She tried again to stop it bleeding but with no success. The fall must have opened the wound up again. Now very weak from the loss of blood, she buried her head in her hands. Even the knife wound was nothing compared to her intense throbbing headache, but she was determined somehow she must pull herself together. Standing gingerly, she collected her things and then, after taking nearly twenty minutes to climb out of the ravine, she moved on. In the distance a small light flickered and Karen headed towards it. Why she'd no idea, somehow she needed to find help, check her injuries in better light and get some food. Even if it meant taking all the occupants in the house hostage, there was no option.

Once at the house she looked inside through a small window. There was an open fire with someone sitting in a chair, their back towards her. She waited but nobody else came into the room. She moved away from the window and around towards the door, which was made more difficult by debris littering the yard. Then, catching her foot on something partially hidden, Karen stumbled; breaking her fall by grabbing the handle of an old farm implement, but it was unstable and went crashing to the ground. Seconds later the door opened and light spilled out, illuminating a corridor of light twenty feet in length.

"Who's there?" a woman's voice shouted in the local language.

Karen understood her question with what little words she'd picked up from listening to Saeed and his mother talking. However, unable to hide, she moved quickly, stepping out directly in front of the woman. The women moved back in surprise. Karen was holding the gun in both hands and indicated her to go back inside by jerking her head up a few times. The woman did as she indicated, with Karen following. Once inside and leaning against a wall after kicking the door closed, Karen surveyed the room, trying to satisfy in her mind that the woman was alone.

The woman didn't say anything, just stood looking at Karen, whose clothes were covered in a mix of both dried and fresh blood on her side, with more blood running down her face from the wound to her head. It was immediately obvious to the woman this young girl was in a very serious condition and desperate for help, to come so close to a property, but even so, still very dangerous with the weapons she was carrying. The woman believed any sort of move towards her would meet with an instant reaction of the girl using the gun for defence.

Plucking enough courage up, but with no fast movements, the woman asked her name in the local language. Karen never answered. Then she tried French. This time Karen seemed to understand her.

"You are alone?" Karen asked in broken French.

"Yes, I'm alone. There's no need for the gun, I'm not going to hurt you. In fact, you look injured. Can I help?" the woman replied.

Karen held her hand up. "Again please, but slowly."

The woman stared at her for a moment then smiled broadly. "You prefer English?" she asked in perfect English.

Karen frowned. "You're English?"

The woman laughed. "Of course! My husband, who is now dead, was local, but I'm English, from London in actual fact and by the look of you, I think you need help?"

Karen shook her head. "I'm alright, just food and something hot to drink. If you've got anything like that I'd appreciate it, then I'll be on my way."

The lady sighed, asking her to take a seat at the table while she brought the food. Karen sat down with her elbows on the table, holding her head. The pain was intense and she felt faint, even to the point of not hearing the woman return and place a dish full of hot soup with bread alongside her.

She touched Karen's shoulder. "Wake up; I have some nourishing soup for you."

Karen woke with a jerk, realising this woman could have taken the gun easily. She grasped it quickly, holding it tight.

The woman laughed at her actions. "I assure you, you're perfectly safe here, I mean you no harm. So please put the gun down and eat your food, I think you need it."

Karen did as she asked, feeling better as she ate her first cooked meal in days.

The woman returned to her chair and sat watching her. "My name's Martha, what's yours then?" she asked, after Karen had finished.

Karen looked at her for a moment. "It's best you don't know, for your own safety, but I needed this food and I can pay."

"I don't want your money. You're welcome to stay as long as you want, but I think I should look at that wound on your head. Also the one on your side, it hasn't stopped bleeding since you arrived, but only if you want me to? The last thing you need is anymore loss of blood. That will stop you in your tracks."

Karen was very aware that the bleeding must be stopped and was not even sure just how much she had already lost, except she constantly felt dizzy, and her reactions were slow. "I'd be grateful if you could stop the bleeding for me," she said quietly.

Martha left the room and returned with a bowl, cloth and a small bottle. She quickly cleaned the head wound and wiped Karen's face. "This wants more than a plaster, it needs a stitch, could you take the pain if I did it for you? I've no pain killers."

"Just stitch, I'll take the pain," Karen replied, perhaps

too bravely.

Martha went to a drawer and brought back some scissors, also a needle with gut attached. She cut a little hair from around the wound and dabbed it with antiseptic. Karen flinched, it stung.

"Soon be finished, hold your breath. I've done this many times when I was in the army hospitals during the war," Martha said confidently.

Five minutes and a lot of pain later, Martha stood back. "There, it's all done. Now let me help you remove your t-shirt and I'll take a look at the wound on your side?"

Karen did as she asked and Martha set about cleaning the wound. "This is a knife, not a fall, have you been in a fight then?"

Karen shuddered at the pain as Martha cleaned it.

"Just do what you can, I don't want to answer any questions," Karen replied.

It took three stitches and a great deal more pain, before Martha sat back satisfied. "That will sort you for now. You should see a doctor in case of any internal damage, but for the moment you need rest, lots of it."

Karen shrugged indifferently. "Thank you for your help but I'd better move on. I need to be somewhere by late tomorrow and I can only move at night." She pulled out a twenty dollar note from her bag and placed it on the table. "I'd appreciate it if you didn't mention I've been here. It's for your own safety. I have a feeling the people searching for me would not take kindly to someone giving me help."

Karen stood somewhat unsteadily and began to move to the door. She stopped and glanced at a cross attached to the wall.

Martha moved over and touched the cross. "Are you Catholic?" Martha asked quietly.

Karen nodded.

"Would you like to pray with me?"

Karen turned and looked Martha in the eyes. "Why would I want to pray?"

"For his help in your time of need."

Karen stepped back, her features hardening. "Time of need?" she retorted, "I was brought up Catholic and prayed every day, besides going to church. What did God do for me? I'll tell you how he repaid my devotion. He allowed me to be abducted, raped and abused. I've killed to survive, killed for revenge. Even if I still believed he loved me, I've broken his most important commandments and God won't forgive that." By now tears were running down her face. "So I've blown it with God; I'll never pray again, what's the use, he's not a good God. He's no compassion and don't say he's testing me. He's not. He's abandoned me."

Karen fell silent, looking down at the floor, then up at Martha. "I'd just like to know what I've done that's so wrong, would that be too much to ask of him?"

Martha didn't know how to answer; the girl was rambling, perhaps because of the strain she was under and loss of blood? However, she knew whatever she said would have no effect. Her faith and her trust in others was shattered, convinced she'd nobody to turn to for help.

Karen sighed, pulled the gun over her shoulder, and rubbed her wet eyes with her hand before moving towards the door, holding onto the wall for support. Pulling it open, she glanced back, thanked Martha for the food once more, then left the house.

Martha followed. Outside she could see Karen leaning heavily on the small front wall and staring out across the fields. As far as the eye could see, there were lights bobbing about. She went over, stopping at Karen's side. "What's wrong, I thought you were going?"

Karen pointed to the lights. "I'm too late," she whispered, her voice trembling.

Martha looked away from the lights towards Karen, a

final realisation of what she suspected since the girl arrived at her door. "You're Sirec's girl, aren't you?" she asked.

Karen spun round, her eyes wild. "I'm no girl of Sirec's, in fact I'll kill the bastard if I ever meet him for what he's done to me," Karen shouted. She put her hands to her head, the pain intense, tears running freely down her face once again.

Moments later she'd composed herself and looked back at Martha. "Please go inside now. All those lights are soldiers looking for me. I've probably got less than half an hour before they come. I need to plan and find somewhere to wait."

Martha cut in. "But you can't escape, with your injuries you'd not get a couple of miles without collapsing, so why not just come back inside and wait?"

Karen laughed. "I don't intend to escape; I intend to fight, unless you've a car to get me out of here?"

"A car wouldn't get you out of here. There's only one road and by the position of those lights, there's vehicles already on it. Anyway, it's foolish to say you're going to fight. There's an army out there, you'd have no chance, they'd kill you," Martha persisted.

She shook her head. "No, they won't kill me. I'll kill some of them, that will be certain, but they won't kill me. I wouldn't give them the satisfaction, or the opportunity."

Martha grasped her shoulders. "What are you saying?"

Karen shook her off, becoming fed up and annoyed with Martha. "Listen, you stupid woman, go back to your house and lock every door. In fact I'll give you a present." She pushed her bag into Martha's hands. "There's thousands of dollars in there, it's all I have in the world, but it's of no value to me anymore. I'd intended it for buying retribution but now..." she hesitated, looking away, unable to face Martha, her voice shaking. "I'll be dead within the hour, so even that's been thrown in my face by your so-called God.

Now I'd like some time alone before I die."

Martha stepped back and stood looking at this proud girl finally accepting there was no place to run and the inevitable. "You really want to die then?" she whispered.

Karen turned and looked at her, tears still running down her cheeks. "No, I don't want to die; I'm only just eighteen for God's sake. In fact, if the truth was known, I'm scared to death even thinking about it. How I'll face the Almighty, try to explain my actions, I've no idea. I don't even know if I've got the guts to put the bloody gun to my head, that's how confident I am. But I'll tell you this, after what I've been through, death may sound an easy cop-out to you, but is far more preferable to what's waiting for me out there." Karen leaned against the wall, her head throbbing, the injury in her side sending shots of pain through her body every time she moved. "Now please, just go will you? I don't want to talk anymore," she pleaded, her voice shaking.

Martha persisted. "But you belong to Sirec, whether you accept it or not. Nobody will dare to hurt or kill you. He'd have them shot, so let them take you to him. Talk to Sirec, explain everything and he'll understand."

Karen had no more fight left in her to argue, again looking out across to the fast approaching lights, shaking her head from side to side slowly. "Sirec would understand would he?" she asked quietly. "Would you understand if your home had been destroyed, your friends killed? Would you understand I had to kill or be killed? No, I don't think you or even he would. And you're asking me to lay down my arms, beg him for forgiveness and maybe he'll let me go home?"

Martha grabbed her arm gently. "He will, I'm sure of that."

Karen shook her off and turned to face Martha, her voice low, resigned to her fate. "Have your beliefs if you want. I'm not prepared to take that chance. These weapons are all I trust now. They won't let me down; perhaps I'll even take a few men with me? Who knows or even cares?"

Martha looked horrified. "I care. I care, not just for you, but the young men you'll kill. They have mothers, fathers, perhaps even a young family. No matter how much bitterness you have against God, you wouldn't want to face the Almighty with those deaths on your conscience."

Karen looked at her for a moment, tears trickling down her face. "I have a mum and dad as well, you know, I've even a sister and my cat. Those men you are so keen to protect, took it all away from me, ground my cross into the dirt. Now I'll never see my family again, never be able to tell them how much I love them." Then, drawing her handgun from the inside of her jeans, she offered it to Martha.

She looked alarmed, pushing it away. "What use have I for such a weapon?"

Karen shrugged. "You care for the men, don't you? Bothered about what havoc I'll wreak? Believe me this gun I'm holding will rip them to pieces. So do them a favour, kill me before they arrive, then perhaps your precious menfolk will live to fight another day."

Martha stared at her, unsure as to what to do or say, the girl was deadly serious and no matter what she said, it would not dissuade her from the actions she proposed.

Karen sighed. "Forget it, I can see you're not prepared to kill me. Just go. All I want to do is wait and spend a short time thinking about my family, my friends. The good times I had before all this. Then when the time comes and I can no longer think, I'll squeeze the trigger myself."

Martha grasped her arm gently. "What is your full name?"

"Karen, Karen Marshall. What's my name matter?"

"Well, Karen Marshall, I, like you, was brought up in the Catholic faith. I don't want to see you die, the same as I don't want any of those soldiers out there to die. When you came into my house I'd a feeling you were the girl Sirec was looking for. Even without your injuries, other girls would have given up; you hardly flinched when I stitched them. I've seen men pass out with that sort of pain. That's determination. Then when you left to move on I couldn't believe it. You're one of the bravest girls I've ever met; even through the war I met nobody like you. You've given Sirec a run for his money like no other, and should continue. So if you want to go home, and now I really believe you should, come with me."

Karen stood there confused. "What are you saying?"

Martha looked at her, her face serious. "My man was in the Hasher group who fought for years in this country. He was hunted many times and I suppose those days I, too, believed in the cause. But to cut a long story short, we've a hide-out; it's dark, damp and very uncomfortable, besides not being used for years. Believe me, in a few hours this search party will have moved on, so are you coming or dying?"

Karen never moved.

Martha frowned. "What's wrong, I'm offering you a chance to live?" she asked.

"How do I know? Many people have offered to help me, but there's always a cost, so what's yours?" Karen replied.

Martha grinned. "You're right, of course. You don't know me and I don't know you, but unless you want to die, Karen Marshall, we have to meet in the middle. Where I'm going to hide you, they couldn't get in without you knowing they were coming. So what's the difference, you fight here and die, or go in my hiding place and have a chance to live?"

"And the cost, what will it cost me?"

Martha sighed. "I'm seventy-eight, what need have I for money? So what else could I possibly want from you, you're probably thinking?" She fell silent and looked across at the approaching searchers. Karen never said a word, then

Martha grasped her hand, tears in her eyes. "I want nothing, Karen, except to see a young girl have a chance to live and not die in a hail of bullets alone, without a mother or father to hold her hand and give her comfort. I want to convince you that not all people in the world expect to receive some sort of monetary value for helping a fellow human who's either fallen on hard times, or is in some sort of danger. My man would want me to do this, no matter what the danger. So please, no more arguing, come with me."

Karen stood silently, looking at her, but didn't move.

"Come on, Karen, this is a chance to live. Snap out of it," Martha urged.

"I'll come so long as it doesn't endanger you? Otherwise I fight and die here."

Martha shrugged. "What can they do to me, I've had my life? Take the chance, Karen; perhaps you'll get to go home? If they find you, and believe me they won't, you've still got your gun as a final resort."

Karen followed Martha into the house and through to the small kitchen. She pushed a bottle of wine into her hand, half a loaf of bread and some cheese. Then, after grabbing a blanket, urged her out to the back.

They crossed the yard to what was, at one time, a stable, but now a crumbling building. Martha pushed the open door shut after they entered the stable. Behind was another small half-door set flush to the wall; this she opened and pulled a matchbox from her pocket, quickly striking a match. The room was small with a mattress on an old wooden bed.

"The art of hiding someone, Karen, is don't overlook the obvious. Many people had rooms hidden under the floor, the entrance covered with a mat. Every searcher worth his salt knows that. My man was clever. A door, old and open, into a dilapidated barn, is an invitation to search inside. Nobody, let alone a searcher, shuts the door after coming in. Why should he? After all, he's not there to shut doors or tidy up, so you'll understand then, this room will not be found. Keep quiet; in fact sleep if you can. Anybody trying the door will waken you. Provided when you're inside you prop the bed behind it, you'll not be caught unaware. I'll come for you tomorrow, then we'll see if we can't get you home."

Karen thanked her, then went inside. Using the torch she still carried in her bag, she moved the bed against the door, as Martha had said, before lying down and pulling the blanket over her. Within minutes she was asleep, oblivious to what was going on outside.

Chapter 22

Sirec listened to Khan's report without saying a word. When he'd finished Sirec banged the table in frustration.

"Khan, we're talking about a girl only just eighteen here, not an S.A.S. soldier. A girl two of your men actually captured and now one's dead and the other badly wounded. By all accounts Karen's also wounded. You then tell me she was traced to an old farm where the owner says she demanded food at gunpoint, then moved on. This farm, Khan, is not on the line I drew to the pick-up point of Tiala, which tells me one of two things; either Karen's lost, but I don't think so, after all, she's not made any mistakes yet, alternatively Farrow's confession of Tiala is also wrong. Either way, she couldn't have got far because the kid's on foot and she's certainly not a ghost or some super being."

Khan shuffled uneasily. "It's not my fault, you said not to kill her. The men were inexperienced soldiers looking after her, waiting for their captain. She produced a gun from somewhere and that was it, they couldn't fire back."

Sirec stood and grabbed his lapels. "She had a gun. She had a gun!" Sirec screamed. "Why didn't your soldiers search her? For them to have not checked that she'd no more weapons on her person would seem very stupid, even for a conscript. So, my dear friend, let this be a warning as to just how dangerous Karen is, perhaps next time you take her, bring her in naked and bound if you want, but don't let her near even a glass of water. Do I make myself clear?"

Khan nodded, clearly shaken with Sirec's reaction.

Sirec returned to his chair and studied the map, shaking his head in confusion. "I do not understand what's happening here," Sirec began. "It would seem that if she's turned east then the logical location would be Sharma not

Tiala. What are your thoughts, Khan?"

Khan, relieved Sirec had composed himself again, looked down at the map. "It's possible, but risky. We've a military base less than twenty miles from there. They would risk detection from our normal security operations in the area."

Sirec rubbed his chin in thought. "You might be right, Khan, but I think not, they'd be in and out before the base could mobilise. The problem I see is, if we saturated the area, she'll not come. We need to keep a way open for her to enter the trap. The point is, which direction will she come in from?" Sirec said, still studying the map.

"That's assuming that it is Sharma she's heading for, Sirec," Khan said bravely.

Sirec looked up at him. "Why shouldn't it be? After all, she's turned off and is heading straight for it."

Khan smiled with satisfaction. "But more the point, Sirec, why did she turn off? I suggest she turned to avoid the road and intended to loop back round. It's logical for any soldier to do that."

Sirec sighed. "But we're not talking about a trained soldier; as I said this is a school kid, Khan."

Khan stopped him. "This school kid, as you like to make us all believe she is, has had some training, she must have. She helped take over a helicopter, disabled and killed the occupants of three Land Rovers, overcame two soldiers, escaped a net even a mouse couldn't hide in and is still free. No, Sirec, no matter how you want to pull her down, she's as good as anyone we have out there, in some ways better. I say this because for her, it's freedom or die. That, Sirec, is like fighting a suicide bomber; you can never win because in the end they will commit suicide. Besides from our experience, she's very capable of retaliating if cornered."

Sirec glanced over to him. "So if I hear you right, you don't think we can take her alive then?"

Khan shrugged. "Who knows, if we're lucky and catch her unaware maybe? But if you want my opinion, 1 don't think that will happen, and if cornered, she'll take her own life."

The room went silent, Sirec deep in thought. The last thing he wanted was her death. "Right, let her go. Pull all your forces out and let her go."

Khan stared at him. "What are you saying?"

Sirec grinned. "Tell me this, where will the British take her?"

Khan shrugged. "Cyprus is logical, before shipping her back to England."

Sirec threw his hands up. "There you are then; I'll arrange to have her snatched in Cyprus or the UK. She'll be disarmed, that's certain. She'll have a false sense of security, thinking she's made it, even more so with the press everywhere. Can you give me a better plan?"

Khan couldn't and lifted the telephone. Ten minutes later he sat down opposite Sirec. "It's done; she'll get through without a problem. Even if they see her, they'll just report it."

By now Sirec had lit a cigarette. "I've been thinking about your suggestion that Karen intended to take a circular route. I agree with you, that's probably the case. So Farrow's location is, I believe, correct. The pick-up's tomorrow night. You take personal charge and deliver the remaining S.A.S. officers to the same location. Get the bloody lot of them out of the country in one go. It'll be certain then, with the injured, they'll head for Cyprus, so use it as insurance. I suggest you set off tomorrow and get them there perhaps an hour or so before. If she's around, she'll recognise them, even possibly joining up again when you've gone. That too will convince her we've given up."

With this plan agreed, Khan left Sirec alone. Sirec picked the telephone up and dialled quickly. "Halif, the local search has been called off..." Sirec listened then replied. "Yes it's too dangerous; you must see Assam now and tell him to set a course to Cyprus. I'll have my contacts snatch the girl and Assam can bring her back."

Halif, on the other side of the phone asked a question, but Sirec discounted it. "No, Halif, I still want the contact in England to inform us when the parents leave. This will give us further conformation she's arrived in Cyprus."

When Khan left Sirec, he made his way to the barracks. In the wardroom a number of officers were sat around. Khan closed the door and looked around. "Sirec's called off the hunt for the girl. He's got some stupid plan of snatching her in Cyprus, but it's a pipe dream. She'll be well guarded until she leaves for England. Anyway, that girl killed our comrades; she'll kill again unless we kill her first."

One of the officers in the room frowned. "How do you expect to do that, Khan?"

Khan lit a cigarette slowly before answering. "She's been very astute turning east, perhaps trying to make us believe she's going to Sharma, but I don't think so. She's on the way to Tiala."

"Why Tiala?" another asked.

"It's obvious; if you mark on the map the sightings of her, then draw a straight line, it ends up there. Besides, even the British in their arrogance, wouldn't pick up less than twenty miles from one of our bases."

Many in the room agreed and Khan opened a map. "She's caught this time. There's only one way in and one way out. We just go down and collect her."

He leaned forward and looked around their faces; "Between you and me, this girl will not come out of Tiala alive. Either she dies trying to defend herself, or we execute her there. Let her escape and we've lost her forever. Are we agreed?"

They all mumbled agreement.

"Then we move at eighteen hundred tomorrow. Form a small troop of five good men; it will be enough to flush this scum out. The ship's not due in the area until dark at twenty hundred. They will find a body, and no more."

Chapter 23

Sirec walked over to the Karen stirred as Martha banged on the small door. "Karen, open the door please," she called.

Eventually, she woke enough to climb out of bed, then with great difficulty was able to pull the bed away from the door.

Martha burst inside. "Come, follow me. I've good news and a hot dinner for you," she said excitedly.

Karen didn't feel that well, but followed her into the kitchen. "Sirec's called off the hunt for you, Karen. According to local sources he's withdrawn the reward and all soldiers have been returned to barracks."

Karen's eyes narrowed. "So that means they know where I am?"

Martha shook her head. "They don't, believe me. Last night they searched this place completely. I told them you'd come but moved on after food. They thought you were injured, but I said you weren't or if you were, you didn't show it. In fact I even told them a white lie, saying you were pretty fit, just hungry." Martha stopped for a moment then frowned. "I was lucky though, the lounge was splattered with your blood and I'd only just enough time to tidy before they came knocking. Anyway, they left at about three in the morning; they were still searching just before leaving. I'm surprised you didn't hear them, they pulled everything out," she grinned, "but they never closed the barn door. Anyway suddenly it was all off. Some say you're dead, others say you've been caught and Sirec's not admitting it, to save his reward money. What I can tell you is there are no soldiers for miles this morning, that's certain. I've spoken to some of my neighbours who've also been searched."

Karen said nothing and began eating the food Martha

had laid out, but she felt worried. Why had Sirec pulled out? This wasn't the impression she'd formed of him. He wasn't, she was sure, a man to give up so easily, unless he'd other plans, but what?

When she'd finished, Martha left the room and brought back a dressing gown. "Right, Karen, get out of those dirty clothes. I've filled the bath so it's about time you turned back into some sort of reasonable human being. Apart from stinking, you must feel awful yourself?"

This was a demand Karen didn't object to and soon she settled down in a warm bath, finally rubbing the congealed dirt from her hair. Eventually she returned to the kitchen in the dressing gown Martha had given her.

"Out here," Martha called.

She was sat on the small balcony overlooking the entire area. "Bless me, you really are a very beautiful girl," Martha said, as Karen came out and settled in a chair at her side.

She gave Martha a weak smile. "It's good of you to say, to tell you the truth I don't feel very beautiful. In fact, since this all started I've only felt dirty and abused but the bath was very welcome. Thank you."

Martha touched her hand gently. "It'll get better, Karen, believe me, I know. It'll take time and don't, as I did, believe every man is a rapist. Just live your life and put this behind you."

Karen looked at her strangely. "Are you telling me you were raped?"

She smiled at her and put a finger to her lips. "We all have secrets, Karen. Mine are from a long time ago and time heals. Later I was lucky enough to meet a man I not only loved, but respected. Mind you, you'll find men are fickle. They like to believe they are the only one. It's stupid I know, but always remember a little deception makes for a quiet and happy life. Anyway, enough of me, how are we getting you home?"

Karen told her of the cove she was supposed to be at later that day.

Martha sat for a moment and scratched her head. "It's not far as such. To tell you the truth, it's an area where locals don't go; used in the past for illicit drug shipments. Some locals lost their lives under strange circumstances. I could take you as far as where the track meets the main highway. Beyond that my old car wouldn't cope. For that matter, neither could I. You'd have to go on alone from there."

Karen grinned. "That isn't a problem, Martha, I'd be thankful for the lift to the start of the track. At least it's a chance of freedom, even if it's tough going getting down."

With this agreed they both fell silent. Martha drifted off to sleep; Karen watched the horizon, still not convinced Sirec had given up. Later that day after a late lunch they were ready to go. Karen dressed in clean jeans, t-shirt, hair tied back, and her blue eyes shining for the first time in ages.

"My word, now you're dressed in clean clothes you really look so different. And nothing like the girl who came into this house last night."

Karen smiled, she felt good inside. "It's all your doing, Martha. It was you who saved my life, you who sorted my injuries. I can't thank you enough."

Martha shook her head. "No, that's not true really. I've helped a little, everybody needs help sometime but it's you, Karen, you've pulled yourself together and I'll take no credit for that. So let's stop this silliness and get you on your way?"

They talked very little on the ride to the beginning of the track which led down to the cove. The car, while functional, had seen better days and it coughed and spluttered all the way. At times Karen was convinced it'd give up but Martha nursed it on and eventually she pulled off the road.

The engine died and she turned to Karen. "This is it. Two miles and you're on your way home," she said sadly.

"I'll miss you; it's been a day I won't forget."

Karen hugged her tightly then broke away, opening the car door. Martha rummaged in her bag and pulled out a piece of paper, pushing it into Karen's hand. "Send me a card to say you're home, will you? Don't say much, just 'wish you were here' sort of thing."

"Martha," Karen began, but Martha held her hand up. "No, Karen, we've talked ourselves out, say nothing, love. Just get on your way and be careful. I'm not one for sentiment; my husband always thought it bad luck."

Karen said nothing more, just pulled the ammunition belt across her shoulder and tightened the strap holding the handgun round her waist. Then she slipped the rucksack on and grabbed the machine-gun. Slamming the car door she walked away, only turning to give Martha a final wave, before setting off down the track.

Martha had watched as she'd readied herself, tears coming to her eyes. How often her man had done the same. Karen could have been him at that moment. A soldier ready for action, rather than a young girl just trying to get home, but unlike her man, who one day never returned, Martha knew Karen would return home. She'd the determination like her husband first had. However, Martha had a strange feeling this would not be the last she saw of this girl. Why? She didn't know, just a feeling.

The walk down the track wasn't, as Martha had suggested, too hard. For Karen, her only real concern was her vulnerability. It was narrow but not narrow enough not to take a vehicle. In fact she could see the tracks close to either side that showed, in the past, a vehicle had been down. But odd areas where rain must have washed the tracks away also told her the tracks were not recent. However, about half a mile from the end of the track she stopped and looked carefully around. Somehow she felt she still needed to hide, yet be close enough to see any small boat arrive in the cove.

The track at this point was very narrow, to one side completely sheer to the rocks below. The other side was steep with a few thick shrubs clinging precariously to the side. Further along the track it opened wide enough to allow a vehicle to turn. Beyond this turning circle it was only a footpath falling steeply down to the cove. Karen decided this was where she would wait, hiding in the shrubs to one side. In this position she could see anyone or anything coming down the track, besides having a reasonable view of the cove.

***

Time went on and for the twentieth time she glanced at her watch. It was coming up to seven fifteen, less than an hour and she'd be leaving this place forever. It would be a country she wouldn't miss; besides the S.A.S., the only person to help her was Martha, and probably because she was English and understood. The rest... it wasn't worth thinking about. At that moment Karen held her breath. There was the distinct sound of a labouring vehicle engine, as it worked itself slowly down the track. Her heart sank. No boat would come if they were here. Now she was trapped with no way out, they had her this time, she was certain. This must have been Sirec's plan to trick her into believing she'd escaped, when all the time they just had to wait until she came to them. She looked up at the track; it would be ten or twelve minutes before they'd be here. A small but desperate plan was forming in her mind. The risk was enormous if it went wrong, she'd have no escape and nowhere to run. All that was left then, would be to put the gun to her head.

Finally deciding to take the risk, she first checked her handgun, this was her final solution and it must work. Then she walked back up the track to just before the turning circle where it was narrow with a sheer drop to one side and looked over the edge. Going over to the opposite side of the narrow track, she crouched low behind a shrub. In this position the driver, or even a passenger in the vehicle, wouldn't see her, only as they passed would she be in view. She then unclipped two hand grenades from her belt, placing them carefully on the ground in front with her machine-gun. Now she waited, the noise of the truck becoming louder every second. Karen took the two grenades from the ground, holding them firmly. She began to shake in fear, involuntarily holding her breath as the truck went slowly past only feet away from her. Clutching the two grenades, she pulled the pins with her teeth, counting under her breath.

By now the truck had passed and she jumped down onto the road, running towards it before throwing the two grenades into the open rear of the vehicle. Not waiting to see the result, she ran back to the shrub and grabbed her gun, falling flat on the ground, waiting for the explosion. She could hear shouts and screaming as, whoever was in the back, realised what she had thrown. All these actions were measured in seconds before the two grenades exploded.

The truck lurched from side to side on the narrow track; a front door burst open just before the truck lost its tenuous grip on the track and plunged as if in slow motion off the edge, down to the rocks below. Karen lay there for a moment before looking up. The truck was gone and there was complete silence until a sudden explosion. Then nothing.

She stood and walked to the edge, looking tentatively over at the mangled remains below. Then she heard a noise and swung round, gripping the gun she held even tighter. A soldier dressed as an officer, who must have either jumped or been thrown out of the truck, was standing further down the track brushing himself down with his hands. For some reason he'd not seen Karen until the moment when he heard the click of the safety going off. Khan stood there looking at her. Karen was also standing watching him.

He gave a sickly grin. "So you must be the famous Karen Marshall, then? My name's Khan."

"What's it to you? Anyway you're in my way. I want to go down that path," she responded.

He looked her up and down. She was taller than he'd imagined, attractive in a European way, but not the type of girl he'd fancy. He could understand Sirec wanting her and he could also understand why they'd not found her. She was clean, even her hair was combed. Someone had helped her all along, probably hidden her until now. He also understood why the other soldiers, both around eighteen, had not heeded their captain's orders on how dangerous this young girl stood in front of him was. She portrayed weakness, femininity and naivety. Even her get-up of sporting an ammunition belt and holding a gun was as if a photographer had set her up for a photo shoot. However, Khan was not that naive, and the girl who stood in front of him was not weak, he'd no doubts about that in any way. He was all too aware of her capability and just how dangerous she really was. Even now, to have taken a truck on alone without knowing what was inside, was either sheer stupidity, or a very brave and calculated action. This girl, he knew, was not stupid.

He glanced at his watch. "You're not due out for another hour or so at least, so why don't we talk? After all, I've been looking for you for some time now and you've been very elusive. I must congratulate you though. I don't have a man in my command who'd have taken on a truck full of troops. That would be worth a Victoria Cross if it happened in a war."

He made to put his hand in his pocket, but Karen raised her gun. "Don't think about it, you'll be dead before your hand touches whatever's in there," she said curtly.

He laughed. "Only a cigarette, just a cigarette. Do you

object even to that?"

She said nothing but allowed him to pull the case out very slowly. Then he opened it, showing her the contents, before putting one in his mouth. "I don't suppose?" he asked, offering her the case. She shook her head and Khan lit the cigarette slowly. "So, Karen Marshall, where do we go from here? Or is it your intention to kill me?"

His question was for her, a problem. Where did she go from here? "Do you want me to kill you?" she asked.

He shrugged. "Of course not, but you're renowned for killing, aren't you?"

"I've killed no one who hasn't attacked me first, every time has been self-defence," Karen retorted.

Khan laughed. "I suppose Assam's friends tried to shoot you, did they, or the farmer in the field? Then there's the two conscripts, one dead and the other in hospital?"

Karen cut in. "One of those conscripts tried to kill me," she pulled her jumper up a little to reveal the knife wound. "What do you think this is, Scotch mist? So don't give me the 'holier-than-thou' bit. I'd have been happy just to let them go, I'd no argument with them," she protested.

Khan noticed she'd avoided Assam's friends and the farmer but he'd another card to play. "What of your own people who came to save you? Did you need to kill them, as well?"

Her face changed, a look of surprise written all over it. "I don't know what you're talking about, who's dead?"

Khan grinned. "Why, Karen, the S.A.S. officers who were going home tonight on the same ship you're waiting for. They were in the back of the truck you sent to the bottom of the ocean."

Her eyes narrowed. "You're lying, trying to get me to panic or something, but it won't wash. That was full of your men. They'd come for me. Perhaps to kill me or take me to Sirec?"

"No, Karen, we'd not come to get you, but send home the people who came to help you. They're all dead on the rocks below, but that's your way, isn't it, shoot before you think. You're really just a killer out of control. Even you can't claim self-defence anymore. I suppose if the truth was known, you enjoy it... Enjoy seeing people die."

Karen stood there confused, this man couldn't be right, could he? However, the long walk down here, then the attack on the truck and now having to stand and talk, had tired her. The wound in her side was beginning to give her pain again, her head, although aching before, had become worse in the last few minutes. Then with the effort of keeping concentration on a prisoner, who'd kill her if she wavered, she was fast losing her grip on the situation.

Khan, on his side, could see her becoming more confused, not realising it wasn't the conversation that was doing this, but her injuries, so he persisted in his interrogation. "I was surprised the people who've harboured you all these days didn't mention we'd given up and decided to let you go?"

"What are you talking about?" she asked.

Khan puffed on his cigarette. "Well someone must have helped you otherwise you'd not have avoided us for so long. So who was it then?" he asked.

Karen frowned. "Nobody helped me, even though, if anyone had, it's nothing to do with you. Besides, I'm perfectly capable of looking after myself without risking help from your race."

"I suppose you washed in a stream last night? Cleaned your clothes and lay in the sun while they dried? Come off it, Karen, even I'm not stupid enough to believe nobody helped you."

She laughed, but wanted to discourage any possible link with Martha. "Well that's where you're wrong. I did get here by myself, except last night I was lucky enough to find a house, the occupants were away. So I washed, found some spare clothes in a drawer and made my way here. Simple when you know how," she said haughtily.

"Think a lot of yourself, don't you?"

"Why shouldn't I? After all, I'm told I'm attractive and men want me, well my body at least, so why should I care what you think?" she retorted.

Khan sighed to himself. The girl was right, people did want her. But why was it only he could see a born killer stood opposite and others saw just an attractive young girl to have some fun with?

Karen glanced at her watch; she needed to make her way down to the beach. "It's time I was out of here so if you please, I'd like you to remove all your clothes."

Khan's face suddenly lit up. "Why, Karen, do you think we have the time? I'm flattered Sirec's girl would want me," he teased.

Her features changed. "I'm nobody's girl, as many of your countrymen have found out to their cost. Even Sirec will find this out, if I ever meet him. Anyway, I've been caught once with a hidden weapon from one of your lot and I've no intention of falling for that again, so take your bloody clothes off or die. It's of no interest to me either way, except dead you're no threat," she replied curtly.

Khan looked at her for a moment, then began to remove his clothes. She was clever this girl, she'd no idea if he had a knife or gun hidden. This would tell her instantly. Soon, stood in his pants, he looked at her. "So what do I do now?"

"The pants as well. Then you can start down the track."

He stood his ground, indignant at her demand. "I've got no hidden arms, Karen. The pants stay; I'll not remove my pants in front of a young kid."

She grinned at his embarrassment. "You know, I've had the same problem."

"What are you talking about?"

Karen laughed. "Well nearly every person I've met recently kept demanding I took all my clothes off, particularly my pants. Mind you, I only did it to avoid a beating; you're to do it on pain of death. So drop the pants or die. You've got nothing I've not seen before you know. I've even felt them forced inside me. So don't come with your objections. Exposing your sexual organ will not have an effect on me; but I'll try not to laugh."

He did as she asked before walking down the path, Karen followed at a distance. However, what looked a short walk wasn't, and it took a lot out of her, just to keep going. Finally they arrived in the cove and she leaned heavily against a large rock, breathless, her head spinning, now unable to concentrate properly.

Khan looked at her for a moment; there was something wrong, he was sure of that. Could she, as he'd heard, have been injured more seriously than she was admitting? Had the old lady been lying, was it her who'd looked after Karen last night? Were they so close that if they'd searched properly, they'd have found her? He was now certain that must have been the case.

"You feel faint, Karen? Maybe you're injured? Should I call the boat for you?" he asked very softly.

She looked at him, he didn't seem in focus. Panic was beginning to set in. What if she fainted? How could she keep him prisoner until help arrived? Khan also was convinced something was seriously wrong and began to move very slowly, so as not to alarm her. Closer... Closer he came towards her.

"Perhaps I should help you, Karen. You're going home; you don't want to miss the boat, do you?" he kept saying softly, every second that little bit closer.

By now Karen could no longer hold herself together, but her will to go home was strong. This man was offering help, except he terrified her. Everything about him represented all she despised about these people. Suddenly she panicked, seeing everything she'd fought for being taken away by this man and she instinctively squeezed the trigger. The machine-gun shattered the silence. Khan was suspended briefly, shock written all over his face, then he collapsed slowly to the ground.

Karen dropped the gun, putting her hands to her head. She felt sick and dizzy as she collapsed to the ground herself.

Peace had returned to the cove, the only sound was the sea crashing into the rocks to each side. Khan, his eyes open, staring lifelessly up to the sky. In his haste he'd panicked her. If he'd just stayed where he was, rather than move towards her slowly, she'd have been his now. But like a fool he'd tried to take her before Karen had lost control of the situation completely.

***

When she came to, it was very dark. She lay there for sometime, unable to think straight. Her body was shaking, the pain in her side intense, her head pounding. Then slowly it all came back to her. She pulled the torch from her bag, sweeping it round until it rested on Khan. He was a mess. The gun at such close quarters, switched to maximum output because she believed she was going to have to fight whoever was in the truck, had cut him in half. Karen felt sick and turned the light away quickly. Then she removed the radio and pressed the send button, praying she wasn't too late. Nothing happened, so she tried again. This time the radio broke into life; the relief inside her was overwhelming. She gave the password and waited. Seconds later the reply came, they were coming. Not wanting them to find Khan, she dragged herself up, leaning heavily on the gun for support. Then after collecting her backpack, she made her way slowly down to the edge of the water. Once at the edge, she threw the gun into the water then removed her ammunition belt, and did the same. Finally she took out the handgun from her pocket, looked at it for a moment, then threw it in as well. Now she was just Karen; injured, yes, an armed civilian, no. She pointed the torch out to sea, flashing it once every five seconds as Chapman had told her. Minutes later someone was grasping her hand and asking her where everyone else was?

"There's only me, no one else is coming," she heard herself saying, while they helped her into the small craft.

Karen gazed back at the shore as it melted into the darkness. Somehow the last weeks seemed like a nightmare, not reality. Now she was going home. But for her it would never be the same. She'd grown up, lost her innocence. But more importantly she had money and there were scores still to settle.

Chapter 24

Sirec walked over to the edge of the cliff and looked down. He could see a number of soldiers standing on the narrow beach using long rods with hooks, pulling to shore what looked like a body. There were already four body bags alongside them, zipped up and ready to be taken away. He sighed, then continued along the narrow track towards the beach, glancing at a heap of clothes by the side of the track as he passed.

An officer saw Sirec and hurried up the track to meet him. "Sirec, the name's Jived. I was told you were coming and to leave everything as it was found. We have, of course, been continuing to pull the dead from the water after finding the army truck. It had gone over the edge."

"Do you know what happened here yet?" Sirec asked.

"We don't know for certain. I believe our troops came upon smugglers, perhaps moving drugs or weapons, and a fight ensued. We've one dead on the beach, besides four others already pulled out of the water. The one on the beach must have been an officer, judging by the clothing left up on the track. We expect to find at least six bodies. That's how many are missing, according to the local military base, who'd reported the vehicle hadn't returned from an operation. Why they stripped the officer then took him down to the beach before shooting him, is a mystery. Unless, once they were on the beach, he tried to make a run for it?"

"Perhaps you can show me?" Sirec asked without comment on Jived's analysis of what had happened.

They both walked down to the beach and Sirec looked at the corpse for a moment when one of the soldiers pulled back a cover laid on top of him. It was Khan, now Sirec was beginning to understand.

"You can see he was shot at very close range by an automatic weapon," Jived began. "He didn't have a chance; it literally cut him in half. We've also found the weapon we believe killed him, besides a handgun and an ammunition belt thrown into the water. This is all very strange because these weapons were not his. His handgun was still with the clothes on the track, why were these left, I don't know? We can find no footprints that might tell us just how many people were here and if they left by boat."

Sirec took out a cigarette and lit it slowly, before walking over to the guns and ammunition belt still lying where they were found. He bent down and looked at the belt carefully. The first thing he noticed was that the ammunition, still on the belt, could not be used for either gun, and the straps on the pouches that held grenades, were unfastened, as if they'd recently contained grenades.

He stood and then looked at Jived. "The truck, was it damaged beyond what could have happened if it had slipped over the edge?"

"There was an explosion, possibly a grenade, inside the back of the truck, if that's what you're thinking? We know that for certain, because the bodies inside were blackened from it, with some of the dead in pretty bad shape, being in close proximity to the explosion. Is that important, Sirec?"

He shook his head. "No, I'm just trying to piece together a picture in my mind, that's all. Probably it was one of the soldiers' own grenades that exploded when the truck went over the edge and hit the rocks."

"I thought that as well, Sirec. Can we take the bodies now? I don't think we can glean much more from here? But we will be looking for the killer, or killers. They shouldn't be too difficult to find."

"Yes that's fine with me, keep me informed as to your progress in the investigation, will you?"

With this agreed Sirec walked further down the beach

then stopped and gazed out across the still water. He took a last draw on his cigarette and threw the remainder into the sea, watching it floating on the surface. He was trying to visualise just what had really happened in this cove. However, with Khan dead on the beach, for Sirec it didn't take much imagination to suspect that this was the work of Karen. The description by the farmer, of the weapons Karen carried, were similar to the weapons left on the beach. Everything was there; the machine-gun, the handgun and more importantly, the belt worn by someone knowing little about guns, because neither gun lying on the beach used the ammunition still attached to the belt. Finally, there were the grenades the farmer mentioned. With the straps open and the grenades missing, this meant the explosions inside the lorry were deliberate and not accidental. The only error she seemed to have made was not to realise that the weapons would remain hidden by the water. Unless, he thought for a moment, she was trying to hide them from the rescuers and was not really concerned if they were found later?

However, Sirec was very impressed with how she'd taken on a truck full of soldiers and how she must have insisted Khan stripped to be sure he carried no weapon. This was a simple but effective act for someone alone and unable to search him. But what made her shoot Khan? Did the foolish man try to take her? Did she panic, or did she intend killing him anyway? Sirec didn't think the latter was the case; after all, unlike Saeed, who she had a real hatred for, she'd never met Khan and only had to wait with him for her rescuers. So he surmised Khan went for her, a hasty and costly mistake on his part.

Sirec began to laugh, at last he owned a girl who was his type. Even against formidable odds, she was not only very good, but had been a true adversary, not afraid to fight and more importantly, she was not to be underestimated.

"Well, Karen," he said quietly, at the same time looking

out across the water towards Cyprus. "It would seem the first round is to you. The next round will be mine. Enjoy your short freedom, girl, before I bring you home. You've earned it."

Then he turned and walked purposefully back up the track, pulling his mobile telephone out of his pocket and beginning to press numbers; it was time to call in some favours.

Lightning Source UK Ltd.
Milton Keynes UK
UKOW02f0053240816

281370UK00001B/15/P